Dear Diary,

I am so happy! Dad's welcome-home party was a great success. There were plenty of tears, of course. After all, twenty years in prison is a long time—but mostly there were smiles and hugs and lots and lots of laughter.

Mom and Drew and I are thrilled our family's together again, and soon Julia and baby Jeremy will join the clan. (Okay, I couldn't have been more wrong about my future sister-in-law, but at least I admit it.) And now that our dear friend Alexandra is working with Hannah and me at Forrester Square, life couldn't be better.

Running a day care is so rewarding, although every night I check for gray hair. If I find any, I'll know who's responsible—those precocious twins, Kevin Taylor and Kelly Bassett. I never knew two kids could get into so much trouble. Kevin was mischievous enough on his own, and now with his sister... They're such cuties, though, and it's beyond me how their parents could have separated them as babies.

For that matter, why did Meg and Brody divorce in the first place? Anybody can see they're perfect for each other. I honestly think it's Meg who's resisting, but why? Brody is handsome, successful and such a good dad. I really hope they're not going to miss this chance to be together again. After all, it's too much of a coincidence that they enrolled their kids in the same day care without knowing it.

Fate is at work here—I can feel it. I just hope Meg and Brody do, too.

Till tomorrow, Katherine.

CATHY GILLEN THACKER

is a full-time wife, mother and author who
began typing stories for her own amusement
during "naptime" when her children were toddlers.
Twenty years and more than sixty published novels
later, Cathy is almost as well-known for her witty
romantic comedies and warm family stories as
she is for her triple-layer brownies, her ability to
get grass stains and red clay out of almost anything,
and her knack for knowing what her three grown and
nearly grown children are up to almost before they
do! Cathy's books have made numerous appearances
on bestseller lists and are now published in seventeen
languages and thirty-five countries around the world.

Forrester Square

LEGACIES . LIES . LOVE .

CATHY GILLEN THACKER
TWICE AND FOR ALWAYS

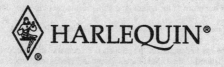

HARLEQUIN®

TORONTO • NEW YORK • LONDON
AMSTERDAM • PARIS • SYDNEY • HAMBURG
STOCKHOLM • ATHENS • TOKYO • MILAN • MADRID
PRAGUE • WARSAW • BUDAPEST • AUCKLAND

HARLEQUIN BOOKS
225 Duncan Mill Road, Don Mills,
Ontario, Canada M3B 3K9

ISBN 0-373-61269-9

TWICE AND FOR ALWAYS

Cathy Gillen Thacker is acknowledged as the author of this work.

Copyright © 2003 by Harlequin Books S.A.

Visit us at www.eHarlequin.com

Printed in U.S.A.

Dear Reader,

When my husband and I started our family years ago, we were overjoyed at the prospect of having children together. And we had no idea how much having three children would change our priorities and enrich our lives. Our careers were—and still are—very important to us. But when it comes down to making a choice between work and the needs of our family—bottom line, we choose family every time. We realize our greatest happiness comes from taking care of those we love.

Meg Bassett and Brody Taylor have come to this realization also, albeit the hard way. You see, initially, when their twins were born, they figured their lives wouldn't have to alter one iota. Meg would continue her stage career—in New York City. Brody would fulfill his long-held dream of starting his own computer software company—in Ireland. Only the realization that they couldn't do both simultaneously split them apart. So they did what they thought was the most sensible thing two divorcing parents could do—they each took an infant and headed off to fulfill their individual destinies.

Now, five years later, they realize parenting is not nearly as simple as it seemed. And living without each other is much lonelier than they ever could have imagined. Still, they have their pride. And they don't want to upset what has turned out to be a very workable—if initially ill-thought-out—situation. But when fate puts them back in Seattle and has the two of them and their twins coming face-to-face, the sparks ignite once again. And soon Meg and Brody are asking themselves—is it ever too late to love?

I hope you enjoy reading this story as much as I enjoyed telling it. And I hope you'll visit my Web site at www.cathygillenthacker.com.

Best wishes always,

Cathy Gillen Thacker

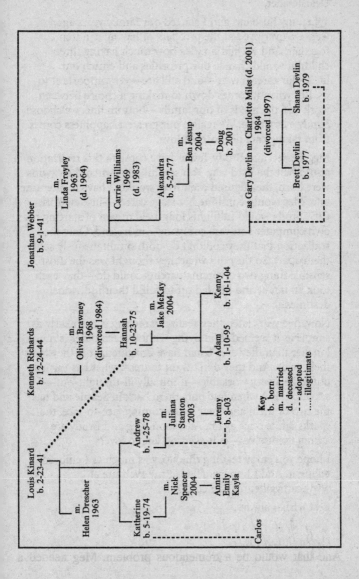

Louis Kinard
b. 2-23-41

m.
Helen Drescher
1963

Katherine
b. 5-19-74

m.
Nick
Spencer
2004

Annie
Emily
Kayla

Carlos

Andrew
b. 1-25-78

m.
Juliana Stanton
2003

Jeremy
b. 8-03

Kenneth Richards
b. 12-24-44

m.
Olivia Brawney
1968
(divorced 1984)

Hannah
b. 10-23-75

m.
Jake McKay
2004

Adam
b. 1-10-95

Kenny
b. 10-1-04

Jonathan Webber
b. 9-1-41

m.
Linda Freyley
1963
(d. 1964)

m.
Carrie Williams
1969
(d. 1983)

Alexandra
b. 5-27-77

m.
Ben Jessup
2004

Doug
b. 2001

as Gary Devlin m. Charlotte Miles (d. 2001)
1984
(divorced 1997)

Brett Devlin
b. 1977

Shana Devlin
b. 1979

Key
b. born
m. married
d. deceased
- - adopted
......illegitimate

CHAPTER ONE

MEG BASSETT HEARD a man's low, husky voice as she stepped through the arched front door of the sandstone building in Seattle's Belltown area.

"I'll be back at the office as soon as I get this cleared up. Yes, it's a nuisance, but I've got to have my pager. No. Tell the managers I'll be there. I want to have that staff meeting today, no matter how late we all have to stay."

Spoken like a true workaholic, Meg thought. And she ought to recognize one. In fact, if she didn't know full well that Brody Taylor was in Ireland now, she'd even think that man sounded like her sexy, successful—workaholic—ex-husband.

Not that he was of any concern to her now. Her priority was deciding what to do about the mischief her five-year-old daughter Kelly had been getting into with another kindergarten student. No two children should be causing this much trouble, Meg thought firmly as she walked down the cheerfully decorated front hall of Forrester Square Day Care. It was only Kelly's second week in the school, and already she had conspired with another student to disrupt storytime with an impromptu song and dance routine, take off down the street in the day care's pedal cars and, last but not least, switch Meg's and another parent's beepers. If the troublemaking continued at this rate, her daughter and her equally precocious partner in crime would be asked to leave the prestigious new school before the end of the week. And that would be a tremendous problem. Meg needed a good, safe place for Kelly to attend kindergarten while she taught musical theater classes at the university. She had to meet with the other child's parents and the day care staff to resolve this quickly and amicably, Meg thought as she entered the office and came face-to-face with the man talking on the cell phone.

For a moment, the only thing they could do was stare at each other in stunned amazement. It had been five long years since Meg had laid eyes on Brody Taylor, yet nothing much had changed. He was still as tall and fit and ruggedly appealing as ever. Broad shoulders and a sinewy chest filled out his olive tweed sport coat. Long legs and lean hips made the most of his stone-colored dress slacks. His thick black hair was conservatively cut and combed straight back. And his dark brown eyes had zeroed in on her with mesmerizing accuracy.

"What are you doing here?" Meg demanded, aghast.

Brody's strong jaw took on the familiar, stubborn tilt. Using the flat of his palm, he smoothed his silk tie against his crisply ironed shirt. "I came to get my beeper. And I could ask the same thing of you!" he challenged. "You're supposed to be in New York."

Meg squared off with Brody, trying not to notice the way he was hungrily drinking in the sight of her, too. As if it had been too long. Far too long. "And you're supposed to be in Ireland," she accused, her heart turning cartwheels in her chest. She had always known she would see Brody again—she just hadn't expected it to be so soon. And certainly not without warning. But he was here now, and Kevin, too. With more strength than she knew she had, Meg suppressed the flood of maternal love that rose within her at the knowledge that her little boy was so close. First she had to find out what Brody was up to.

Brody blinked, his glance roving over her casually upswept hair and parted lips before returning to her eyes once more. "You didn't get my letter?" he asked in a low, piqued voice.

Folding her arms in front of her, Meg dug in her heels and regarded him just as contentiously. "You didn't get mine?"

"Someone want to fill me in?" Katherine Kinard asked dryly as she walked into the office to join them.

Meg and Brody turned in unison toward the driving force behind Forrester Square Day Care. At twenty-nine, Katherine was a beautiful woman with silky chestnut-brown hair and a big wide smile.

"We used to be married," Meg explained uncomfortably, not sure Katherine would understand just how far awry cupid's arrow had been when it joined her and Brody together.

"We split up five years ago, when Kevin and Kelly were just two months old," Brody continued matter-of-factly. "We each took one of the twins with us."

"I went to New York to pursue a stage career on Broadway," Meg added, "and Brody went to Ireland to begin a computer software company."

"Do Kevin and Kelly know they're twins?" Katherine asked, a faintly disapproving look coming over her face.

Meg and Brody exchanged uneasy glances. "They know they have a sibling their age who lives with their other parent, but that's all, so far," Meg said. "We thought our arrangement would be too much to try and explain to a young child."

About that, Katherine Kinard seemed to agree.

"We planned to introduce them and tell them everything when they were old enough to understand, say around twelve or so." Brody frowned, his expression troubled. "We hadn't expected to do it so soon."

Katherine sat down behind her desk. "Why didn't you

list each other as next of kin on Kevin and Kelly's applications?"

"Brody and I don't have joint custody," Meg explained. "We each assume total responsibility for the twin in our care." And they had done so for a reason, she thought as she sat down in one of the chairs along the wall opposite Katherine's desk. Her own parents had divorced when she was very young, and Meg had spent her entire childhood being volleyed back and forth between them, to the point where she'd ended up feeling insecure and torn apart inside, as if she really didn't belong either place. She had also felt terribly disloyal to both her parents and was extremely conflicted about that. It had been a sad, unhappy way to grow up. She hadn't wanted to inflict similar pain on their twins.

Brody settled his six-foot-two frame into the chair next to Meg's. "Given how far apart the two of us were going to be living," he elaborated in his usual all-business tone, "Meg and I felt it would be too hard to arrange visitations. So we each took one of the twins, and promised we would let them get acquainted when they were twelve."

"In the meantime, all we've ever told Kevin and Kelly is that they each have another parent and a sibling living an ocean away," Meg said. It had been like a fairy tale, or a faraway dream that brought only happy thoughts, and not the pain and heartache of divorce and a family split in two. "Of course," she sighed, looking back at Brody, "now that Kevin and Kelly have met, we're going to have to tell them the whole story and go from there."

Brody looked just as daunted by the possibility of doing that as Meg felt.

"Maybe I should give you two a moment alone to sort all this out," Katherine said kindly.

"Thanks." Brody stood and began to roam the office restlessly. "We'd appreciate that," he said distractedly.

Katherine stepped outside, shutting the door behind her. Meg and Brody were left alone.

"I guess we've both got some explaining to do," Brody said reluctantly.

Meg crossed her legs at the knee and looped her clasped hands around one. "You first. What brought you back to Seattle?" He couldn't have been here for very long. She had just spoken to him five weeks ago, and he had still been in Ireland then.

"I'm opening a U.S. office of Taylor Software here in Seattle. I just moved a few weeks ago. I had my attorney send you a formal letter of notice, shortly after the last time we spoke on the phone, but I guess the letter didn't reach you."

Meg knew why it hadn't. "I wanted to see if I could get a job out here before I made the decision to move. When they offered me the position teaching musical theater at the University of Washington, it was contingent on me starting right away and teaching fall term. So I said yes and made arrangements to have my apartment in New York sublet and all our belongings shipped. Kelly and I spent the last month or so driving cross-country on vacation, then finding a place to live out here and moving in."

Brody looked surprised but pleased. "What happened to your stage career?" he asked curiously. He braced a shoulder against the wall and folded his arms in front of him. "The last I heard they had offered you the starring role in the Broadway production of *Annie, Get Your Gun.*"

Feeling unbearably restless, Meg rose and walked over to the windows overlooking Sandringham Drive. The restored historic district of Belltown, near the Seattle waterfront, was bathed in the late afternoon sun. "I turned it down," Meg told Brody seriously. "Kelly was starting kindergarten, and if I took the part of Annie, she and I would literally never see each other. She would be gone most of the day, and I'd be working every evening, plus all day Saturday and Sunday. That was okay before she started school, but I didn't want to spend that much time away from her. So I decided to head back home, to Seattle, and look for a day job." Meg studied Brody's face, noting the healthy golden glow of his skin, the blush of sun across his nose and cheeks. "Why did you relocate to Seattle?" she asked curiously.

"Same reason as you." Brody smiled with unabashed sentiment. "It's home. And although I loved Ireland, and my family there, I wanted Kevin to grow up in the States. Plus, we did want to open a branch of the company here, and Seattle is a great place for software development."

So it wasn't just his heart bringing him back. It was also the welfare of his beloved business. Trying not to feel resentful of the ambition that had driven them apart, Meg asked, "How has Kevin adjusted?"

Brody's brow furrowed. "Not as well as I would've liked. I haven't been able to find a nanny."

"What happened to the one he had in Ireland?"

Brody paused just a second too long before answering, "Her family is in Ireland. I couldn't ask her to accompany us to the States, although she probably would have."

"Even just for a short time?"

"I figured I could handle Kev until I found someone else. Of course—" Brody shoved a hand through his hair "—that was before I knew how difficult it was going to be to get a replacement he liked."

"I take it you've been interviewing?"

"Oh yes. But Kevin hasn't liked any of the women I've met with so far." Brody paused and gazed at Meg hopefully. "You wouldn't happen to know of anyone here in the Seattle area, would you?"

Meg shook her head. "How long do you have to find someone?" Meg asked gently, her heart going out to him.

Child care was both the saving grace and bane of every single parent.

"Truthfully?" Brody tapped his foot restlessly. "I needed one yesterday. Since the move, I've adjusted my work hours and curtailed all business travel, but that can't last forever. Anyway..." he massaged the muscles in the back of his neck "...I know the disruption in our home life is probably partially responsible for this chaos today."

"And the rest?" Meg prodded curiously.

"Is just Kevin being Kevin."

Eager for more information on the child she had been separated from for so long, Meg leaned toward Brody earnestly. "He has a mischievous streak?"

Brody made a seesawing motion with his hands. "I prefer to think of it as a tendency toward higher-level thinking. He's always coming up with these bright ideas. You know, imaginative solutions to real-life problems. The difficulty is his maturity and judgment are still those of a kid."

That sounded like trouble. "Give me an example," Meg urged.

"Okay." Brody didn't have to think long to come up with one. "Just last night he wanted his own car to drive around, so he tried to build one for himself out of plastic building blocks and bed pillows. He needed wheels, so he decided to use a metal trolley from the kitchen, and nearly totaled himself and the kitchen. I'm used to dealing with his innovativeness. In fact, I think it's kind of cute. But this—" Brody pointed to the beepers "—is for the record books. Getting the two of us together this way. Do you think they did it on purpose?"

"Who knows? It's an amazing coincidence—not just about the beepers, but for us both to enroll our kids in the same school at the same time." What were the odds for such a thing to happen?

But Brody, as usual, seemed to take the unexpected in

stride a lot more easily than Meg did. "Maybe not," he said casually. "Forrester Square Day Care is the hottest new child-care center in the city. It's only been open a short time and already it's got a phenomenal reputation. We would both want our kids to have the best, so it makes perfect sense that we would enroll them here."

Oh, Brody, Meg thought wistfully, *if only it could be that simple.* "What are we going to do?" she murmured, wishing the two of them had never gotten themselves in such a mess.

"First," Brody stated firmly as he unclipped the black transmitter from his belt, "we're going to give each other our beepers."

A rap sounded at the door, and Katherine Kinard walked in, a twin on either side of her. For a moment, Meg couldn't breathe. She'd seen pictures of Kevin, charting his progress as he grew from infant to toddler to little boy, but nothing prepared her for the impact of seeing her child in person after five long years. He was so incredibly cute she couldn't take her eyes off him. And his twin sister, Kelly, was just as adorable. Not that they looked anything alike. With her jet-black hair, cut in a pageboy style, and dark eyes, Kelly looked a lot like her father and nothing at all like Meg. Whereas Kevin, with naturally curly, reddish-brown hair, green eyes and freckles, took after her. It was no wonder no one had put two and two together and realized they were twins, fraternal or otherwise.

"We're sorry," Kelly said.

"Yeah, we are," Kevin added earnestly in a sweet Irish accent.

"We didn't mean to mix up the beepers." Kelly bobbed up and down, unable to stand still even for a second. Intent on talking them out of trouble, she failed to notice the tears Meg was blinking back, and instead focused on Brody, who, Meg noted, was struggling to control his emotional reaction at seeing Kelly.

"I was just showing Mommy's beeper to Kevin this morning." Kelly pointed to Brody. "You were out in the yard, and Mommy was talking to that other lady. Mommy's going to be our new music teacher," she finished proudly.

Meg drew a shaky breath. It was all she could do not to gather her little boy into her arms and hug him to her chest. But given the fact he still didn't have a clue who she really was...

"You're teaching here, too?" Brody's brow rose.

Meg swallowed hard around the lump of emotion in her throat. "Part-time, to the older classes, in exchange for reduced tuition for Kelly." Since she'd recently bought a small, cozy home in Seattle after forgoing a paycheck for most of the summer, her finances were tight. "I start later this week."

"And then my daddy came back in, and we put the beepers back in his briefcase and your purse and we got 'em mixed up." Kevin continued his explanation with an exuberant array of hand and arm motions.

"We won't do it again," Kelly promised, an angelic expression on her face, "'cause we know beepers aren't a toy. Right, Kevin?" She elbowed her brother dramatically.

Kevin nodded vigorously in response.

So, Meg thought a little shakily as she slid the correct beeper back into her purse, that much was settled. As for the rest... With a heart that was filled to overflowing, she looked at the child she had given up shortly after birth. What were she and Brody going to do? She was still precariously close to tears, wanting to take her little boy in her arms and hold him tight, yet knowing that would scare him. The overwhelming love and joy pouring out of her heart made it hard for her to hold on to her composure.

Meanwhile, Brody—who seemed to be struggling with

the same feelings—finally tore his eyes from Kelly and looked back at Meg. His dark eyes were glimmering with tears. "I don't know about you," he said in a low husky tone that seemed to come straight from his soul, "but I'm thinking it might be a good idea to leave early for the day and go somewhere and talk."

Meg nodded, knowing Brody was right. They had to get things settled, and fast. "Why don't you and Kevin come over to our place for dinner this evening?" she asked casually. Knowing how much of a take-charge guy Brody could be, she wanted to have this family meeting on her turf.

"Yippee!" Kevin and Kelly held hands and jumped up and down. "We get to play together!"

Brody caught Meg's eyes and his face split into a wide grin. "Sounds good to me, too," he said, already pulling out his cell phone. "Just let me call my office and tell them to reschedule a meeting for tomorrow."

"ARE YOU NERVOUS, Mommy?" Kelly said.

Meg put down her hairbrush and turned away from the mirror in her bedroom. "Why would you ask that?" she said as she sat down on the edge of the bed to put on her sneakers.

Kelly perched beside her on the bed and bounced up and down, as if she were on a trampoline. "'Cause your cheeks are all white and you're frowny-faced, and your hands are shaking. You look kind of like before you go onstage where you're doing something new and you're a little bit scared." Kelly paused and asked curiously, "Whatcha call it when that happens?"

"Stage fright," Meg supplied, thinking her little girl knew her too well. And her little boy—well, he didn't know her at all.

"Yeah, that's what you look like you got," Kelly announced loudly.

Meg drew a deep breath. Out of the mouths of babes…

Kelly was right. She was frightened and on edge. And for no logical reason. She was a professional actress. She would hide her nerves and lingering feelings for Brody Taylor and act as if he meant nothing to her except as the father of her children.

"It's just been a long day, honey," Meg explained with a weary smile.

"For me, too," Kelly said. She curled her lithe little body into a ball and did a slow-motion somersault across the bed.

Her daughter looked no worse for wear, Meg noted affectionately. In fact Kelly was more exuberant than ever as she hopped back down onto the floor.

"Can I take Kevin outside to play on my new swing set when he and his daddy get here?" she asked.

"If you promise to stay in the backyard and not be too rambunctious," Meg cautioned.

Kelly abruptly came to a halt, folded her arms at her sides, stood stiff as a little toy soldier and regarded Meg seriously. She flattened her chubby little hand over her heart. "I promise I'll behave."

Meg smoothed the hair from her daughter's face and bent to kiss her cheek. "That would make Mommy very happy."

Kelly vaulted into her arms and hugged her back. "Me, too."

The sound of car doors slamming had them both turning and looking out the window. Meg caught her breath at the sight of her ex-husband and son in a shiny new, forest-green SUV.

"They're here!" Kelly shouted. Looking as if she had

just gotten the best gift in the whole world, the little girl threw up her arms in excitement and raced down the stairs toward the front door.

BRODY CLIMBED OUT OF the SUV and circled around to help Kevin out of the rear seat. "Don't forget the cake!" Kevin reminded his father, as soon as his feet hit the drive-way.

"I won't." Brody reached past his son to grab the two bakery boxes on the other side of the bench seat.

"Do you think Kelly likes German chocolate cake as much as we do?" Kevin asked.

Brody knew Meg did. "I don't know," he replied. "But if she doesn't, she can always have one of the vanilla cup-cakes. Those are good, too."

Kevin happily fell into step beside Brody as they walked up the curving flagstone sidewalk to the cozy, two-story home Meg had purchased for herself and Kelly. The pale pink brick Tudor with slate-gray shutters and roof, and white trim, was small—Brody guessed it to be about sixteen hundred square feet, if that. But it had special touches, like a bay window and a pretty etched-glass and wood front door. It was located on a shady, quiet street, not far from Brody's place and the day care. Two shade trees graced the front yard, and flowers had been planted in neatly tended beds that rimmed the shrubs and porch, providing a riot of color against the manicured lawn. It all seemed to fit Meg's personality.

Before they reached the porch, Kelly threw open the door. The sight of his little girl standing next to Meg brought a lump to Brody's throat. He'd told himself for so long that he and Meg were doing the right thing, separating the kids and remaining so far apart, but now it felt as if they had made a gigantic mistake, allowing each other to miss so very much of their children's lives.

"What's in the white boxes?" Kelly skipped out to greet

them, while Meg lingered, smiling uncertainly, in the portal. Gone were the formal teaching clothes she'd had on earlier in the day. In their place was a pair of old jeans and a pale yellow oxford cloth shirt that, although comfortably loose, did nothing to hide the sensational figure beneath. Reluctantly, Brody tore his gaze from her full breasts, slim waist and curving hips, and returned his attention to her face. As he studied her lovely features, her emerald-green eyes and long, reddish-brown hair, something else stirred in him, as well. His whole body tightened and his heart began to race. This was no good, he told himself sternly. Thinking like this would only make him want to take her to bed again. And that was damn well not going to happen. Not when there was still so much discord between them, simmering just beneath the surface of cool civility they had forced themselves to adhere to ever since their divorce.

"We brought dessert!" Brody said, surprised at how casual and carefree his voice could sound, when he was all torn up inside.

"Yeah, we got cupcakes and cake," Kevin added excitedly.

As Brody stepped into the house and handed Meg the two boxes, their hands brushed, sending a current of awareness shooting through him. He turned away quickly, watching instead as Kelly took Kevin's hand and announced, "Mommy said we can swing on my swing set in the backyard."

Meg looked up at Brody. "Is that all right with you? The yard is fenced, and the kitchen windows overlook the play area, so we can keep an eye on them while I finish preparing dinner."

"Sounds good," he said, before turning to caution Kevin. "No rough stuff, okay? I don't want any skinned elbows or knees."

"I promise," Kevin said as he raced after Kelly.

"Bye!" she shouted, throwing up a hand.

They barreled out the back door, across the flagstone patio and onto the grass. Meg and Brody followed as far as the kitchen window, where they stood for a second, watching the twins climb onto the child-size wooden play fort, which had two swings hanging from one end and a slide on the other. Brody couldn't help but note that Meg looked every bit as emotional as he felt.

She turned to him briskly. "What are we going to do?"

Inside, all Brody felt was wistful. And he wasn't a wistful kind of guy. He swallowed, forcing himself to put his emotions aside, and asked in the most disinterested voice he could manage, "Do about what?"

"The kids." Meg drew a deep breath and held his eyes as she plunged on in a low, rusty-sounding voice. "Now that they've met—"

"We can't keep it from them." Brody cut her off abruptly, guessing what she was about to say.

"The question is," Meg said, as cautious as ever when it came to anything emotional, "how do we break it to them?"

Without sounding like completely untrustworthy parents, Brody mentally added.

"How about straight out?" he suggested matter-of-factly. When Meg made a face, he shrugged. "Maybe if the two of us don't make such a big deal of this, or act as if our meeting was anything out of the ordinary, the kids won't perceive it that way, either."

Meg looked at him as if to say *Fat chance.* "Aren't you being a bit too pragmatic?" she responded coolly.

Brody edged closer, trying all the while not to notice how deliciously feminine she smelled. Like fresh-cut flowers on a warm and sunny day. "The twins are going to respond according to our cues, Meg," he said quietly. "If we act like it's a horrible emotional ordeal, then that's the way they'll feel.''

Meg's lush lower lip quivered slightly. ''Our splitting up *was* a horrible emotional ordeal,'' she said throatily.

No joke, Brody thought. He had been miserable for months and months afterward, and he suspected from the too-cheerful tone of Meg's letters back then that she had been, as well. ''But they were too young to know that,'' Brody reminded her as he braced a hand on the counter beside her.

''I just don't think it's going to be so simple,'' Meg said, slumping back against the counter and folding her arms in front of her.

Giving in to impulse and the need to comfort Meg, Brody touched a hand to the side of her face. Her skin was as silky and warm as he recalled. Her lips looked just as kissable. ''It's going to be as simple as we want it to be,'' he told her softly. Feeling her lean into him, feeling her yearn as much as he was for their lips to touch, he bent his head, determined to explore the physical heat still simmering between them.

And heard the back door slam.

His whole body thrumming with frustration, Brody reluctantly moved away. As he did so, he saw the disappointment in her eyes, too. Like him, she was wishing they had kissed. Just to see... But it was too late. The moment of near intimacy had passed.

''Hey, whatcha doing? Is dinner ready yet? Can we have Popsicles?'' Kevin and Kelly asked excitedly, both talking at once.

''Mommy and I are having a conversation. And the answer is no. And no.''

''Huh?'' Kevin blinked.

''Sit down, kids. We have something we want to talk to

you about.'' Brody patted the backs of two chairs at the white café table with a decorative ceramic-tile top.

"Wait a minute, Brody…'' Meg's delicate hand curved around his biceps.

Deciding swiftly that absolutely nothing could be gained by drawing this out any further, and that things were likely to get a lot worse if they made a big emotional production out of it, Brody ignored the mixture of wariness and hesitation in her eyes. "I know what I'm doing here, Meg,'' he murmured quietly. Determinedly, he ushered her into a chair and sat down before turning his attention back to the kids. "You know how we told you that you both had a twin and a parent living on the other side of the ocean?'' he asked casually.

Kevin and Kelly nodded vigorously, clearly having no clue as to what was coming next. "Well, Kevin, Meg is your mommy and Kelly is your twin sister. And Kelly, I'm your daddy and Kevin is your twin brother.''

They blinked at him, and Meg looked as if she was about to slug him.

"We can't be twins,'' Kevin protested immediately.

"Kevin and me don't look the same. To be twins, you have to look the same,'' Kelly explained, as if Brody were a total dunce.

"You two are fraternal twins,'' Meg clarified gently. "That means you were born at the same time, but you don't necessarily look the same. Twins that look exactly the same are called identical twins.''

To Brody's amazement, the twins appeared as if they couldn't have cared less. Or maybe the information was too much to deal with. At least there were no tears, no recriminations. "Can we go back outside now?'' Kevin demanded impatiently.

"Yeah. And can we take Popsicles with us?'' Kelly pleaded.

Once the kids were outside again, Brody turned to Meg. "Well, that went well, don't you think?" he said, feeling both satisfied and relieved.

Meg glared at him. "You autocratic know-it-all." She pushed the words through gritted teeth. "How could you?"

CHAPTER TWO

BRODY, MEG NOTED, had the grace to blink at her in stunned amazement.

"How could I what?" he echoed.

She strode forward until they were standing toe-to-toe. Hands on her hips, she glared up at him contentiously. "Just barge on ahead and tell them without first discussing it with me!"

"We did discuss it," he reminded her with easy familiarity.

"No, Brody," Meg corrected sternly, warmth climbing from her neck into her face. She turned so her back was against the kitchen counter. "You gave your opinion and decided that was that, without even listening to me."

A muscle worked in his cheek as he shifted around to stand directly in front of her. "Someone had to take charge of the situation," he countered heatedly, his gaze narrowing in silent challenge.

"Then why not me instead of you?" Meg demanded even more emotionally.

Brody squared his powerful shoulders and started to speak, then stopped. No matter. Meg had an idea what he had been about to say, and she didn't like it one bit. "Because you're always right and I'm always wrong?" she asked in a saccharine tone meant to irk.

Silence fell between them as Brody continued to stare at her without an ounce of apology. Finally, he shook his head. "Delaying the inevitable would have only made it harder."

Meg shrugged. "Says you."

"Says anyone with a lick of common sense," Brody countered even more firmly. He stepped closer, so their bodies were less than an inch apart, and braced a hand on either side of her.

Meg tilted her head back and they stared at each other in mute dissatisfaction.

"I don't believe this," she murmured cantankerously at last. They were so near she could feel the heat and strength emanating from his body, see how closely he had shaved before coming over. Worse, she could feel how much she still wanted him and he wanted her. But then passion, fierce physical passion, had been the one constant between them. Their desire for each other had thrown them headlong into a tempestuous love affair and marriage. And it was plainly persisting, even after their divorce and five long years apart.

Brody arched a brow and regarded her for a long, thoughtful moment. "Believe what?" he prodded softly.

Although she flushed and tipped her head back, Meg didn't move away. "Five years have passed and you haven't changed one bit!" He had never taken her feelings or ideas seriously.

"Like you have?" He scowled, every bit as annoyed as she was. "You're just as stubborn and determined to do things your own way and nobody else's."

Meg released a long, tremulous breath. "Well, so much for any attempts at peace," she said grimly.

"We could get along if you would just listen to me and stop making a mountain out of absolutely everything."

"I've been making my own decisions for the past five years and have managed very well, thank you," she retorted resentfully. "I don't need anyone dictating to me." That was the problem with her ex. Although he could fuel her emotions like no one else ever had or ever would, Brody had always insisted on having the final say in everything. And she hadn't been able to live that way. She had needed an equal voice in their marriage. She'd needed Brody to listen to her, and she wasn't sure he had ever done that. When it came to the bottom line, it was simply his way or the highway. And while his natural leadership abilities had given him the guts to go out and start his own software company from scratch, and made him a great CEO of Taylor Software, it had also made him a lousy husband.

"Okay," Brody conceded reluctantly, "maybe I should have let you do some of the talking to the kids just now."

Meg was sure he was just saying that because he thought it would bring some peace. She tossed him a wry smile and moved away from him. "And you should have consulted me about exactly when and what to tell them."

"But the bottom line is that it worked out okay," Brody continued. "They weren't the least upset."

On the surface, anyway. "Or even curious, really," Meg added aloud, not bothering to hide her puzzlement. Knowing how precocious their children were, she had expected dozens of questions and lots of interest on their part. Perhaps even resentment or anger at all that had been denied them. Instead, the twins hadn't seemed to care that they were all related.

The back door banged again, interrupting Meg's thoughts. Kelly and Kevin came inside carrying their sticks and paper wrappers. Their faces, hands and forearms were smeared with cherry Popsicle.

Kevin marched right up to Meg and tilted his head to look up into her face. "Does this mean you're my mommy, too?" he demanded.

Meg's throat constricted unbearably. If he only knew how much she had longed to be able to claim him these past five years. Her heart aching with the loss she had felt, she nodded, unwelcome tears filling her eyes. "Yes," she said raggedly. "I am." And because of her and Brody's stupidity, she had already missed so very much of her young son's life.

"Good." Kevin launched himself at her, wrapped his arms around her middle and held tight. He buried his sticky face in her clothes. "'Cause I always wanted a mommy all my own," he told her.

That did it; the tears Meg had been holding back rolled down her cheeks. Meanwhile Kelly marched up to Brody, tilted her own head back and gazed up at him.

"Yes," Brody said, his voice sounding abruptly tender and sentimental, "that means I'm your daddy, too."

Kelly smiled, albeit a little more shyly than Kevin. Her eyes shining with happiness, she wrapped her arms around Brody and clung tightly. "Goody," she said. "'Cause I always wanted a daddy, too."

The four of them stood together like that for a long blissful moment, then the kids grinned. Grabbing hands, Kelly and Kevin let out wild yelps of glee that resounded in the cheerful kitchen. "Now we get to be a family!" Kelly said.

KELLY'S ANNOUNCEMENT hit Brody like an arrow to the heart. How he wished life were that simple. But it wasn't, and he couldn't let the twins jump to any erroneous conclusions that would end up hurting them.

"Whoa," he said calmly, holding up a hand, even as he caught the discreet I-told-you-this-wasn't-going-to-be-so-easy look in his ex's eyes. He hunkered down so he could be on eye level with both twins. "We're all related, but…"

"But what?" Kelly asked, when Brody didn't continue immediately.

For once, Meg was not the least bit eager to take charge of the conversation. Instead, giving him a look that let him know this was his mess and he would just have to get out of it on his own, she walked calmly to the drawer beside the kitchen sink, wet two clean washcloths and brought them back over to the kids. She handed one to each of them and watched while they washed the stickiness off their faces and hands.

"But we're not going to live in the same house," Brody explained as gently as he could.

"Why not?" Kevin demanded in acute disappointment.

Pulling out a chair, Brody sat down and lifted Kevin onto one knee and Kelly onto the other. As he looked down into their cute little faces, he resolved to make this as easy as he could for them. "Because your mother and I are divorced," he explained kindly.

Kelly and Kevin took a second to mull that over. "Can't we get un-divorced?" Kelly suggested somewhat timidly as Meg stepped in to finish the job the kids had started, washing first Kevin's face and hands, then Kelly's.

"It doesn't work that way," Brody said in a calm voice. His glance followed Meg as she took the damp washcloths back to the sink, then returned to pull up a chair and sit down with them.

"How come?" Kevin asked. He slid off Brody's lap and onto Meg's.

Hell if I know, Brody thought, feeling discouraged and disgruntled, too. At the time of their split, divorce had seemed like such a sensible idea. And for a while, it had been, because he and Meg had been so bitter and angry and disillusioned with each other. Staying apart had been the only way to maintain any serenity in their lives. And by the time he had begun to have regrets and realize what a mistake they had made, well, it was too late. He and Meg had both moved on. And they were living an ocean apart. So he had done the honorable thing and kept to the promises he had made, and Meg had done the same.

Only now, Brody could see the loss suffered by all of

them because of his and Meg's selfishness. If he could undo it, go back and try to save their marriage for the sake of their kids, he would. But he couldn't. So they had to find a way to go on, as happily and contentedly as they could. Because there was no way, Brody decided, that he was going to let them all sink into the lifelong bitterness and resentment his own mother had, after his father left them.

Noting that Brody was struggling with what to say next, Meg cut in, speaking gently to both children. "We can't be a family and live in one house together," she said, "because sometimes it works better for a mommy and a daddy to each have their own home. That's the way it is for your daddy and me. But now that we're all living in the same city, and you two are going to the same school, we'll be seeing a lot of each other. And that's a good thing."

Brody thought so, too—if he and Meg could get their own emotions under control.

Kevin pushed himself off Meg's lap. Kelly vaulted off Brody's. "Can we go back out and play on the swings now?" Kevin asked, looking as bored with the discussion as his sister.

Meg nodded even as she cast a worried glance Brody's way. "Dinner's going to be awhile," she told the kids with a smile.

Kelly and Kevin ran outside, slamming the door after them.

Brody looked at Meg. Her emerald eyes were gleaming with emotion, her cheeks were flushed pink, but the anger was gone. In its place was a simple sincerity.

"Did you mean what you just said?" he asked her quietly.

Meg turned to face him. "About what?"

"About us seeing each other a lot."

Momentarily panic-stricken, Meg stared at Brody. Then, quickly regaining her poise, she turned away from him. "Of course I meant it," she said crisply in that no-nonsense tone she always used when she wanted to keep him at arm's length. "Now that they know—now that we're all here—we have to spend time together. It would be wrong to do otherwise."

Brody breathed a sigh of relief. "I agree. We are going to have to behave like a family, albeit a highly functional broken one, at least for a while." He had been afraid she would give him a hard time about this.

Avoiding his gaze, Meg headed for the refrigerator and continued her own list of stipulations. "But we're going to have to have some new rules."

Brody lounged against the counter, his arms folded in front of him. "Such as?" he prodded, when she didn't go on immediately.

Meg brought out the makings for a salad. "We discuss everything first. And I mean *everything*," she declared. "No more just jumping in and acting on our mutual behalf without clearing it with me first."

The contentiousness of her tone made him wary. "Or…?"

"We'll fight," she said plainly, her voice surprisingly soft as her gaze meshed with his, "and the kids will suffer. And neither of us wants that."

No, Brody thought wearily, they didn't. "Agreed," he said. It would be a pain, hashing out every decision ad nauseum, but for Kelly and Kevin's sake, he could do it.

"Good," Meg said.

Brody's gaze drifted over the slender curves of her hips as she turned her attention to the stove. "I know we've never had a formal visitation schedule…"

"And I don't want one now, either," Meg declared as she gave the simmering spaghetti sauce a stir.

Brody could understand that—he didn't particularly want to get lawyers involved, either, if the two of them could avoid it. "I want to spend time with Kelly, get to know her. And I want you to spend time with Kevin," he said.

"Absolutely."

"We could do it as a foursome," Brody suggested, wondering how far her new spirit of cooperation went.

Meg shook her head, her eyes darkening worriedly. "That might give them a false impression of togetherness where you and I are concerned. I think it would be better if we took turns having both kids at the same time. We could even call it play dates, to make it casual and non-threatening. The last thing I want is for the kids to feel like they're torn between the two of us."

"That sounds fine," Brody said, trying not to show his disappointment that Meg obviously had no interest in spending time with him. But he wouldn't give up, because it would be good for their children if the four of them did things together once in a while. The only problem was, he'd have to come to terms with the attraction he still felt for Meg. They had enough challenges ahead of them without adding sex to the mix.

"I STILL DON'T GET what you mean when you say we're frat-nell twins," Kevin said as they sat down to dinner in the breakfast nook in Meg's kitchen.

Meg smiled at her son, her heart bursting with happiness at the chance to spend time with him again. "Fraternal. And it means you were both in my tummy at the same time and you were both born on the same day."

"So me and Kelly's birthday is the same day," Kevin surmised. "And we're the same years old?"

"Yes," Brody said firmly. "You were both born on July fifth and you're both five years old."

"My daddy has a birthday in October," Kevin told Meg and Kelly.

Meg remembered with a touch of nostalgia. She had always loved celebrating with Brody. "I know. It's on the eleventh."

Not to be outdone, Kelly piped up. "My mommy had a surprise party at the theater on her birthday. They had a cake and flowers and everything!" She turned to Kevin. "Maybe we could give your daddy a surprise birthday party."

It's our *daddy*, Meg corrected silently, wondering just how long it would take before Kelly would really feel that way, and Kevin would accept her as his mother.

Brody spooned spaghetti onto Kevin's plate. "I want to play a game while we eat our dinner," he said, as if this little get-together was the most normal occurrence in the world. "Anyone want to play with me?"

"Yeah, me!" Kelly said.

"Me!" Kevin echoed, just as enthusiastically.

Brody looked at Meg. "Of course," she said, smiling, not about to be the spoilsport.

"I want to know what everybody's favorite thing to do is," Brody said. "I'll go first, and then we'll all take turns. I like to do things outside in the sunshine, like take long walks and ride bikes."

Kevin sat up really straight. "I like to go to parties and sing songs and dance and clap hands."

Looking handsome as all get-out in a long-sleeved, charcoal-gray knit shirt and jeans, Brody grinned over at Meg. "My Irish family had a lot of those."

Meg had surmised the Taylors were a lively bunch, close and loving. They were also overly helpful, in the sense that they were always meddling in Brody's business, she recalled resentfully. And in fact, if Brody's uncle Roarke hadn't taken it upon himself to help make all Brody's dreams come true by giving him the money to start his own computer software firm, with the caveat that the firm had to be based in Ireland, she and Brody might never have come to the loggerheads that led to their divorce.

"And I like to take walks on the village green with Fiona," Kevin continued.

Brody caught Meg's look. "Fiona is—was—Kevin's nanny."

She nodded. There was no reason to feel jealous about the fact that another woman had taken her place in her son's life. In fact, she ought to be happy Kevin liked his former nanny so much.

"I like parties, too," Kelly stated, getting the conversation back on track as she speared a bite of lettuce with creamy ranch dressing. "But I 'specially love computers, only we don't have one at home."

Meg smiled as she buttered a hot roll for each of the children. "The good news about that is we're going to be getting a computer honey. The university insists teachers be able to communicate with our students via e-mail, so I'm going to have to learn how to do that, too."

"Daddy can teach you how to e-mail," Kevin said. "He taught me so I could send messages to my uncle Roarke and my cousins. 'Cause they all have computers, too. But they can write fancier messages 'cause they're older and they know how to spell more words and stuff than I do." Kevin looked at Kelly. "It's fun. You can say 'hi' and 'bye' and 'I went to school' and stuff like that."

Brody looked at Meg, then Kelly, before he warned, "You have to be able to read, though."

"I can read!" Kelly propped her hands on her waist and looked insulted. "Mommy taught me phonics last year. And we read every night before we go to bed."

Meg nodded approvingly. "The writing is coming a little slower. Probably because we haven't worked on that as much, but Kelly can write simple sentences like 'I love you' and her name."

"I know my numbers, too, and I can tell time as long as it's divital," Kelly added proudly.

"Digital," Meg corrected absently.

"I think I'm too full to eat my dessert," Kelly said, pushing away from the table.

"Me, too." Kevin patted his tummy.

They'd both done a pretty good job with their dinner, Meg noted. "That's okay. We can always have it later, after the dishes are done."

Kelly slid off her chair. "Can I take Kevin upstairs and show him my room?"

"Sure," Meg said.

Once again, she and Brody were alone. "Excellent dinner," he said. "Thanks for fixing it."

Meg flushed with pride at his unexpected compliment. She hadn't cooked much when they were together—she hadn't known how—but she had gotten to be a pretty good cook in the time they'd been apart. "You're welcome." They suddenly sounded like awkward strangers, not two people who'd had children together.

"Kevin and I are going to have to return the favor and have you and Kelly over to our place," Brody continued casually.

She shouldn't be letting them get this cozy this fast, given all the reservations she still had, Meg realized, but she was reluctant to give up the chance to be with her son again. And right now that meant being with Brody, too. Doing her best to keep things on an even keel, she asked with forced cheer, "So? What else don't I know about Kevin, besides the fact he can do e-mail and type out simple messages?"

Brody shot her a contemplative look, aware she hadn't responded to his implied invitation, then stood and began to help clear the table. "He can use the phone and operate just about anything he's seen me use."

Their shoulders bumped as they fought for space at the dishwasher. "So can Kelly." Meg kept her attention diverted as she scraped the plates.

Brody fitted them in the dishwasher. "He has a photographic memory."

Meg smiled at that. "So does Kelly," she murmured, wondering why something as pedestrian as doing the dishes together should feel so exciting.

Brody put the salad dressings, Parmesan cheese and butter back in the refrigerator, then turned to her and grinned. "Kev wasn't kidding when he said he likes to party. The kid can really sing and dance. Put him in a room full of people and he thinks he was put there to perform for them." Brody paused and leaned against the refrigerator door, his gaze roving over her appreciatively. "He must get that from you," he murmured softly.

Meg tingled at the mixture of affection for Kevin and admiration for her in his low tone. Unable to help herself, she smiled, touched that although she and her son hadn't been together during his early years, they still had something in common. "Well, Kelly gets her love of computers and anything and everything electronic from you," she confided. "When I was trying to hook up our VCR and DVD players after we moved in here, she was the one who knew which cable went where."

"Sounds like she gets that from me, all right," Brody said cheerfully.

"They're awfully quiet up there," Meg observed as she prepared to take the kitchen garbage to the can out back.

"They're fine," Brody said with a look that implied she was ridiculous to worry. He held the door for her and followed her outside. He nodded at the wooden swing set in the backyard and walked toward it. "This is really nice." When he was close enough, he ran his strong, capable hands along the support beams and the swings and slide. "It looks brand-new. Did you put it up? Or was it here when you bought the house?''

Content to enjoy the cool, misty evening air, Meg edged closer. It would be dark soon, but right now everything was cloaked in dusky light. The air smelled fresh and clean. ''I called and had it put up.'' Leaning against the support post, she tilted her head up to look at Brody as they continued catching up parent to parent, instead of woman to man. ''I had promised Kelly when we moved here that I would get us a house with a backyard, and her very own climbing fort and swings. She was deliriously happy to realize that if she wanted to play outside, she could simply go into our very own yard.''

Nodding approvingly, Brody braced a hand just above Meg's head and leaned toward her. ''It must have been tough rearing a kid in New York City.''

Meg's heart raced at his nearness, yet pride kept her from drawing away. She shrugged her shoulders. ''It wasn't bad. Just different.''

Brody's gaze dropped to her lips once again, before returning ever so reluctantly to her eyes. He seemed to be struggling to understand her. ''Are you glad you're here?'' he asked quietly.

''Yes.'' Meg found herself unable to draw her gaze from his. The easy familiarity of the moment, reminiscent of their happier times, combined with the stillness of the approaching night to hold her momentarily spellbound. Knowing he was still waiting for an answer, she confided in a low, intimate tone, ''I was shuffled around so much when I was growing up. I want Kelly to have as normal a childhood as possible. She could have had that in New York had I not been working in the theater, or if we'd still been married and you were home to take care of her in the evenings.'' Meg paused, before straightening and moving away. ''But that wasn't the way it was, so, this is better. She'll be able to go to school and come home at night, not to a sitter, but to me.''

Brody caught her arm above the elbow and gently drew her to him. ''That's a heck of a sacrifice you're making for her, giving up the lead in a Broadway play after years of working in the trenches.'' He searched her face, nothing but admiration for her in his dark eyes. His voice dropped a notch as he continued, ''She doesn't realize the enormity of it now, but one day she will, and she'll thank you for it.''

Meg knew how much Brody had coveted being welcomed into the large, loving clan of the father who had deserted him years ago. His own mother had been so bitter after Brody's father had walked out on them, leaving her to bring up Brody alone, that she had barely been able to give him any attention or love. After his mother had died, in the early months of his marriage to Meg, he had done a genealogy search and discovered and then gotten to know his extended family in Ireland. When he found them to be wonderfully warm and loving, he had been over the moon. And Meg had understood and been happy for him. Family love was something she had yearned for, and not really received, in her own childhood.

''What about you?'' she asked gently as she let her guard down and leaned into his touch. ''Was it hard for you to leave Ireland and all your family there?''

''A little,'' Brody said. Taking her by the hand, he led her over to one of the bench swings. Meg sat down on the wide plank seat, and he took the other swing. ''Although I plan to take Kevin back and visit as often as we can, and I'll be returning alone on business. But I knew if I wanted Kevin to feel more American than Irish, he had to grow up here. So it was a sacrifice I willingly made.''

''We've changed in that regard, haven't we?'' Meg murmured as she tightened her fingers on the chains of the swing.

"Grown up?" Brody shrugged and twisted in his swing so he was facing her. "I think so."

Meg dug the toe of her sneaker in the grass. "When we were together before…"

One side of Brody's mouth crooked up in a remorseful smile. "It was our individual careers first, the marriage second."

She released a sorrowful breath and chose her words carefully. "I thought success in my career was the key to happiness."

Brody nodded, his handsome face reflecting his own regrets. "So did I."

"But once I really got into mothering," she admitted seriously, looking deep into his eyes, wanting—needing—him to know this, "I realized it was a lot more complicated than that."

"Same here," he replied huskily.

There was a growing tightness in Meg's throat. She was feeling sentimental again. Vulnerable in a way she didn't like. Nevertheless, there were things that had to be laid out on the table. "We have to make sacrifices for the sake of our kids."

Brody's eyes were so full of concern, she found herself wishing they could find it in their hearts to somehow make things right between them once again. To be, if not lovers, at least friends.

"The funny thing is, I don't mind it as much as I thought I would," Brody murmured conversationally. Slowly he got back on his feet and stood looking down at her.

"I don't, either," Meg remarked in honest surprise. Reluctantly, she pushed out of her swing, knowing they should go back inside the house, even if she didn't yet want to.

"Because," Brody said, catching her hands in both of his, "Kevin's happiness is everything to me."

Meg swallowed as Brody's warm grip tightened. "And Kelly's is everything to me," she confided sincerely.

A comforting silence fell between them. Meg felt closer to Brody than she had in years. Maybe ever. His head lowered, and she rose up on tiptoe. The next thing she knew, she was in his arms and they were kissing each other as if they had never been apart. Gently and tenderly at first, then hotly and rapaciously, until her mouth was opening to the plundering strokes of his tongue and desire flowed through her in waves. He kissed her until she moaned softly and clung to him. Until every inch of her was tingling. Heating. Wanting.

It had been so long since she had felt like a woman, instead of just a working single mom. So long since she had been loved, touched, kissed, held. So long since she had wanted to take someone into her bed and into her life, Meg thought as she strained against him, driven by a passion long held at bay.

But Brody was no easy man, she reminded herself. And the kind of unflagging devotion he wanted from her, and indeed any woman he chose to become involved with, was not easy, either.

Meg had had difficulty standing up to him, making her needs and wants known before. Without a child.

Now, with two…and a new job and a new home in the balance…she knew she'd be a fool to let her life become any more complicated than it already was.

Flattening a hand on his chest, she called on every ounce of willpower she possessed and pushed away from him. "No, Brody. We can't," she said breathlessly.

Brody let go of her arms and threaded his fingers through her loosely upswept hair. "Why not?"

She turned her head and felt his lips skim her temple,

softly, seductively. Damn, but she wanted him. "The kids—"

He kissed the exposed nape of her neck. "Are taking the news better than we could have ever dreamed."

"Exactly my point." Meg wedged her forearms between them, hoping that would halt the flow of sensations. But all it did was remind her of the warmth and solidity of his much larger body, and how it felt to be held against the muscled length of him, her heart pounding, her feelings in an uproar. She didn't want to be this susceptible. And especially not with Brody—the man who had given her everything she had ever dreamed of, and then broken her heart.

He lifted his eyebrows curiously. "Are we talking about the kids now?" he murmured, his expression gentling even more. "Or you?"

Meg gulped in air as she began to tremble. She forced herself away from him, trying not to notice the smooth muscles of his chest bunching beneath the cotton knit shirt. Forcing herself to think about the children, instead of the passion she still felt for their father, she said, "Kevin and Kelly are taking this a little too well, Brody. This was potentially devastating news you—we—delivered to them tonight. Especially now they can see what they've been missing all these years."

"So?" Brody became calmer as her emotions rose.

"So," Meg replied just as bluntly, "I think the big reaction we both sort of expected from them—the temper tantrums or acting out in some way—is yet to come." In fact, now that she really thought about it, she was sure that was the case. And she knew they had to be prepared.

Brody scowled and ran a hand through his hair. "Don't you think you're overreacting here?" he demanded unhappily.

"Borrowing trouble?" Meg queried, selecting one of his oft-used catch phrases from their time as husband and wife.

He clasped her arms lightly and looked down at her, his gaze intense. "Making a calamity where there is none. Yes."

"Well, kissing me just now didn't help." Meg moved away from him.

Brody followed her to the edge of the porch, leaning against the railing and regarding her, his eyes alight with a mixture of humor and desire. "I don't know about that," he drawled. "I felt a cease-fire there for a few seconds."

So had Meg. Which was precisely the problem. She had made a complete and utter wreck of her life by getting involved with him once, and she wasn't about to do it again. But how to tell Brody that, and get him to believe it, after the passionate way they had just kissed, she didn't know. She looked up at him. He looked down at her. And she had the feeling he was about to forget what she had just said, reel her in and kiss her again—until they suddenly heard a commotion in the vicinity of the back door. They both turned in unison to see Kelly and Kevin stick their heads out.

"You just stay right there and wait for your surprise!" Kevin called out.

The door slammed after them. And then clicked.

"Oh, no," Meg said.

Brody stared after the kids, looking as if he had just won the booby prize in a raffle. "Tell me they didn't just lock that door."

Meg slanted him a glance. She only wished that were the case. Too bad she couldn't feel victorious for being the one with the right prediction. "So much for them not acting out," she said.

CHAPTER THREE

"KELLY! KEVIN!" Meg commanded in her most authoritative voice. "You open that door right now!"

"We can't, Mommy!" Kelly shouted back just as determinedly.

"Yeah," Kevin added. "We're fixing you and Daddy a surprise."

Meg turned to Brody. He was standing right next to her, an equally displeased look on his face. "Well," she said, "this is the kind of emotional acting out I was expecting. It looks as if we're going to have to have a talk with them."

"Through the door?" Brody narrowed his dark eyes at her. Obviously, he didn't agree with her plan.

She tossed him a rueful look. "What choice do we have?"

Brody tucked his thumbs into the belt loops on either side of his jeans. "We order them to come out, that's what."

"We tried that," Meg said, exasperated, wishing Brody didn't look so capable when she felt so completely inept. "It didn't work," she explained dryly.

"Then we'll try again." Brody shouldered her aside and stood close to the door. "Kids!" he ordered in a booming voice. "Your mother and I are not fooling around here. We want you to unlock the door right this second!"

Meg could just make out the muted sounds of a lot of commotion and small quick footsteps on the other side of the door.

"Daddy, we told you," Kevin said after a minute, sounding peeved. "We can't."

"Yeah, you're just gonna have to wait until we're done in here." Kelly seconded her twin brother stubbornly.

"Done?" Meg echoed, thinking of the disastrous possibilities of two unsupervised five-year-olds in a fully equipped kitchen. Visions of overheated burners and sharp knives filled her mind. "What are they doing in there?"

Brody read her thoughts. "Kevin knows not to touch the stove," he reassured her firmly.

"So does Kelly," Meg said miserably, her worry increasing by leaps and bounds with every second that passed. "She also knows better than to do something like switch our beepers and disobey her teachers at school but that didn't stop her. Face it, Brody, moving has been very hard on both our kids, whether we want to admit it or not. And that was before they knew about us." Suddenly Meg had a very bad feeling about this, and her maternal instincts were almost never wrong. She rushed around to the front door. "Damn," she said as she rattled the doorknob. It was locked, too. But then she knew that. She was the one who'd locked it after Brody and Kevin had walked in.

She rushed back around to the rear of the house. Because it was already getting dark and she hadn't expected the kids to go into the yard again, the miniblinds in the breakfast area had been lowered for the night. All that left was the window over the kitchen sink, and she couldn't see into that from the ground. "You're going to have to lift me up," she said. Brody cupped his hands together in front of him and Meg slipped her foot into them. With both hands anchored on his broad shoulders, she hoisted herself up. To her dismay, she couldn't see what the kids were doing from that vantage point, either, but she could hear them very well, and they were completely hyper.

"We've got to get in there!"

Brody looked just as frustrated as she felt. "You don't have a spare key hidden somewhere?"

"No," Meg said, chastising herself silently for the lack of foresight, even as her next idea hit. "But there is a window open on the second floor, in my bedroom," she suggested brightly. "We could get through that."

"If we could get up there." Brody eyed the window thoughtfully, then appeared to come up with a plan of his own. "I'll be right back. You stay here and continue trying to talk them out." Giving her no chance to argue, he raced off.

Meg spoke through the door to the kids, but to no avail. Either they were making so much noise they couldn't hear her, or they had just decided to ignore her. She couldn't tell which. She was about to give up when Brody rounded the corner, an extension ladder tucked under his arm. Not bothering to mask her amazement, she asked, "Where did you get that?"

"Your neighbor across the street. I spotted one in his garage when we drove up."

"Good thinking." Her heart filled with a mixture of gratitude and relief, Meg watched as Brody propped the ladder against the side of the house and climbed up. It took him no time at all to get the screen off and push it into the bedroom ahead of him. Then he was gone. Not about to be left behind, Meg climbed up after him, slid her leg over the windowsill and followed him down the stairs. She reached the kitchen hard on his heels, and gaped at what she found there—Kevin and Kelly and the biggest mess she had ever seen.

"We're fixing everybody dessert," Kelly announced.

And they hadn't, Meg noted, stopped with vanilla cupcakes and fat slices of German chocolate cake positioned sloppily on dinner-size plates. They had gotten out the ice cream, whipped cream, cherries and chocolate sauce and were in the process of making giant, messy ice-cream sundaes in the center of the plates. The good news was they had used an ice-cream scoop, and the blunt-edged cake server instead of a knife. The bad news was they had gotten more frosting, cake and ice cream on the table, the floor and themselves than the actual plates.

"Oh, Kelly," Meg sighed. Kelly had never misbehaved so much in her entire life as she had with Kevin.

Brody scowled at the two of them. "Kevin, you're having a time-out, just as soon as we get home tonight."

"Fiona wouldn't have made me have one," Kevin pouted.

"Well, Fiona isn't here," Brody countered.

Tears of disappointment welled in Kelly's eyes. "Don't we get dessert?"

"Yeah. We worked real hard," Kevin added in their defense. He looked more put out than upset.

"And besides," Kelly complained in a low, choked voice, "it was Kevin's idea. He said—" She stopped abruptly when her twin glared at her.

"What?" Meg prodded.

Kelly looked back at Meg. "That if we made dessert, you'd pay attention to us and you wouldn't tell any more secrets. So we did!"

"Well, Kevin, we have a rule in this house." Meg looked at her son gently but firmly. "If you make a mess, you have to clean it up." She slid the ice cream back into the freezer, along with the dessert plates, then handed the kids paper towels and the spray bottle of dish soap and water she kept for quick cleanups. "So you two get started while your dad and I go in the other room and discuss what we're going to do about this. And there better not be any misbehaving this time. Got it?" She looked at both twins. They nodded solemnly.

Satisfied all was calm for the moment, Meg motioned

Brody into the living room. He looked at her, unimpressed. "Before we decide on a punishment, we have to talk," Meg told him.

He shrugged his broad shoulders. "I've already decided what I'm going to do. Give Kev a time-out." He gave her a telling look. "And I suggest you do the same."

Meg smiled tightly. This dictatorial manner was so typical of Brody. He might be a CEO at work, but he was not the executive in charge here. She perched casually on the piano bench, her back to the keyboard. "I'm not really into time-outs as much as teaching responsibility. They make a mess, they clean it up. They say something mean, we find out why and they apologize."

Brody studied her as he paced back and forth. "More cause and effect."

"And reparation, yes," Meg said in the softest voice she could manage. She watched as Brody pulled up an ottoman to sit directly in front of her. "I want our children learning that if they're part of the problem, they have to be part of the solution. It's a much more proactive approach than simply putting them in a corner. It makes them think and helps them learn about actions and consequences and putting things to right."

"Sounds...effective," he admitted grudgingly.

Meg smiled, encouraged by the fact he was at least taking her seriously. "It is."

"Okay, then—" Brody started to get up.

Meg caught his arm, propelling him back onto his seat. "We don't need to help them, Brody. They can do this by themselves."

Brody looked skeptical. Clearly, Meg thought, he was not in the habit of giving their son much responsibility. "They'll use that whole roll of paper towels," he warned.

It was Meg's turn to shrug offhandedly. "I don't care. I want to talk to you about Kevin and what he told Kelly about getting your attention.'' She paused to search Brody's eyes. ''Exactly how long has he been acting out like this?''

Brody's mouth tightened. His expression became evasive. ''To this degree? Six months or so.''

Meg's heartbeat picked up. ''Do you know what prompted it?''

''I have an idea.''

Frustrated that he was being so uninformative, Meg said, ''Do you want to share it with me?''

Brody straightened. ''There were a couple reasons.''

Still Meg waited.

''For one thing, I was traveling a lot.''

''And another?'' she prodded.

''There was a lot of tension between me and his nanny, Fiona, and I think Kev picked up on it,'' Brody admitted reluctantly.

Now they were getting somewhere. ''Why were you quarreling with his nanny?'' Meg asked.

''We weren't fighting,'' he replied irritably.

''Then what was it?''

Looking guilty and reluctant, he did not enlighten her.

''Just how old was this nanny?'' Meg asked curiously when it became apparent her query was going to go unanswered.

''Twenty-three,'' Brody muttered. He scanned her face. ''But it's not what you're thinking,'' he added hastily.

Meg certainly hoped not. Her own father had been a well-to-do executive with a penchant for seducing the household help, both before and after his divorce from her mother. Meg had never expected Brody would behave in the same manner. On the other hand, whenever people lived under the same roof, a certain intimacy inevitably sprang up. And Brody had always been a very physically passionate man. ''Is Fiona pretty?'' Meg asked, figuring the answer to that would lead her to the rest of the story.

"What does that have to do with anything?" Brody demanded.

In other words, Meg thought ruefully to herself, the answer to that question was yes.

"Mommy?" Kelly abruptly appeared in the doorway, a contrite look on her face. Kevin was right beside her. He was also very subdued. "We're done cleaning up. And we're really sorry. You and Daddy want to come see?"

Meg nodded. "Yes, I do, honey." And she also wanted to know precisely what had happened between Brody and Fiona to create such "tension." But judging by the closed look on Brody's face, that information would not be forthcoming this evening.

ACROSS TOWN, a dinner party was going on in honor of Louis Kinard. Alexandra Webber wasn't quite sure what to expect as she arrived at the small, lovely home where Helen Kinard had moved twenty years earlier after her husband, Louis, was sent to prison and she was forced to give up the expensive, stately old home in Forrester Square in the Queen Anne district. Would the mood of the party be ebullient or subdued? Happy or simply relieved?

As a young child, Alexandra had also lived in Forrester Square, near the Kinards and their other friends, the Richardses. Back then, of course, they had all been more family than friends. But that had been before the fire that had claimed Alexandra's parents' lives and sent her to live with relatives in Montana. She still had nightmares about the fire, and being here again in Seattle, she felt uncertain and on edge. But Katherine Kinard and Hannah Richards had cajoled, flattered and persuaded Alexandra to join them as a partner in their new day care, and she had finally relented. She hoped the nightmares and anxious feelings would pass once she was among friends again. Smiling, she braced herself to ring the doorbell.

And was greeted promptly by Helen Kinard, who was dressed in a beautiful long-sleeved amber sheath. Now sixty, Helen was a little heavier than Alexandra recalled, but as lovely as ever. Her gray-brown hair was styled in neat waves, and her hazel eyes were alight with warmth. "Alexandra!" Helen engulfed her in a warm, maternal hug. "It's so good to see you, dear!"

Relief flowed through Alexandra, for this was indeed easier than she had thought it would be. She returned the embrace fondly and kissed Helen's cheek. "Thank you. It's good to see you, too."

Louis Kinard came up to welcome her, and Alexandra's heart went out to him and his wife for all they had been through. The twenty years he had spent in the Northwest Correctional Facility had left him thin. His dark hair was graying, but his brown eyes were alert and proud. Although the criminal case against him was airtight, he had always maintained his innocence. His wife, Helen, and his two children had stood by him firmly, knowing there was no way Louis would have stolen software technology and embezzled money from the company, Eagle Aerotech, which he had founded with Alexandra's father and Kenneth Richards. Alexandra really respected the Kinards for that. It couldn't have been easy, holding their heads up high amid all the ugly gossip and public scandal. But they had stuck together and gotten through it, their love for each other intact.

"How did the move go?" Helen asked cheerfully. "Did you get settled at Katherine's?"

"Yes," Alexandra was pleased to report. "And your daughter's home is really lovely." It was a small cottage in a quaint, quiet neighborhood, attractively maintained. The exterior was of gray slat siding, and flower-filled boxes adorned every window. The interior was filled with chintz furniture and lots of sentimental mementos, including photos from Katherine's childhood. "But then you know what a talented homemaker she is," Alexandra continued.

"As well as a foster mom." Helen beamed proudly as the front door opened again and Katherine came in, carrying an armload of fresh flowers from her own garden with her twelve-year-old foster son, Carlos Vega, by her side. Tall and gangly, he was dressed fashionably in clothes that were loose enough to go skateboarding in.

"Hello, everyone!" Katherine smiled happily at the assembled group of family and friends who had come to celebrate Louis's release from prison.

She was followed by her brother, Drew, and his fiancée, Julia Stanton, who held her baby, Jeremy, in her arms. Warm welcomes were exchanged, then Helen and Katherine went off to put the flowers in vases, while Drew disappeared with Carlos to check the latest baseball scores.

Olivia Richards, Hannah's mother, approached Alexandra to say hello. A stylish woman with light brown hair highlighted with gold, she looked as elegantly garbed and perfect as she had when Alexandra was a child. Katherine had told Alexandra that Olivia had recently had plastic surgery and it showed in her taut, unwrinkled face. The older woman looked thirty-six, not fifty-six.

"Alexandra!" Olivia took her hands and kissed both her cheeks. "Where are you staying?"

Alexandra disengaged her hands from Olivia's grip and took a step back even as she plastered a sociable smile on her face. "I've moved in with Katherine for now."

Olivia lifted one well-shaped brow. "I take it that's not a permanent situation?" she queried smoothly.

"No." Since reaching adulthood, Alexandra had never really wanted to live in any one place for long—least of all Seattle, the city where her parents had died. But Katherine and Hannah needed her help, as well as the expertise of her business management degree from Northwestern. She would stay here until she had made good on her commitment to her friends, then she would sell her share of the partnership back to them and move on again.

"I heard you're going to be working at Forrester Square Day Care, too," Kenneth Richards said as he came up to greet Alexandra and hand her a glass of wine.

Alexandra knew Kenneth had believed in his friend Louis's innocence. His wife, Olivia, did not, however, and that was one of the factors that had led to the Richardses' eventual divorce. Nevertheless, the two were acting civil to each other this evening, Alexandra noted with relief. And that was good. The Kinard family had been through a very difficult time. She hoped now that Louis had finally been released, they would be able to put the tragedy behind them.

"Yes, I'm really looking forward to getting to know all the children," Alexandra said. Although too much of a restless spirit to connect with anyone for long, she had always loved kids, loved being around them. Maybe because they were so innocent and pure of heart. Not all adults were.

"Well, we hope you decide to settle here permanently," Katherine said, coming back to join them. She smiled at Alexandra. "We've all missed you."

Alexandra had missed them, too, in her own way. But as to whether or not she would stay on permanently—that would depend on her nightmares. If they worsened while she was here, it wouldn't matter how much Katherine and Hannah needed her at the day care. She would have to leave again, go back to contract consulting jobs in various cities, and once again assume the lifestyle of a rolling stone.

"MOMMY?" A pajama-clad Kelly appeared in the doorway to Meg's bedroom just as Meg climbed into bed. Her dark eyes were clouded with worry. "Are you still mad at me?" she asked softly.

Meg shook her head. Her exasperation had long since faded. "No, honey," she said gently.

"Just disappointed," Kelly guessed unhappily as she spread her arms wide and touched her fingers to either side of the door frame.

"And frightened." Knowing this was a situation that needed further discussion, now that emotions had cooled, Meg motioned her daughter closer. "I didn't like being unable to get to you that way."

"In case of an emergency." Kelly yawned sleepily and crawled into bed beside Meg.

"Right."

"And Kevin and I need to be supervised."

"Yes, you do."

Kelly rested her head on Meg's breast and wrapped her arms around her. "We won't do it again," she promised, cuddling close.

"Good," Meg said. She buried her face in her daughter's hair, breathing in the sweet baby-shampoo scent.

"Do I get to tell everyone tomorrow that I have a daddy now?"

Meg's lips curved into an ambivalent smile. She was happy that Kelly's dream of having a complete family, albeit a divorced one, was coming true, yet sad that things hadn't worked out better for Brody and her and their children in the first place. "Yes," she said, rubbing Kelly's back with soothing, circular motions.

"And Kevin can tell people he has a mommy?"

"Yes."

Kelly released a contented sigh. "That makes me happy, Mommy. I always wanted a daddy. And Kevin says he always wanted a mommy, too. "Except…""

"What, honey?" Meg prodded.

"He had Fiona," Kelly murmured, even as she struggled to keep her eyes open. "She was just like a mommy, even if she wasn't really his mommy, and he still misses her lots.''

They cuddled some more, until Kelly was nearly asleep, then Meg took her back to her own bed and tucked her in for the night. Her thoughts in turmoil, Meg returned to her own room and reached for the treasure box of cherished mementos she had driven across the country herself, rather than trust to movers. On the top were photos of Kevin and Brody in Ireland—Kevin sitting on Brody's shoulders at age two, riding a tricycle at age three, climbing a backyard jungle gym at four. Both Brody and Kevin looked healthy and happy in all the pictures.

But then, Meg thought as she sorted through the box for a single black videotape with a pair of silver wedding bells on the cardboard sleeve, she and Kelly had been happy, too.

A little lonely at times, though, she admitted to herself as she popped the tape into the VCR in her bedroom and pressed the play button. But that was to be expected. Being an actress and single mom hadn't left much room for anything else. And she had expected—or was that hoped? she wondered with self-effacing honesty—it had been pretty much the same for Brody.

The wedding arbor set up on the shores of Lake Tahoe came into view. Music played, and there were smiles all around as Meg walked down the aisle toward the waiting, tuxedo-clad Brody. Meg couldn't help but note how young and pretty she looked in the antique white lace Gibson girl gown, with her hair done up and adorned with flowers. Her pregnancy had not been evident at that point. She and Brody both seemed happy and full of hope for the future. They'd thought at the time they would be able to work things out, that the two of them would always be together.

But it hadn't happened that way, Meg recalled sadly. It had taken little less than a year for their marriage to fall apart. They had told themselves and everyone they knew that they were splitting up because of career conflicts. But deep in their hearts they had both known they were divorcing because they had realized that physical passion and an unexpected pregnancy were not enough to base a marriage on. They had needed love, the enduring kind of love between a man and a woman, and that was the one thing Meg and Brody had never been sure about.

Now, having achieved the theatrical success she had always yearned for, Meg knew there was more to life than simply work, just as she knew that she and Brody had entered their marriage with a lot less determination than they had needed to succeed over the long haul. She regretted that now. She wished they had tried a little harder to find the kind of love and understanding to make their hasty marriage last. Or at least found a way to keep themselves in both their children's lives.

But she couldn't turn back the clock. She and Brody simply had to soldier on, despite their past mistakes. They had to concentrate on being good parents to Kelly and Kevin. To give their children the security of a family, which they'd both obviously longed for, yet at the same time maintain the independence that both she and Brody valued.

It wouldn't be easy, given the chemistry still flowing freely between them. But it could be done. And anyway, Meg told herself fiercely, her thoughts straying to the passionate way Brody had kissed her after supper, and the abandoned way she had kissed him back, it didn't really matter that her desire for Brody was as strong as ever. What counted was that the two of them had never been able to make their relationship work on any practical day-to-day level.

But, oh, how she wished they had been able to do just that, Meg thought wistfully.

Because everyone knew a loving, intact family beat a broken one any day.

CHAPTER FOUR

MEG WAS JUST PUTTING AWAY the music when Julia Stanton walked in, her infant son, Jeremy, cradled in her arms. Though Julia had recently survived a murder attempt by her uncle, a well-known senator, she was now looking forward to her upcoming marriage to Katherine Kinard's younger brother, Drew.

"How did your first music class with the kindergartners go?" Julia asked, her blue eyes sparkling with encouragement.

"Great, actually." Meg wasn't sure which group she liked teaching best, her college students or the kindergarten kids. Both were challenging in ways she found very exciting. "The kids couldn't have been more cooperative today."

"That's great to hear." Julia smoothed a hand across Jeremy's downy, white-blond hair. "Listen, I was just in the office talking to Katherine and Alexandra."

With effort, Meg tore her gaze from Jeremy's angelic little face. "And you heard about Kevin being my son." Meg guessed where this conversation was leading, since she'd had more or less the same one ever since she'd arrived at the day care center early that afternoon.

"And Kevin Taylor's father, Brody, is your ex-husband!" Julia continued, perching on the tall swivel chair Meg had been using.

Meg picked up the rhythm sticks and slid them into a cloth sack. "It's true."

Julia shook her head in amazement. "What an astounding coincidence to have both twins turn up at the same school."

Or fate, Meg thought wistfully, wishing that hopelessly romantic dreams could come true in real life as easily as they did in movies or plays.

"Everyone's saying it's destiny."

"Well, whatever it is, I'm sure it will be a good thing, because our kids will now have two parents."

Hope shone on Julia's pretty face. And why not? Meg thought. Jeremy's father had been killed before Jeremy was born, and now, instead of facing a future as a single mother, Julia was about to have everything she had ever dreamed about when she married Drew at the end of the month.

"Are you and Brody going to be able to work this out?" Julia asked.

That depended, Meg thought dryly, on what she meant by "work out." "I think we can be civil to each other for the sake of the twins." Meg finished putting things away, then turned back to Julia. She knew she hadn't sought her out just to probe about the latest developments in Meg's life—she wasn't that kind of person. "What's brought you in here?" Meg asked curiously.

"A couple of things." Her son began to fuss a little, so Julia stood up to walk the floor with him. "First, I'm going to be working here, too. That way I'll have a job I love and great day care for my baby."

"That's wonderful." Meg knew how much it had meant to her to have a job that let her be near Kelly as much as possible.

"And Drew is beginning proceedings to legally adopt him."

Meg had spent a fair amount of time talking to Drew Kinard the day she had come in to sign her teaching contract. "He'll make a great father and husband," she said.

"I think so, too." Julia beamed as she brought out a pacifier for Jeremy to suck on. "Anyway, you know we're getting married next month."

"Right."

"On the morning of Saturday, October eleventh."

Brody's birthday, Meg thought.

"And Drew and I would like you to sing at our wedding."

Meg gave Julia a hug, delighted to have been asked. "I'd be honored. Let me know when it's convenient for you and Drew to meet with me and we'll select the music you want me to sing."

No sooner had Julia left than Amy Tidwell walked in. The eighteen-year-old part-time teacher's aide looked at Meg expectantly. "Katherine said you needed to talk to me?"

"Yes, Amy, I do," Meg said urgently. "It's parents night for the kindergarten students and I really need a sitter for Kelly. The person I had lined up fell through. I know Katherine's arranged child care here, but I think I'd prefer Kelly to be at home."

Amy played with the sandy braid that fell nearly to her waist. "I've already accepted a job—with Brody Taylor. But if you want," she suggested enthusiastically, "I could watch both Kelly and Kevin at the same time. It'd be no problem."

BRODY SAT DOWN to have a talk with the twins before he left for the kindergarten's parents night.

"We promise we'll behave," Kevin told Brody as he prepared to leave both children with Amy Tidwell.

Beside him, Kelly nodded vigorously. "Mommy says I have to. So we're not gonna get in any trouble tonight *whatsoever.*"

That certainly sounded like Meg, Brody thought. He

looked at Amy. Unlike most kids her age, she had eschewed the tight and revealing clothes fashionable these days for a pair of baggy jeans and an oversize sweatshirt, bearing the name of the high school where she was currently a senior. "You have my beeper and cell phone numbers?"

Amy nodded. "As well as Meg's. And the fire department and the EMS. And both pediatricians. I'm sure we're going to be fine." She pointed to the game of Candyland on the coffee table. "But if you get worried about us, Mr. Taylor, you can call. A lot of parents do that, especially when they have a new sitter for their kids."

Brody was impressed with Amy's businesslike approach to the evening ahead as he continued down his list of do's and don'ts. "No boyfriends."

"Absolutely not."

"And I don't want you chatting it up on the phone, either."

"Of course not, Mr. Taylor. I would never do that. My friends don't even have this number."

"And of course you are not to leave the house or drive the children anywhere. I don't want any running out to the video store on the spur of the moment or anything."

"No, sir. I promise you that will not happen."

Kevin tugged on the hem of Brody's sport coat. "Daddy, you better go or you're going to be late."

Kelly nodded solemnly, every bit as concerned about Brody as her brother. "Mommy left a long time ago."

Unfortunately, Brody hadn't been home when Meg had dropped Kelly off. He'd been out picking up a pizza for Amy and the kids. "All right," he said reluctantly as he bent down to kiss and hug each child in turn. "I'll see you later."

Amy looked relieved when Brody finally walked out the door. After the fifteen minutes of very detailed instructions he had given her, Brody could hardly blame her. He knew he was being ridiculously overcautious, but he couldn't help it. He was accustomed to leaving Kevin with a live-in nanny he knew he could trust, not a teenager. But that problem would be solved as soon as he found another nanny. In the meantime, he would have to do what Meg did—adapt an abbreviated work schedule and manage with the help of baby-sitters.

When he arrived at the day care, Brody went to the kindergarten classroom first. Meg wasn't there but he accepted a handout from the twins' teacher, Carmen Perez, and learned about the impressive curriculum the kids would be studying. A question and answer session followed, then all the parents in attendance were directed to the events room next door, where story hour and music and theater classes were held.

Meg stood behind the podium, looking lovely in a vibrant blue dress with a matching bolero jacket. As he walked in, her eyes met his. He wasn't sure what he saw in them. Wariness? Pleasure? Whatever it was, it was quickly shuttered as she turned back to the other parents in the classroom. As soon as everyone was seated, she began to speak in the gentle lyrical voice that had fueled his fantasies and haunted his dreams.

"As most of you know, I've been hired to teach music and dancing and basic theater performance to the two older classes, the four-year-olds and the five- and six-year-olds. We'll be doing several musical programs throughout the year, and the first will be held later this month. So we look forward to seeing you all there."

Meg spent the next ten minutes steadfastly avoiding eye contact with Brody again as she went over some of the songs the kids would be singing, the activities and games they would be doing, and then took questions for another ten. Brody began to feel a little irked. He didn't want special treatment just because they had once been married, but he would like to be acknowledged, rather than invisible to her. Was this how it was going to be when they were both at the day care? He hoped not. He had never liked being summarily dismissed.

As soon as Meg had finished, Katherine Kinard came in, holding up a list in her hand. "As you all know, the success of any school depends greatly on the level of parental involvement. Therefore we're asking every parent to sign up on at least one volunteer sheet before you leave this evening. The lists are in the hallway on the tables we've set up, so if you could do that on your way out, we'd greatly appreciate it. In the meantime, we invite you to look around, go to the dining area and the kitchen, where you can have some cookies and punch, and check out the play yard. As always, the other staff and I will be available to answer any questions you might have."

The parents chatted with each other, spoke to Meg again, then filtered out a few at a time. Seeing Meg was busy, Brody ambled out to take a look at the sign-up sheets. Then he went out to check the play yard, stopping first to partake of cookies and punch and chat with other parents. By the time he came back inside, the school had pretty much emptied out. Meg was standing next to the table with the sign-up sheets. She looked up at him, and she wasn't pleased.

"I see you signed up to help me," she said, her tone feisty, her green eyes glimmering with obvious resentment.

Brody nodded. Not wanting anyone else to overhear what they had to say to each other, he stepped even closer.

"That's very sweet," Meg continued in a brisk, businesslike tone, "but wouldn't you be of more use training the children in the computer lab?"

In other words, she didn't want him hanging around her. He wondered what she was afraid of—another kiss? Or that one kiss would lead to more? No matter what happened between them, he wasn't going to run from it. He didn't intend to let her do so, either. As far as he was concerned, they had already done enough of that. "I signed up there, too."

Meg tossed her head imperiously and color swept into her cheeks. "You'll have time to do both?"

Something about her attitude urged him on, dared him to teach her a thing or two about trying to dictate what he did. At home or at the day care. "I'll make time," he told her evenly.

Without replying, Meg turned and walked back into the events room. Ignoring the fact that he was right behind her, she gathered up the extra information sheets she had prepared for the parents. Brody shut the door to the classroom. "You're obviously displeased," he said. And he wanted to know why. He'd thought—erroneously, it seemed—that she would appreciate his willingness to become friends again and help her with her job.

Meg swung around to face him. With her riot of curls smoothed into an elegant chignon at the nape of her neck, she looked very slim and chic and pulled together. It made Brody want to take her hair down and unzip her dress…and make her his. Only she wasn't his. And she was doing her darnedest to remind him of that.

"I'm confused," Meg countered in the low, soothing tone Brody had heard her using with other parents. "I just…" she paused, drew a deep, bolstering breath, and looked him straight in the eye. "Brody, you don't sing or dance or build scenery. You've never had any interest in those things."

True, Brody thought, studying the flush of color in her cheeks. The same blush that appeared whenever she was physically close to him. The same blush that appeared when they kissed. Finally assured of her attention, he moved even closer. "I can create programs with the desktop publishing software made by my company, print the programs out in color, e-mail parents to remind them of the performances, and do any other publicity-related tasks you might have for me.'' All those were things she would have difficulty doing, given her lack of computer expertise.

''I hadn't thought of that,'' Meg said ruefully.

''Is there some reason you don't want me working with you?'' Brody asked, tracking the rapid rise and fall of her breasts and the agitated sparkle in her eyes.

''No, of course not.'' Meg ducked her head.

Liar, Brody thought. He tucked a hand beneath her chin, forcing her gaze up to his. ''You wouldn't, by any chance, be afraid I might kiss you again, would you?''

Meg's eyes darkened in that hands-off way he recalled so well from the waning days of their marriage. She gave him a brisk smile and stepped away. ''Trust me—there is no chance whatsoever of that happening again,'' she said in a low, quavering voice.

''Sure about that?'' he taunted.

Meg cocked her head, considering. ''It wouldn't be wise.''

''But it would be fun,'' he countered softly. Not to mention pleasurable.

When Meg walked out of the room without another word, he realized she was only interested in protecting her heart from further damage. And that would be best accomplished by keeping all the barriers between them—physical, emotional, intellectual—as firmly in place as they had been since the day they had foolishly agreed to divorce.

HER HEART STILL POUNDING from the passion in Brody's eyes, Meg followed him to his house to pick up her daughter.

It wasn't that she didn't want to kiss him again. She did. More than he could ever know. She was just afraid that if she did end up in his arms again, she would soon find herself making love with him. Which might have been okay, if she could have separated her feelings from the physical act of sex. But she couldn't. For her it was one and the same. And right now she wasn't ready to have her emotions in an uproar once again. She wasn't prepared to be in a situation where she was constantly waiting for the ax to fall, as she had been when they were married. Precariously happy to have the family she'd always yearned for, but at the same time, scared it would soon be taken away. There'd been so little in her life she felt she could count on. Kelly was one, her work another. Meg didn't want either disrupted by renewing a romance that was guaranteed to have no future.

As for Brody, he tended to act quickly and take the most expedient path in his personal life. That was why he'd rushed her to the altar. Neither of them had been ready for marriage at that point in their lives. They should have looked for another solution that would have worked for the long-term. But they hadn't—and their hasty action had ended up hurting them both terribly.

So, like it or not, Meg reassured herself firmly as she pulled over to the curb behind Brody's SUV, her ex-husband was going to have to put his own needs aside and understand that she wanted to focus on their children's happiness right now, not their own....

Brody's new home was located in the exclusive Forrester Square section of Seattle's Queen Anne district. The sprawling white Victorian with pine-green trim sat on a beautifully landscaped two-acre lot. Amy's car was parked in the driveway. Behind it was a sleek black limousine.

Meg lifted a curious brow in Brody's direction as she joined him on the sidewalk leading up to the leaded glass front door. "I have no idea who it might be," Brody said. "I wasn't expecting any company."

Meg frowned thoughtfully. "It could be Amy's father, I

guess." Amy's mother had died years before, and her father, a wealthy businessman, kept a pretty tight rein on his daughter, according to Katherine. Possibly Russ Tidwell was checking up on Amy.

"Well, there's one way to find out." Brody slid his hand beneath Meg's elbow, unlocked the door and guided her inside.

The interior of his new home was as beautiful as the outside. The foyer rose two stories and was graced with an elaborate chandelier and a circular staircase grander than anything Meg had ever seen. To the left was an enormous living room. Two large jade-colored sofas and a pair of coordinating wing chairs flanked the marble fireplace. A game board was set out across the mahogany coffee table, and three pairs of shoes were scattered here and there, but no children and no baby-sitter were in sight.

From the rear of the house came the sound of boisterous laughter. "They must be in the kitchen." Brody led the way past a formal dining room, and media room to a big country kitchen with white cabinetry, a stylish black-and-white tile floor and black marble countertops.

Kevin and Kelly were seated at a large round table in front of the bay window, next to a tall, barrel-chested Irishman in an ivory fisherman-knit sweater and gray flannel slacks. His cheeks were filled with color and his eyes sparkled as he laughed with the children.

Amy was on the other side of the counter, taking a fresh pot of coffee off the warmer. "You're just in time!" she told Meg and Brody cheerfully. "Mr. Taylor brought scones for everyone! From Ireland, no less!"

"Baked fresh this morning," their unexpected guest said.

"Look, Daddy, Uncle Roarke's here!" Kevin announced happily.

"I can see that." Brody smiled, his own affection for his uncle clear.

Roarke swept a hand through his thick black hair and stood. "Meg, sweetheart, good to see you, too." He crossed to Meg and kissed her cheek. Mindful of Amy and the twins' eyes upon her, Meg returned Roarke Taylor's hug with mixed feelings. She was glad Brody had the warm and loving family he had always coveted, but she did not like Roarke's unabashed meddling, and never would.

"Hello, Roarke," she said quietly.

"Still pretty as ever, I see," Roarke continued.

"Thank you." Meg accepted Amy's offer of coffee with a grateful nod. "You look to be in fine health, too."

Roarke slapped his thigh. "That I am, girl. That I am."

"You should have let me know you were coming. I would have met you at the airport," Brody said.

His uncle shrugged his beefy shoulders. "I knew you were busy tonight. I didn't mind hiring a car for myself. And it gave me time to spend with both the children, for a change."

Meg winced at the dig. Not that she was surprised by it—she and Brody both knew how much Roarke had resented her decision to split with Brody, and deprive Brody—as well as the Irish Taylors—of contact with Brody's only daughter.

Roarke looked at Meg. "I understand you're teaching now."

"Yes."

"I may be speaking out of turn here—" Roarke continued.

"Then perhaps you shouldn't," Brody interrupted, stepping between the two.

"But you really don't have to work nowadays," Roarke said anyway. "Brody makes more than enough money to support all four of you in a style any woman would love to become accustomed to."

"Uncle Roarke," Brody cautioned in a low, warning tone.

He shrugged. "Just telling her the way it is."

Determined not to put their children in the middle of the conflict between her and Brody's uncle, Meg forced a smile and said in the sweetest voice she could manage, "Thank you for letting me know that, Roarke, but I prefer to support myself, and Brody is aware of that."

"I'm sure he is."

Amy looked uncomfortable. Meg couldn't blame her.

"How's the rest of the family?" Brody asked cheerfully, changing the subject as he attempted to defuse the tension between Meg and Roarke.

"Splendid," Roarke said, helping himself to another scone. "They all send their love. And so does Fiona, by the way." Roarke paused and looked at Brody meaningfully. "She asked me to tell you and Kevin both how much she misses you."

"I miss her, too," Kevin declared. "She makes really *really* good scones. With dried cherries and apricots and raisins."

Roarke smiled at Meg thoughtfully. "A man like Brody is very much in demand with the ladies, you know. Especially the young and pretty ones, like my grandnephew's former nanny." The look he sent Brody was chastising. "Matrimony is still very much a possibility, you know. All it would take is a ring and a proposal."

"Uncle Roarke..." Brody shook his head.

Roarke shrugged. "It's not like you two don't know each other. Four years under the same roof, in the most intimate of circumstances."

Brody looked at Meg. "Nothing untoward happened," he stressed.

"A man would have to be daft to turn away from such a devoted beauty," Roarke continued.

"Is that so," Meg murmured, her own temper rising right along with her suspicions.

"What are you talking about?" Kevin asked.

With an unconcerned air she couldn't begin to feel, Meg left that question for Brody to answer later, and looked at Kelly instead. "Honey, it's late. We really have to go. I imagine Amy needs to get home, too, since tomorrow is a school day."

"You're right. I do." Amy put the coffeepot back on the warmer. She smiled at Kelly. "Come on. I'll help you find your shoes." The two of them took off hand in hand for the living room.

"I'm stayin' right here with Uncle Roarke," Kevin announced as he slid onto the burly Irishman's lap.

"I'll walk you out," Brody told Meg.

She took a final swallow of coffee, then set her cup on the counter and murmured her goodbyes to both Kevin and Roarke. Disappointed that she had been deprived of any time alone with Kevin, she turned on her heel and headed out. She was halfway to the front door when Brody caught up with her and, giving her no chance to protest, steered her wordlessly into the library.

"You're upset," he said, "and I don't want you to be."

Can you blame me? Meg thought. After what his uncle had implied? "You know Roarke and I have never seen eye to eye on much of anything, Brody."

"Starting with my move to Ireland," Brody recalled.

Meg knew she had been right to be irritated with Roarke about that. "I never begrudged him the offer to help you start your company, you know that."

"You just resented the stipulation that the company be located in Roarke's village in Ireland."

"He knew I was a stage actress," she countered, her frustration rising despite her efforts to stay calm.

Brody gave her a steady look. "He thought you'd stay home after the twins were born."

"He was wrong." Meg folded her arms defiantly. "And so were you, if you really believed that." She had made it plain from the get-go that she intended to go back to work.

They glared at each other, and a muscle worked in Brody's jaw. Finally, he jammed his fingers through his hair and said, "Roarke is an old-fashioned guy. He believes a woman's place is in the home."

And Meg knew just who the meddlesome Roarke had in mind. "Like the young and beautiful Fiona?" she blurted out resentfully, before she could stop herself.

Brody's dark eyes narrowed in irritation. "Leave her out of this," he warned tightly.

Unaccustomed to the jealousy pouring through her, Meg retorted, just as cantankerously, "Why? Roarke didn't." And neither, Meg noted even more painfully, had their son. Her heart ached at the notion that Kevin cared more for another woman than he did his own mother. But that was the situation she and Brody had created when they'd decided to rear the twins separately, rather than move them back and forth across the Atlantic like pieces on a chessboard. "Roarke said Fiona is very devoted to you."

For once, Brody didn't argue. Which meant what? Meg wondered anxiously. Had the two been close to marriage? And if that had been the case, why had Brody left Ireland?

Amy appeared in the doorway to the library, Kelly at her side. "There you are! We wondered where you had gone."

"Are we ready to go, Mommy?" Kelly asked as she ran into Meg's arms and held on tight.

Meg looked down at her daughter's weary face and nodded. The truth was, she couldn't wait to get out of there.

CHAPTER FIVE

MEG HAD JUST PUT KELLY to sleep and gone down to the kitchen to make their lunches for the following day when the doorbell rang. Wondering who it could be at that hour, she rushed to the front door. When she looked through the viewer, she switched on the porch light. Brody was standing there, still dressed in the clothes he had worn to kindergarten night.

Meg opened the door. "What's wrong?" she demanded quickly, certain something must have happened. "Where's Kevin?" She looked behind Brody anxiously.

"Nothing's wrong," he told her with exaggerated patience. "Kevin is with Uncle Roarke. I just need to talk to you."

Piqued because he had scared the wits out of her, showing up unannounced that way, she replied with more coolness than she'd intended. "I think whatever it is can wait until tomorrow."

"No, it can't." Squaring his broad shoulders, Brody walked in without waiting for an invitation. He shut the door behind him. "We're not going to leave things unsaid."

"Fine." Meg rolled her eyes and blew out an exasperated breath. Knowing he wasn't going to leave before he'd had his say, she went back to the kitchen to resume making lunches. "What do you need to tell me?" she asked impatiently.

Brody lounged with his back against the counter, facing

her, his arms folded in front of him. "First, I know what you think, Meg, but Uncle Roarke did not try and break up our marriage."

Meg layered thin slices of mesquite-smoked turkey, Havarti cheese and lettuce in a pita for herself. "Then why did he offer you the chance to start your own company, but only if you did it in his village?" she demanded.

"Because the village was dying," he explained, obviously proud of what he had done. "There were no jobs for the people, no opportunity. My coming in and starting the company, and training the locals to help run it, saved the entire community, Meg. It attracted other industry and businesses. And the tax laws in Ireland are more conducive to starting a business than they are here in the States."

Meg felt small for having so strongly resented his decision. And she was infuriated that he hadn't explained all this to her—in detail—much earlier, instead of leaving her to think the worst about him. "You could have said no."

"And given up my dream?"

Finished with her own lunch, she began making Kelly's. "You knew I'd been offered a supporting role on Broadway, that it was my big shot at a career in theater."

"Not," Brody reminded her succinctly, "until after I had already told Roarke yes."

Back then Meg had hated the way he'd put others first, ahead of her. She spread cream cheese on a bagel and tucked it into a sandwich bag. "So it was easier to disappoint me and tear apart our family than to tell him no thanks?" she asked sweetly, feeling the heat of her indignation climb from her chest up into her face.

Brody sighed as Meg added celery and carrot sticks to another bag.

"It doesn't matter, anyway," she continued. "We've both moved on. You with Fiona." *And me with…absolutely no one.* Because despite how much she'd tried, Meg seemed unable to find a man to equal her ex-husband, at least as far as her affections were concerned.

"I did not have a romance with Fiona," Brody insisted, scowling.

That wasn't the way Roarke told it, Meg thought to herself. "Really," she countered dryly, managing to avoid Brody's eyes.

He took her by the shoulders and forced her to face him. In a low, sexy voice that sent shimmers of awareness skimming over her, he said matter-of-factly, "She just wanted it to be more."

"And you knew—"

"That she had a crush on me?" he interrupted. "Yes. But Kev loved her, and she was so good with him, it seemed wrong to try and get someone else in to care for him when everything else was going so well. Plus, I figured Fiona would eventually find someone else to get romantically involved with if I just ignored the way she looked at me and let things run their course. I actually encouraged her to go out on dates."

Meg knew what it was like to be the recipient of an unwanted crush, but she also knew Brody well enough to realize he was leaving out some crucial part of the puzzle. "What happened to change things?" she asked quietly.

He looked less willing than ever to confide in her, but to his credit he said evenly, "Late one night Fiona came into my study after Kevin was asleep." He grimaced unhappily. "She was in this nightgown—I had only to look at her to know what was on her mind."

Oh, no, Meg thought.

Brody shook his head and continued in a low voice, "It was awful. She declared her love for me and tried to seduce me."

And, Meg thought, Brody blamed himself for all the months he had said nothing to discourage her.

He turned to Meg in silent entreaty. "I wanted to fire her on the spot—for her own sake."

"But you didn't," she guessed, able to understand what a thorny situation he had found himself in.

Brody shrugged and slid his hands into the pockets of his slacks. "Had I done that, there would have been a lot of questions. People would have wanted to know why, and if they weren't told, they would have speculated. In any case, I knew I had already hurt Fiona by my handling of the situation." He sighed and ran a hand through the short, neat layers of his hair. "The village is small and I wanted to spare her further humiliation. She was still pretty upset that I was not going to be asking her to marry me or accompany me and Kevin to Seattle when we moved, but she seemed to accept it graciously, and things went back to normal."

"Is that the real reason you didn't bring Fiona to Seattle with you to help with the transition?"

Brody nodded. "I realized I should never have allowed her to stay working for me, knowing how she felt, how sheltered her life had been. She's just very young, Meg. Very starry-eyed and idealistic." His voice was earnest. "I don't love her, Meg. And except for that one night, there was never even a hint of impropriety between us."

"You never kissed her?"

"No," Brody said firmly. "She had no reason to think what she did."

"Then why is Roarke pushing the idea of marriage?" Meg asked cautiously, still trying to understand his uncle's attitude.

Brody spread his hands on the counter behind him. "Because he wants me to have a wife and Kev to have a mother, and he knows how eager Fiona is to fill that role."

Meg was glad Brody didn't love Fiona, but she worried about the pressure he was getting from his Irish family.

Brody cared what Roarke and the others thought. And he cared about Kevin's happiness. Right now, Meg and Kelly were filling the void in Kevin's life that Fiona had left. But what would happen when Brody had to go back to traveling for business once again? Would he reach for what was easy and convenient—namely, Fiona? And why should it bother Meg so much if he did decide at some point to employ Fiona again? He had already said he was looking for a nanny, and hadn't been able to find one in Seattle that Kevin liked. He'd made it clear to Fiona he wasn't interested in her romantically. So why did just the possibility of Fiona reentering Brody's life unsettle Meg? Was she jealous? she wondered uncomfortably. And if so, what right did she have to be feeling that way, given how long she and Brody had been divorced?

"Look," she said, forcing herself to confront the issue. "I never for one minute expected that either of us would swear off romance or relationships with other people when we split up." She had just secretly hoped they would. Hoped that one day Brody would realize what a huge mistake he had made and come back to her. But it hadn't happened. And eventually, she had been forced to move on. Build a life for herself and Kelly—without Brody. Or Kevin. Yes, there had been lonely nights, and days. And rare occasions where she had attempted to date someone else. But those experiments at finding someone new had never worked out. And Meg had felt only relief, because deep down, she hadn't really wanted anyone to take Brody's place in her heart. She had preferred to be alone rather than settle for anything less than what she'd felt for Brody.

"You're telling me you were—or are—serious about someone else?" Brody demanded, looking every bit as jealous as Meg felt whenever Fiona's name came up.

She averted her eyes from his and concentrated on wiping the counter where she had been working. "I'm telling you that you have as much right to pursue happiness with someone else as I do, Brody. And I have been asked out on dates."

"Here in Seattle?"

Meg dropped the dish rag into the sink. "Yes."

"But have you gone?" Brody placed his hands on her shoulders and turned her to face him.

"Not yet," she replied stiffly, wishing Brody couldn't see through to her real feelings quite so easily. "But only because I've been too busy getting settled in," she fibbed.

Brody studied her silently. Meg could tell he was trying to decide just what she was really feeling. He leaned down so that his face was suddenly, dismayingly near to hers. "You didn't answer my question. Have you been serious about another man since we split?"

Meg battled the desire pooling low inside her. "I'm not going to answer you," she told him as she stepped back, away from his tempting presence. "And I'm not going to ask you the same question, Brody. It's really neither of our business." *And more important, she didn't think she could bear hearing his answer.*

"Isn't that just like you." Brody scowled.

Meg let her glance sweep over him as haughtily as possible. "Meaning?"

"Meaning…as much as you say you want to talk things to death, all you really want to do is sweep problems aside rather than come up with any solution that might mean you have to give ground—or in this case, information."

His words stung. Maybe, Meg thought, because they were true. She didn't want Brody to know how truly lonely she had been or how much she had missed him. Their inability to be truly honest with each other had been as great a problem as their unwillingness to compromise. And Roarke saw it. That was why he was pushing Brody to move on, to find happiness with another woman who apparently would give in to Brody's every whim.

Was Roarke right? Meg wondered uncomfortably. Would Brody—and Kevin—ultimately be happier with someone like that? A woman who was a lot more pliant and emotionally accessible than she was?

Meg didn't know the answer to that. She did know that she and Brody had hurt each other enough for an entire lifetime. And there was no way the difficulties between them would magically subside, at least not anytime soon.

"Thank you for coming by and setting me straight on the situation with Fiona, but it's late," she told him practically as she took his arm and steered him toward the door, putting up the force field around her heart once again. "Your uncle and Kevin are waiting for you, so you really need to be heading home."

"So how did it go? The little lady still mad at you?" Uncle Roarke said when Brody let himself back in the house.

Still smarting from Meg's brush-off, Brody went to the bar and poured himself an inch of good Irish liquor his uncle had brought with him. "What makes you think she was mad at me?" he asked casually, wishing that his uncle didn't see quite so much when it came to Meg.

Roarke lifted his glass in a silent toast. "Sonny boy, I know a jealous woman when I see one. She still loves you. Problem is, she's probably not any more right for you now than she was when those babies of your were born. What you need is a woman who will stay home and take care of you."

"Like Fiona?" Brody said dryly, knowing Kevin's ex-nanny was the last person he required in his life. The woman he needed, wanted—and would probably never have—was Meg. Their five years apart had taught him nothing if not that. Because no matter how he had tried, no woman had ever begun to take Meg's place in his heart. Or make him want her the way Brody still wanted Meg.

But his uncle didn't see that, Brody noted.

"You should give Fiona a call," Roarke persisted in his usual all-or-nothing way. "Or better yet, fly her over here for a week or so to help you and Kevin get settled."

Brody had left Ireland to get away from such familial interference in his life. But he owed Roarke a lot. Roarke had believed in him and backed him in a way no one else ever had. Roarke had made Brody's dreams of owning his own business and becoming wealthy—more important, secure—come true. So Brody couldn't give Roarke the bum's rush, no matter how irritating and intrusive his advice on Brody's personal life was. So he simply said, "I'll take your advice into consideration, Uncle Roarke." And he let it go at that.

AWARE SHE HAD a good thirty minutes before she had to teach at the day care, Meg decided to stop in at Caffeine Hy's for a cup of coffee. She had never been in the coffeehouse, located on the east side of the day care, but it looked both charming and welcoming, with its deep mustard and apricot walls, old beaded floor lamps, paper wall sconces and mismatched chairs. A variety of scarves and cloths in different textures and colors were scalloped on the ceiling, along with original origami figures.

"I don't think we've met," said the tall, dark-haired, dark-eyed man behind the counter. "I'm Hyram Berg, the owner of Caffeine Hy's."

"I'm Meg Bassett, a part-time music teacher at the day care next door."

"You've got a child enrolled there, too, don't you?"

"Actually, I've got two." Meg smiled, aware how good it felt to be able to lay claim to both children.

"So what can I get you?" Hy asked as Meg settled on one of the stools next to the service counter.

She studied the chalkboard menu of daily specials. "I think I'll have a double latte, and a couple of those chocolate almond biscotti."

"You got it." Hy filled her order with the ease of a seasoned professional. Because business was slow at the moment, he continued chatting with her, telling her about some of the other businesses in Belltown.

As they were talking, a bearded man in scraggly-looking clothes walked by outside. He had a gentle, almost otherworldly air about him. "I've seen that man here every time I go in or out of the school," Meg said. "Who is he—do you know?"

Hy shook his head. "He's one of the homeless people who were flushed out of the tunnels beneath the city a few weeks ago, during the fire. He's a sweet old guy, but he won't tell anyone who he is or talk about his past much. All he will say is that what happened yesterday or tomorrow is not nearly as important as what's happening today."

Meg sipped her delicious latte, then glanced back at the mysterious stranger. "So he doesn't have any family?"

"Not that I know of." Briefly, Hy looked as troubled about the older man's situation as Meg felt. "Anyway, I feed him whenever he shows up," Hy said. "I've offered to help him, but right now he just isn't interested."

IN AN EFFORT TO DEFUSE the heightening tension between them, Meg managed to avoid talking to Brody directly for the rest of the week, but by Friday her excuses and tactical maneuvering were wearing thin. Brody was obviously aware of what she was doing, and when he came to pick up Kevin that afternoon, he waited until she was free to have a word with him. "Kevin told me that you and Kelly are planning to purchase a computer this weekend,'' he said casually.

Glad the workweek was over, Meg continued packing up her things in the kindergarten room. Carmen Perez and Alexandra Webber were talking over by the window, so Meg smiled at Brody cordially. ''Yes, we are.''

''Maybe Kev and I could help you,'' he suggested as she headed into the events room to finish tidying up.

From a practical standpoint, Meg knew she needed the assistance. She had no one else as knowledgeable about computers and software as Brody was to go to for advice. Nevertheless, she didn't feel she could impose upon him, especially after the way they had parted earlier that week. ''Helping me purchase and set up a computer is not your responsibility, Brody,'' Meg said kindly.

Brody paused to help her put away the kazoos that had been left on the child-size chairs. ''Then how about we call it a favor between friends in exchange for a home-cooked meal for Kevin and myself?'' he suggested lightly, dropping the instruments he had collected into a box.

Meg put the lid on the box. ''You still haven't learned to cook?'' she queried, her cheeks warming slightly as she held his steady, probing gaze.

''Nope.''

Meg hesitated. ''What about your uncle Roarke?'' If he was still in town, it would be rude not to invite him, too, but Meg didn't relish the idea of spending an evening in his company.

Brody moved closer. ''He went to Austin to check out a struggling software company there. He thinks we should acquire it.''

Meg turned and carried the box over to the music supply shelf. ''What do you think?'' she asked casually, wondering just how far Brody's ambition stretched.

He lifted his shoulders in a shrug. ''I want to see the

information Roarke gathers before I decide if I want to consider it."

"And since you're the one who actually runs Taylor Software…" Meg began.

"My decision will be final, either way," Brody told her in a steady voice. "So what do you say?" His gaze drifted leisurely over her face before returning to her eyes. "Kevin has been asking me to spend more time with Kelly outside of school, and I'm dying to get to know my daughter better. It's Friday night. You have something that needs to be done, and I can help you do it. Think about it." Meg's resolve began to weaken as Brody continued to persuade her. "Those desktop models are pretty heavy. I could carry the components, plug in all those cables, help you choose an Internet provider and even get you set up."

"Okay, okay." Meg put up both hands in surrender. "You win. You can help me."

Together, they collected Kevin and Kelly and headed down to the store Brody had selected. To Meg's relief, Brody was able to explain to her exactly what she needed and why. It was all in stock, and the purchase was speedily completed. By five-thirty, they were walking in the door to her home. Kelly went into the living room to help Brody set up Meg's new computer on the desk, while Meg headed to the kitchen to commence her end of their bargain.

"What're you doing?" Kevin said as he climbed up on a stool at the center island.

Pleased to have one of her children taking an interest in what she was doing in the kitchen—Kelly always seemed so bored by cooking—Meg tore her gaze from his handsome little face and said, "First I'm going to dredge this chicken in flour and spices, and then I'm going to sauté it in a little butter and oil in the skillet, until it gets nice and brown." While that was happening, Meg sliced mushrooms and put water on to boil.

Kevin hunched forward and propped his face on his up-turned hands. His green eyes were filled with lively curiosity. "You know how to cook real good, don't you?" he said, obviously impressed.

Resisting the urge to run a hand over his curly, reddish-brown hair, Meg smiled at him. "It's an important skill to have, if you don't want to eat in restaurants all the time."

Kevin let his head fall to one side, then the other. "Fiona used to cook for us all the time. I liked to watch her in the kitchen, too. She explained things to me, too. But Daddy doesn't like to cook, and he didn't like to be in there with Fiona when she was cooking, neither," Kevin stated emphatically. "He liked to work, instead."

And still did, Meg thought disparagingly, as she considered the number of times his cell phone had rung when they were doing their errands. Although, she admitted, he'd kept the conversations short. He was clearly making more time for his family now than he had when the two of them were married. Would that last? She didn't know. The only thing she was certain of was that she didn't want to start relying on Brody, because they weren't married anymore. And she couldn't allow herself to act as if they were.

"Something smells great in here!" Brody said from the doorway. Kelly was perched piggyback-style behind him.

Trying not to think how good it made her feel to see her daughter so thoroughly enjoying time with her daddy, Meg removed the chicken from the skillet, set it aside and added the mushrooms to the sizzling pan.

"Can we help?" Brody asked, as Meg slid the garlic bread into the oven.

Conscious of how easy it would be to get used to this kind of happy family atmosphere, Meg went back to the stove. This all might feel very good to her and the kids right now, she warned herself sternly, but she had to keep her own expectations realistic. This was more an anomaly than a reality. "Aren't you still working on the computer?" she asked casually, aware that Brody had gotten even more ruggedly handsome in the five years they'd spent apart, more at ease and in command of his surroundings. He looked like a CEO now. He looked…content, in a way he never had when they were married.

"It's all set up," Brody said. "The software comes already loaded on it, so all I had to do, once I got the components hooked together, was get you connected to the Internet. I can give you your first lesson on how to use it after dinner."

"Daddy already showed me," Kelly announced proudly, as Brody let her down onto a stool. "He let me play a game."

Brody went to the sink and washed his hands. "It's a counting game for children. Made by my company."

"It teaches me how to add and subtract," Kelly announced proudly. "It was fun."

"So how can we help?" Brody asked, edging closer still.

"Why don't you set the table?" Trying not to notice how sweetly familiar it felt to have him back in her life, Meg poured the prepared salad ingredients into a bowl and added Italian dressing.

With Kelly's help, Brody put out the plates. Kevin helped place the silverware and napkins. Meg smiled at her kids approvingly. This was what she had been missing in her life, she realized. She wondered if Brody had been secretly yearning for it, too. But there was no deciphering his innermost thoughts as they all sat down to have dinner together.

BRODY TRIED TO TELL himself it was just Meg's talent for making even the most mundane activity a special event that he had missed during the years they had spent apart. But as he got up to help her with the dishes, and the kids ran off upstairs to watch a Charlie Brown video on the TV in Meg's bedroom, he had to admit it was more than that. Much more. He had missed seeing the way the light caught her hair, and watching the sparkle in her eyes when she talked about anything relating to her passion for music and art and theater. He had missed the sound of her laughter, the beauty of her smile, the compassion in her eyes. He had missed her.

And he had missed seeing his beautiful daughter grow up during the first five years of her life. Brody knew they couldn't get the time back, but they could make up for it now. And that was precisely what he intended to do. Providing, of course, he could convince Meg to let the four of them spend as much time together as he wanted. But he figured that consent would come in due course. Right now, he just needed to be content with what they had at the moment. In his business he was always looking ahead, planning for the future, but he knew that if he pushed Meg too hard, she would erect even more barriers to keep him out.

"Ready for your first e-mail lesson?" he asked as she hung up the dish towels and turned off the lights in the kitchen.

Meg regarded Brody with a mixture of dread and bravura. "The sooner the better, I suppose," she sighed.

"You don't need to look quite so much as if you're approaching the guillotine," he teased.

"I can't help it," she protested. "You know how much I hate having to deal with electronics."

"Except stereo equipment. As I recall, you're pretty good at hooking those components together," Brody said.

"That's because I need them for my music," Meg explained. "Otherwise, I'd never have forced myself to learn."

"Well, this is just as simple," Brody promised. "You'll see."

Fifteen minutes later, Meg had to agree. "That's it?" she

asked, amazed, after they had sent several test messages to the e-mail address Brody had set up for her.

"That's it," he said. "If you like, I'll set up an address book for you with the names of all your parents and students, and anybody else you'll need to e-mail. That way, all you'll have to do is click on their name, and their address will appear automatically."

"That would be great," Meg said.

Just then, two little bodies came flying down the stairs.

"We saw it, Mommy!" Kelly cried excitedly.

"Yes," Kevin enthused. "We sure did."

"Saw what?" Brody asked, perplexed.

Kelly and Kevin beamed. "The video of you two getting married!"

CHAPTER SIX

BRODY TURNED TO MEG, who was blushing a very becoming pink, and lifted an inquiring brow. He'd figured their wedding video was something she would have thrown out.

"I never seen it before," Kelly continued.

"Never saw it," Meg corrected absently as she got up and walked away from the computer, avoiding Brody's eyes all the while.

"Then how'd you happen to find it?" Brody asked curiously as Kelly slid onto one of his knees, and Kevin, the other.

"It was in the VCR," Kelly explained happily. "I turned it on, and Kevin hit the play button and before I put my tape in, we saw you and Mommy all dressed up."

Brody turned to Meg, who was blushing all the more as she pretended to straighten the music stacked on top of her baby grand piano. "You were watching it?" he asked her softly. That had to mean she was feeling as sentimental, and perhaps even remorseful, about their split as he was lately.

Meg shrugged a slender shoulder, as if it were no big deal. "I saw it the other night. I came across it when I was unpacking, and just out of curiosity, I slid it into the machine. I wouldn't read anything into it," she said hastily.

"Of course not," Brody murmured, although he did read quite a lot into her actions. She wouldn't have been watching it if she hadn't been feeling at least a little in awe at spending time with each other again. The same as he was. "If you're not that attached to it..." he began.

"I'm not," Meg said quickly.

"Then maybe I could take it home with me this evening, take a look at it myself?" he suggested pleasantly.

"Of course you can." Meg continued straightening stacks of music while Brody shut down the computer.

"Are we still gonna get ice-cream cones for dessert?" Kelly asked, cuddling close to Brody's chest.

He looked at Meg. She seemed to have recovered her composure.

"Absolutely," she said.

As soon as the four of them had settled down with their ice-cream cones at a white, wrought-iron table in a corner of the ice-cream parlor, Kelly asked, "How come you're not married anymore?"

"Darling, I explained that to you," Meg said with a reassuring smile. "Daddy and I weren't getting along."

"Sometimes you and I don't get along and you tell me we have to do better," Kelly said. "How come you and Daddy didn't do better?"

"Yeah," Kevin interjected, scowling thoughtfully as he struggled to understand what had happened. "You both had happy faces when you were giving each other rings and kissing and stuff. So how come you didn't stay happy?"

Out of the mouths of babes, Meg thought. She looked at Brody for help.

"It was complicated," he said finally, looking as much at a loss to explain the demise of their marriage as she was.

"Did you love Mommy when you married her?" Kelly asked between licks of her chocolate cone.

Brody and Meg exchanged looks. Had they been in love? Or was it merely infatuation, due to the passionate nature of their affair, as they had later concluded?

"Of course we cared about each other," Brody said firmly.

Good answer, Meg thought, reaching over to dab at the chocolate dripping off Kelly's chin.

Kelly struggled to understand. "Do married people always love each other?"

"Usually, yes," Meg confirmed, aware they were getting into dangerous waters here.

"It's when they get divorced that they don't love each other no more," Kevin explained to his twin.

"Anymore," Brody corrected. "And that's correct."

"So are you going to stop loving us?" Kelly's eyes abruptly filled with tears. Seeing her, Kevin followed suit.

"No, of course not." Meg put down her own cone and hurried to soothe both children. "Your daddy and I will always love both of you," she promised sincerely, looking them each in the eye. "Nothing will ever change that."

"Yes, but you stopped loving each other," Kevin pointed out.

Meg picked up her ice-cream cone with one hand and rubbed at her temples, where a headache was starting, with the other.

"That's different," Brody explained patiently. "The love between a man and a woman is something else entirely. It's a lot more complicated."

Never more so than when applied to the two of us, Meg thought.

Brody exchanged a worried glance with Meg, then turned back to the kids, a reassuring expression on his handsome face. "You'll be able to understand better when you're older. But for now, all you two kiddos need to know is that your mommy and I love you very much and we will always love you, so you don't need to worry about that. Okay?"

Kevin and Kelly were silent, thinking. They looked at each other, seemed to communicate wordlessly, then turned back to Brody and Meg. "If you hadn't stopped loving each other," Kelly said, "would you still be married right now, right this very minute?"

Brody and Meg looked at each other. What could they say to that? Meg finally shrugged and answered for them. "Yes," she said.

"SO IT'S SIMPLE," Kevin explained to his twin when their mother went off to get some damp cloths for their sticky hands, and their father was throwing their trash away. "We want to be a family again, and live together in the very same house. So all we have to do is make Mommy and Daddy love each other again, just like they did when Mommy wore that sparkly crown in her hair and they got married."

"How are we going to do that?" Kelly asked, frowning at him as if he were the biggest dope in the whole wide world. "Mommy doesn't *want* to love Daddy, Kevin."

"But if they got married again, they *would* love each other," Kevin whispered right back, just as urgently. "Because Mommy said all people who get married love each other."

Silence fell between them as they both took a moment to think about that. "Maybe we need a bouquet," Kelly speculated.

"And some rings?" Kevin suggested.

Meg came back to the table. She was all smiles as she ripped open two packets and handed Kelly and Kevin the hand wipes inside. "What are you two looking so serious about?" she asked cheerfully.

Kevin and Kelly turned to each other. They both knew some things were best kept secret. At least for now. Until they figured out how to make everything all right again.

"Nothing," Kevin said, pretending he wasn't up to something.

"Nothing," Kelly echoed.

Meg looked from one child to the other. Kevin could tell she was trying to figure out what they were hiding. So he ducked his head and buried his face in the wet cloth. His daddy always said you could get what you wanted, you just had to try hard enough. He wanted his mommy back. And his twin sister. So he was going to try real real hard to get them.

"CAN WE WATCH the wedding video again before Daddy and I go home?" Kevin asked the moment they pulled up in front of Meg's house. "Please? We've been really, really good tonight."

"It won't take long," Kelly said. "It was over really fast."

Meg knew. The ceremony had lasted less than twenty minutes.

"All right," she said, relenting. She wanted to talk to Brody alone, anyway. The twins raced upstairs, hand in hand. Meg watched them go, then turned back to Brody. "We've got to do something to take the stars out of their eyes," she said firmly.

"You noted those matchmaking looks, too, huh?" Brody said, sounding as if he didn't know whether to be amused or distressed by the twins' attitude.

Meg nodded. "It would have been impossible to miss, Brody. They want us back together again. They think it will solve everything."

"And bring us back together as a family."

"Right." Meg released a breath and rubbed at the tense muscles in the back of her neck. Brody had dropped down in the center of the sofa and was making himself at home. Seeing him, she felt a thrill of excitement mixed with a tinge of wariness. It felt so intimate having him here, so right. And that feeling increased as his gaze slid approvingly over the casual shirt and jeans she'd changed into before cooking supper. "But, you and I know that's not possible," she warned.

Brody's glance touched her lips, lingering briefly. "So why don't we take them down to Lake Tahoe tomorrow and show them what *is* still possible?"

Meg blinked. All she had to do was look at the expression on his face to know he had something up his sleeve. "I don't understand."

Brody shrugged. "They want us to get married to each other again because that way they think they'll have a mom and a dad and a brother and a sister all under one roof. You and I know that's not going to happen." He settled more comfortably on her sofa. "But we also know that good times—family times— can still be ahead for the four of us if we're smart about it."

Meg perched on the end of the sofa. "I agree with that. But, Brody! Tahoe?"

Tahoe was the place where she and Brody had first met and made love. The place where they'd married. The place where they'd decided once and for all that their marriage was over and it was time to get a divorce.

"What better place?" Brody suggested smoothly. "Everything significant in our life together has happened there." He paused, giving her a second to think about that. "Why not begin this new chapter there, too?"

BRODY KNEW MEG HAD ONLY agreed to go to Tahoe with him for one reason—she wanted to exorcise the demons of the past and focus on the practicalities of their future. He was not surprised. Meg had always run hot and cold where he was concerned. During the six months they were dating, she had been touring in a musical. He would meet her wherever she was performing, and she was always wildly passionate and romantic. But once she got pregnant unexpectedly and they felt forced to marry, everything changed. She knew she was going to be fired as soon as her pregnancy began to show, and her dream of heading back to Broadway with the other actors was ruined. It was only too obvious she felt trapped. Whenever she'd looked at him, it was with sadness and disappointment. Or worse, false cheer.

Suddenly, it had seemed as if both of them were trying too hard. Even the simplest conversations were stymied. Awkward. It was as if she'd put up a shield around her heart and forced him to do the same.

Now fate had conspired to bring them back together again. The passion was still there, simmering just beneath the surface. The kisses they'd recklessly indulged in had showed him that. But this time, all he wanted was to be friends—for their children's sake. He had no intention of breaking his heart over her again.

To BRODY AND MEG'S MUTUAL relief, the kids and their endless questions during the plane ride to Reno and the drive up the Sierra Nevada to Tahoe didn't include even a hint of man-woman intimacy. Once they had checked into the lakeside house he had rented for the rest of the weekend, things got a lot more hectic. They took the kids on a gondola ride, so Kevin and Kelly could see the majesty of the mountains surrounding Lake Tahoe. They ate a picnic supper by the shimmering blue lake, and donned sweaters to ward off the chill of the September air when the sun began to set. The kids were delighted to be with their parents on a real family weekend. But as Meg and Brody went to tuck them into the twin beds in the room they were sharing for the night, worry began to crease their faces once again.

"I think I just want to stay here," Kelly said as she wreathed her arms around Brody's neck and held her face up for his good-night kiss. "I don't want to go back to Seattle at all."

"Me, neither," Kevin stated just as emphatically. "I like it right here in this house."

"Oh, kids, I wish we could stay," Meg told them gently, kissing them good-night in turn.

"We have to fly back to Seattle tomorrow afternoon, so we'll be home in time to get rested up for school on Monday morning," Brody explained.

"I'd still rather stay here." Kelly pouted prettily, looking a lot like Meg when she was displeased, thought Brody. "Here I have a mommy *and* a daddy all the time."

Meg perched on the side of Kelly's bed and took her daughter's hand in hers. "Honey, we explained that you do have a mommy and a daddy all the time, even if we don't live together. Now, how about that story I promised you guys?" she said, pulling out her copy of *The Little Engine That Could.*

The twins settled down, displeased that they hadn't effectively made their case, but eager to listen to the story.

Aware that it was beginning to get a little chilly inside the house, Brody went to see about turning on the furnace and building a fire. He had just set the fire screen in front of the grate when Meg came out. She was wearing jeans and a sweater, and her fiery curls were caught up in a loose knot at the back of her head. With the heightened pink in her cheeks, and her green eyes vibrant and alive, she looked so beautiful it was all he could do to catch his breath. "Kids asleep?" he said, the desire he felt for his ex making itself known in the familiar tightening of his body.

"Yes." Meg toed off her sneakers and curled up on one end of the overstuffed sofa, while Brody went to open up a bottle of wine from a San Francisco vineyard that the leasing agent had left for them. "Thank goodness." She sighed. "I don't think I could have explained one more thing."

Brody filled their wine goblets and carried one over to

Meg. "You think we've got a problem on our hands, too, don't you," he noted, studying the anxiety on her upturned face.

Meg breathed in the fragrant cabernet and took a grateful sip. "The kids think that because we were happy today, we can be happy together all the time. They don't understand that the last time we were here, we were so miserable we had no choice but to divorce."

Brody dropped down on the sofa beside her, recalling with numbing clarity the last fateful time they had been to Tahoe. He took another sip of the wine and rested his glass on his thigh. "I remember that time, too. I'd brought you to Tahoe to tell you that everything was all set. I'd signed the papers with Uncle Roarke, and we were moving to Ireland immediately, all expenses paid." Brody grimaced, recalling how stunned he had been to find that Meg wasn't at all happy about what a phenomenal and exciting feat he had accomplished. Instead, she saw his attempt to provide for his family—something his own father had never done—as the ultimate betrayal.

"And I had news that night, too." Meg's lips curved ruefully. She turned toward him slightly, her bent knee nudging his thigh. "After years of doing regional theater, struggling for work, I had just landed my first part on Broadway. And it wasn't a bit part," she recalled sadly but proudly, "it was a supporting role."

Brody was close enough to Meg to breathe in the floral scent of her perfume and the sweet fragrance of her hair and skin. He put his arm along the back of the sofa so they could sit together more comfortably. "You wanted to move to New York."

Meg relaxed against the cushions, her shoulders molding to the curve of his arm. "I had to. Rehearsals were starting the following day. I barely had enough time to get on the plane and check into the hotel room they had reserved for me, before heading on to the theater.''

''I didn't know you were even up for the part,'' Brody said, looking down at her hands. They were soft and slender and very feminine.

''Well…'' Meg took his glass and got up to pour them both more wine. ''I didn't know you were in negotiations to start your own firm, either.'' She looked over at him briefly, accusingly, and hurt flickered in her dark green eyes. ''I had thought what Uncle Roarke said to us on the phone after our wedding was just talk. Pie-in-the-sky, Irish blarney sort of stuff.''

She sauntered closer, handing him his wine, but not sitting down again.

''It *was* all just talk, until the twins were born,'' Brody explained. ''Then Uncle Roarke decided he had to act if he wanted my Irish family to get to know us.''

Meg's face took on a faraway look. ''The timing for that golden opportunity couldn't have been worse for either of us.''

Brody sighed. He put his own glass aside and rose, closing the distance between them. ''It was more than timing,'' he said as he removed her glass and placed it on the coffee table. Putting both his hands on her shoulders, he said, ''We have to face it, Meg. That blowup had been coming for a long time.'' And it would have happened whether Roarke had stepped in to interfere or not.

''Back then,'' Brody continued gravely, ''we were both unwilling and unable to make any lasting commitment to anyone or anything other than our work.'' Work had been safe—demanding but rewarding. As much as Brody was loath to admit it, their marriage had never given them the same satisfaction.

Meg opened her mouth to protest, but Brody pushed on, determined to make his point while she was still receptive enough to hear him out. "Our relationship and our family didn't come first for either of us, Meg. If they had, I would never have gone to Ireland and left you behind. And you sure as heck wouldn't have headed for Broadway." They would have found a way to put their egos aside and keep their little family together, to everyone's benefit.

"Maybe that's not surprising," Meg said with a delicate shrug, "given the only reason we got married was because..."

As her voice faltered, Brody finished, "...you were pregnant."

"Yes."

Brody rubbed at the tense muscles in the back of his own neck. "I admit your pregnancy was a surprise to both of us." Neither of them had ever entertained the notion that the birth control they were using might fail. "But I was happy about it from the get-go." Even more so when he had found out they were having twins.

"So was I, Brody. But we never should have gotten married just to give our children your name or financial support. We could have done that without a marriage."

She was making it sound as if a set of legal contracts would have been better than their marriage vows!

"It was more than that and you know it," Brody objected hotly. He had married Meg because he had wanted to provide her and their children with the loving family he and Meg had both been denied, growing up.

But Meg obviously did not understand or accept that. She marched forward, not stopping until they stood toe to toe. Planting her hands on her hips, she glared at Brody, tears of resentment sparkling in her green eyes. "What I *know* is that if I hadn't gotten pregnant and lost my job in the touring company, we never would've gotten married when we did. Instead, we would have continued a passionate affair. Period. Face it, Brody. At that point in time, we'd only been dating for six months. We were wildly infatuated with each other and we loved meeting in different cities and sleeping with each other, but we also barely knew one another. A combination of fate and physical attraction and pure animal lust brought us together.''

Brody had wondered if she remembered just how wild and hot their time together had been—before the wedding rings were on their fingers, and they both felt so trapped and unhappy. Now he knew.

"And passion like that always fades," she concluded firmly, as if that were that.

He gave her a long, searching look, wondering just who it was she was trying to fool now. "Bull!"

Meg blinked and looked at him as if she couldn't possibly have heard him right, even though he knew darn well she had. "Excuse me?"

Brody stepped closer to her and tucked a hand beneath her chin. She'd had her say and now he was going to have his. He looked her straight in the eye. "Our passion for each other is stronger than ever."

CHAPTER SEVEN

MEG CAUGHT HER BREATH and felt herself flush with an inner warmth she couldn't contain. "You can't mean that."

"Can't I?" Brody continued to survey her thoughtfully. His voice dropped a notch as he captured her wrist and lifted it to his lips. "Then you tell me, Meg, what—besides pride—is keeping us apart."

She dropped her glance to the strong column of his throat and the crisp curling hair visible in the open V of his shirt. "It's different now," she persisted, aware that she had never felt such a sizzling sensation as she did at this very moment.

"How?" Brody let her hand fall back to her lap.

Needing to put some distance between them, Meg moved toward the fire crackling in the hearth. "Back then we couldn't seem to resist each other." She turned her back to the mantel and faced him with as much moxie as she could muster. "Right now, we can."

Brody favored her with a slow, sensual smile and went over to join her at the hearth. "Can we?" he asked in a low voice that sent shivers of awareness racing along her skin. Smiling down at her, he wrapped his hands around her waist and drew her close.

Heart pounding, Meg splayed her hands across the sinewy warmth of his chest and took a deep, bracing breath. "Brody." She meant to warn him off, but his name ended up sounding like a soft caress.

Brody threaded his fingers through the hair at the back

of her neck and looked down at her with understanding and affection. "I'm willing to be honest here, Meg," he told her as a thrill swept through her, head to toe. "Are you? Because this is all I've wanted to do all day and evening," he confessed as his lips molded to hers and he kissed her long and thoroughly, in a way that made her want much, much more.

With a quiet moan of surrender, Meg pressed her body against his and returned the kiss, knowing even as she did that something magical was happening between them. There had always been passion, but never this overwhelming tenderness. Pleasure, but not the love welling up in her heart. For the first time in her life, Meg felt completely safe, protected, revered. And the wealth of emotions turned her world upside down.

Unable to resist his insistence, she moved her arms from a defensive position and linked them around his neck. Still Brody kissed her, as if he had spent years missing her, and—like her—was tired of pretending that he hadn't. Warmth curled inside her, and she rose on tiptoe, parting her lips helplessly under the onslaught and meeting him stroke for stroke. She felt his arousal pressing against her. And his hand reaching for her breast. He cupped her with his palm, through her clothing, and she moaned, aware that she was shaking all over.

"Brody…" she said again, even more desperately. "The kids—"

His lips moved to the sensitive place behind her ear as his hands worked her nipples to aching crowns. "Are upstairs sleeping."

Meg moaned again, aware she wanted him more than she had ever wanted him in her life. But that didn't mean this was the right time or the right place. Or that, given the differences between them, there would ever be a right time and place. Gathering her composure, she drew a galvanizing breath as she lifted her face to his. "They could wake."

Brody merely smiled. He rained kisses down her neck, across her collarbone, his lips forging a fiery path. "Then we'd better be quiet," he teased as he angled his body against her softness and returned his lips to hers.

Arrows of fire shot through her, and she clung to him as everything around them blurred except the hot, hard pressure of his mouth. The slow strokes of his tongue were unbearably sensual, the tantalizing scent of his cologne tickled her senses, and still she could not get enough of him. And that thought was as alarming to her as it was exciting. There was so very much at stake here. And not just for the two of them this time. She drew a shaky breath and, calling on all her willpower, pushed him away.

"We can't do this, Brody. We can't fall into a love affair again just because it's easy or convenient." *Because if we do, it will break my heart. And this time, maybe yours, too.*

"Is that what you think?" Brody asked, hurt flickering briefly in his eyes.

Frustration filled her soul and made her tense. Aware of being more vulnerable now than she had been in a very long time, Meg turned away. She didn't want them using each other to ease their loneliness. Because in the end, that wouldn't work, either. "What I think is we wouldn't even be talking right now, never mind spending time alone together, if we were still living an ocean apart. And it's not just us anymore, Brody," she continued shakily. "We have Kevin and Kelly to think about, too."

He relaxed and smiled with unbearable tenderness. "I am thinking of them. You heard them a little while ago. They want us back together again. They want us to be a family."

They, Meg thought. Not him. Not Brody. "I won't get involved with you for all the wrong reasons, Brody. Not again. Not ever. We've already been this route and it had a disastrous end. We jumped into a love affair before we'd even begun to work on the rest of the relationship. I don't want to make the same mistake twice."

Brody studied her, still struggling to understand. "You want to be friends."

"First," Meg agreed with determination. And if in the process they realized that was as far as it went, then it would be enough. It would have to be.

He sighed, looking a little surly and a lot frustrated. "I don't agree this is the only way to make a relationship work," he said, letting her know with a glance that he had no regrets about their coming together passionately again. "But if that's the way you want it to be…"

"It is."

The brooding look in his eyes was replaced with quiet resolution. "Then we'll just have to talk about what I had originally slated for this evening," he said, segueing into business mode once again.

"And that is?" Meg demanded warily, wishing she weren't still tingling from their kisses. It was hard to keep her resolve when they were enjoying a glass of wine in front of a blazing fire, their children asleep upstairs.

Brody took Meg by the hand and led her back over to the sofa. "I've set up trust funds for you and Kevin and Kelly," he explained as they sat down side by side. He took both her hands in his. "Even if you don't work another day in your life, you'll never have to worry about money again, Meg," he promised her gruffly. "You'll be taken care of."

"Why would you do that?" Meg searched his dark eyes in stunned amazement. "I mean, I understand about the kids—I would have expected that, knowing the kind of wealth you've earned for yourself and the kind of man you are, but for me…?" Her voice faltered.

Brody gazed deep into her eyes. "I did it because you're my family and my responsibility."

When he looked at her that way, he made her feel as if she were still his wife. Only she wasn't. And regardless of how things were going at the moment, she might never be again. Because if she knew one thing about Brody, it was that he prided himself on never repeating his mistakes. Making love to her out of loneliness and physical need was one thing. Marriage, quite another. "We're divorced," Meg repeated, as much for her own benefit as his.

"It doesn't matter." Brody sat back as she drew her hands away. "You're the mother of my children, and I plan to see you're taken care of," he told her firmly.

Wasn't that just like Brody, Meg thought. Acting unilaterally. Never asking her what she wanted or what she thought might be good or right. Only telling her the way things were going to be, according to Brody.

His gaze roved her from head to toe, generating heat wherever it touched. "This upsets you, doesn't it?" he asked.

Meg turned her eyes to the fire crackling in the grate, but she was still powerfully aware of Brody's presence. She swallowed around the sudden dryness in her throat then admitted huskily, "It just reminds me of the way things used to be between us. And even worse than that," she admitted, leaning forward, "it reminds me of the way things were when I was growing up."

Brody kneaded the tension from her shoulders. "Because your parents were divorced and we're divorced, and financial arrangements needed to be made?"

For a second, Meg allowed herself the luxury of enjoying the soothing massage. Knowing she had her own demons to wrestle with on this particular subject, she struggled to put her feelings into words. When they had been together before, she had tried to hide the residual wounds from her childhood. Having had enough personal misery as a kid, she had preferred to present a capable, optimistic front to the world. And while that had helped her in obtaining work, and in her day-to-day dealings with people, keeping her guard up at all times had hurt her relationship with Brody. Perhaps even doomed her marriage.

Meg knew if she wanted her relationship with Brody to be different, she was going to have to be different, too. More open. Accessible. Because only if he knew how she felt about things, and why, would he ever understand her in the way she wanted him to. "Money was always an issue in my family," she explained. "When my parents were still together, they fought about how to spend it. When they split up, they fought because there never seemed to be enough to run two households in the style to which they'd both been accustomed." She shook her head bleakly, remembering. "And even when those problems were ironed out, they still used money as a sort of emotional currency to make up for any hurt or disappointment they had inflicted on me." Her lips lifted in a half smile as she tossed him a glance and acknowledged wryly, "Although in my parents' case, it was a new dress or a used car or two weeks at a coveted summer drama camp instead of a trust fund. But the principle was the same," she explained, her mood turning restless and unhappy once again. "The 'impromptu gift' was used to erase their guilt and make me forget everything that had come before."

Brody's hands stilled. He stopped massaging her shoulders and turned her to face him. "I admit I'd like to make it up to you for any unhappiness I caused you when we were together," he stated quietly, in a way that let her know he sympathized, and more, understood. He reached out and touched her face as he continued explaining gently, "And this is one way to do it. As for your childhood, I know you were bounced around a lot then and used as a pawn between your folks. And that it's made you wary, of both marriage and divorce.''

"I was also told what to do, how to feel, how to react to things." Meg paused and bit her lip, not wanting to hurt him, especially when he was trying to be so good to her. But she knew she had to be honest with him if she wanted them to be close, so she forced herself to plunge on. "When I married you, I thought it would be different, but you did the very same thing to me, Brody. Over and over again, when I didn't like something or didn't agree with something you had done, you told me that this was just the way things had to be. And that you didn't plan to argue about it.''

Brody's color heightened. "I was the head of the household. I was taking charge.''

"Well, I didn't want a boss, Brody," Meg replied emotionally, throwing up both her hands. "I wanted a husband. An equal partner. Someone to discuss things with and make mutual decisions with.''

Brody was silent, seeming to accept the fact that although he had been well-meaning in his take-charge approach, he had also been dead wrong. "And I let you down," he confirmed softly after a minute.

Meg nodded. "Yes, you did.''

"Well, you let me down, too," Brody said, giving her a pointed look.

Her mouth fell open in surprise. Somehow, she hadn't expected him to come clean with his feelings, too. "How?" she demanded cautiously.

His eyes narrowed. "By acting as if our commitment to each other was an albatross you had to bear instead of a promise from right here." He touched the center of his chest.

Emotions she couldn't name filled her. For a guy who seemed to think only in practical terms, this was a revelation indeed. "Is that what our wedding vows were to you?" Meg asked, thunderstruck. "Straight from the heart?"

Brody's expression turned unexpectedly sentimental. "How could you think otherwise?" he asked in astonishment.

"Oh, I don't know, Brody," Meg drawled with a touch of sarcasm. She pushed herself to her feet and regarded him in exasperation. "Maybe because from the moment I told you I was pregnant, you treated our predicament like a business challenge."

Brody bristled at the criticism in her tone as he, too, leaped up from the couch. "If you're criticizing me for being practical..."

Meg threw up her hands. "You didn't even propose to me, damn it!"

"Maybe not directly," Brody replied hotly.

"You simply showed me your company's medical insurance policy and told me the only way the babies or I would be covered was if the two of us were married," she reminded him. He hadn't asked. He had assumed. And because she had been about to lose her job and had no medical insurance of her own, she had swallowed her pride and gone along with his plan.

Brody searched her eyes, and abruptly, his expression gentled. "I also told you we'd find a way to make it work," he reminded her gruffly.

"Only it didn't work, did it?" Meg recalled sadly. She had been devastated by his unromantic attitude, but pride had kept her from revealing her hurt, and so she, too, had begun to act as if their togetherness were a practical necessity rather than a choice based on love. And because of that, she had done everything she could to keep him at arm's length emotionally, even as she put on a gloriously happy performance for everyone else to see. But inside, her heart had been breaking. The only difference was that now she knew his had been, too. He had just been too proud to show it. As she thought about all the misery they had inadvertently caused each other, her heart filled with grief. "I'm sorry, Brody." Impulsively, she took his hands in both of hers. "I never meant to hurt you. And I know you never meant to hurt me."

"We just did," Brody said sadly.

At that moment, Meg felt like crying.

"Well, we can't change the past, that's for certain," he stated flatly. "But now that we've cleared the air, the two of us can start over. Start fresh."

The thought of a clean slate was very tempting, but Meg forced herself to temper her enthusiasm. The last thing she wanted to do was rush things and end up way over her head with him again. And yet the deeply romantic and passionate part of her knew resisting was futile. Because she would always want Brody to love her, always yearn to believe that somehow, some way it would be possible to achieve a "happily ever after" with him. "Do you really think things will be different this time?"

"If we want them to be?" Brody gave her a smile that seemed to come straight from his heart. He leaned forward and gently touched his lips to her temple. "Absolutely."

"SO WHAT'S THE SCOOP with you and Brody Taylor?" Katherine Kinard asked curiously as Meg joined Katherine and her two partners at Caffeine Hy's for an afternoon coffee break.

"What do you mean?" Meg asked warily. She set her purse, briefcase and umbrella down beside her chair and stripped off the light raincoat she was wearing. It wasn't raining yet, but if those dark clouds in the Seattle sky and the weather report were any indication, they were about to have a heck of an autumn rainstorm that would last well into the evening.

Katherine sat back in her upholstered chair at the cozy corner table. "Kelly and Kevin are telling everyone the four of you went away together for the weekend. To Lake Tahoe, the place where you two fell in love, no less."

Oh, no, Meg thought. They had told the kids they had fallen in love there, and gotten married by the lake, but they had skipped the part about deciding to divorce there, as well. Maybe if they had told them that, the kids wouldn't have been so starry-eyed. Obviously, the twins had taken Meg and Brody's attempt to show them that they could still be a family, despite the divorce, the wrong way. That was something she and Brody hadn't considered.

"Is it true?" Alexandra Webber asked with a cheerful wink.

"Are you and Brody Taylor getting back together after all these years?" Hannah Richards added, her light blue eyes sparkling.

"Whoa, whoa!" Meg held up a silencing hand at the barrage of questions. Outside the coffee shop, the homeless man she had seen earlier was sitting at a table, enjoying a coffee and a sandwich despite the fact that rain was threatening at any minute.

Meg looked at Hannah, the day care's accountant. "No one is saying anything about the two of us getting back together," she said firmly, even if, secretly, that was exactly what she was beginning to wish for. Reason, practicality and the differences between her and Brody be damned.

"Well, just so you and Brody know, Kelly and Kevin have convinced themselves it's going to happen." Katherine smoothed a paper napkin over the lap of her conservative blue suit. Though she was only in her late twenties, she tended to nurture everyone who came within her sphere, including Meg. It didn't seem to matter that Meg was five years older than her and had, unlike the single Katherine, been married, divorced and given birth to two children.

Right now Katherine was looking at Meg with the same compassion she bestowed upon Carlos, her twelve-year-old foster son. "I spoke to Carmen Perez a little while ago. She said the kids haven't been able to stop talking about your upcoming nuptials all morning."

Meg knew the twins' kindergarten teacher wouldn't have mentioned this to Katherine were she not a little concerned about the conclusions the twins were jumping to. "Well, we're not getting married!" Meg insisted firmly, aware that an embarrassed flush was climbing from her chest to her face.

"Well then, you and Brody probably better explain that to the twins," Alexandra suggested kindly.

"I will," Meg promised. Then, needing to unburden herself, she filled the women in on the events of the weekend. Just as Meg ended her tale, their waitress, Millie Gallagher, brought them all her signature drink, a double-chocolate latte with skim foam. A petite young woman with chin-length, curly blond hair and unusual gray-blue eyes, Millie worked mornings in the kitchen of the day care center, preparing lunches for the children, then afternoons at the coffee shop.

"Are you sure the kids aren't just picking up on the vibes you and Brody are sending out?" Hannah asked.

Alexandra nodded. "Maybe the twins are seeing something going on between you and Brody that you two just aren't quite willing to admit to yourselves."

Meg blushed to the roots of her hair. "It's true," she admitted reluctantly, looking at the friends gathered around her. "Despite the differences between us—and just to be clear, there are still problems I don't think Brody and I will ever be able to solve—I do still care about Brody as a friend. And I think the feeling's mutual." Whether their relationship would go beyond that was something that would only be discovered with time.

"Then maybe," Katherine surmised with a gentle shrug, "that's what your kids are picking up on."

But what to do about it, Meg thought as she headed over to the day care center. She couldn't just tell Brody how she felt. It might make him uncomfortable or even make things worse. It could also cause him to jump to the wrong conclusions about the possibility of reconciliation. Because Meg knew how Brody was. He still desired her, just as she still desired him—the heat of their recent kisses had proved that. And if he thought Meg still harbored deeply romantic feelings about him as well, Brody might charge on ahead to make Kelly and Kevin's dream of a happy family life, with all four of them living under one roof, happen. He would do it with the best intentions, of course, because he wanted their children to be happy in a way Meg and Brody hadn't been when growing up. And he would do it because he wanted to be with her again, more than he wanted to be alone. There was no chance he would simply be content with a love affair that was secret from everyone, including their children. Brody was too forthright a man to indulge in such a deception. Nor would he be comfortable carrying on an affair with his children's mother without eventually adding the commitments, both practical and emotional, that went along with it.

So that could only mean one thing. If she slept with Brody again, he would eventually want them to be married. Period. He wouldn't think about all the things standing in their way. He would set that as his goal and find the most expedient way to go after it.

That might not even be so bad, Meg thought wistfully, as the rain began to come down, if it were just the two of them who stood to get hurt. But it wasn't. They now had the kids to consider. And speaking of the kids, Meg realized as she paused to close her umbrella before heading into the day care center, she was going to have to talk to Brody about what their twins were telling everyone.

The opportunity came at the end of the day, when Brody arrived to pick up Kevin.

Meg was helping her daughter put her rain slicker on. "I want to spend the night with Kevin," Kelly said. "At our house."

"Yeah." Kevin chimed in. "Daddy, I want to spend the night with Kelly and Mommy at their house."

"Me and Kevin missed each other last night," Kelly said as she and her brother put their arms around each other's waists and held on tight.

They looked so hopeful standing there together, so connected in the way only twins could be, that Meg felt hard-pressed to deny them anything. After all, she realized sadly, thanks to her and Brody's foolish decision to separate them two months after birth, they had already been denied so much. She turned to Brody and saw he was just as touched as she was by the twins' heartfelt request.

"Normally, it would be fine," Meg said to Brody. "But I've already scheduled a meeting at my place tonight, with Drew Kinard and Julia Stanton. They're going to pick out the music they want me to sing at their wedding. I'm not sure I can handle both kids and do justice to their wedding music at the same time."

"We'll be quiet," Kevin promised. "We'll stay upstairs in the playroom and go to bed all by ourselves."

Beside him, Kelly nodded in sober, hopeful agreement. "Yes, Mommy, we'll be very, very good."

Meg could see they meant what they said. Still, she hesitated. This was a professional job. Julia and Drew deserved to have her complete attention, but with two lively kids together under one roof... Meg hated to let down either party.

"Look, I can come over and baby-sit the kids upstairs in

the playroom while you have your meeting downstairs,'' Brody said with an offhand smile as the twins raced off to collect their lunch boxes and backpacks. "Then, when you're done, and they're asleep for the night," he continued matter-of-factly, "I'll head to the airport."

Meg blinked, not sure she had understood correctly.

"I've got to go to Texas to check out that software company Roarke wants me to look at," Brody said. "He's sending me his jet. I promised I'd be in Austin by tomorrow morning. But it's no problem. I can help you out this evening."

"What were you going to do if I couldn't have watched Kevin tonight?" Meg asked curiously.

Brody lifted his broad shoulders in an unconcerned shrug. "Take him with me. And then leave him with Roarke at the hotel while I was in meetings."

Well, at least he hadn't said, "Call Fiona."

"Are you still interviewing nannies?"

Brody frowned, his expression faintly troubled. He shoved a hand through his rain-dampened hair. "I haven't had time. But once I start traveling again, I'm going to have to find one."

Not necessarily, Meg thought, as her next idea hit. "Why not let me care for him whenever you have to be away or have evening meetings?" she suggested impulsively.

"You wouldn't mind?" Brody asked cautiously, searching her eyes.

Meg shook her head, her heart swelling with love as she thought about the opportunity this presented. "I'd love to have Kevin with us, and I know Kelly feels the same way." It would give Meg a chance to get closer to her son and give her plenty of excuses to see Brody more, too.

"Then that's what we'll do," he decided, looking every bit as satisfied with their new arrangement as Meg felt.

"DADDY, are you ever going to leave me and move far, far away again?" Kelly asked several hours later. The three of them were settled in the upstairs playroom at Meg's house while Meg met with Julia and Drew downstairs.

Out of the mouths of babes, Brody thought guiltily. He sat on the floor playing Barbies with Kelly, while Kevin busied himself drawing and coloring a picture for Meg on Kelly's easel. "No," Brody said, as Kelly handed him a Ken doll to put into the Barbie convertible. "I'm staying right here."

"That's good." Kelly smiled at him angelically. "Because I like playing Barbies with you."

Brody grinned, aware it was the first time he had ever found himself with a doll in his hands. Even harder to believe, he was enjoying the experience. But here he was… "I like playing Barbies with you, too, Kelly." Just as he liked spending time with her, listening to what she had to say, hearing what irked her. Making her laugh.

Kelly put her doll down and slid over to Brody's lap. She rested her head on his chest as casually as if she had been doing it for years. And she had been, Brody realized, only not with him, with Meg. "Did your daddy ever play with you?"

Brody tensed at his little girl's question, then shook his head. "My daddy wasn't around when I was growing up." He had walked out when Brody was seven. Brody had never forgotten the explanation his father had given. *I just don't belong here. I don't love your mother and I'm a lousy father. Trust me, you'll both be better off without me.* Brody's father had acted as if he were doing them a favor, and Brody didn't know, maybe he had…. Certainly, from what he recalled, there had been no love lost between his parents.

"What about your mommy?" Kelly asked curiously. "Did she play with you?"

Brody found himself frowning again. With effort, he kept the resentment out of his voice, as if the lack of parenting and tender loving care had been no big deal. "She was pretty busy working."

"But did you ask her?" Kelly persisted.

As if that would have changed anything, except to make his mother even more irritable than she already was. "Yes," Brody replied patiently.

"And what'd she say?" Kelly leaned forward eagerly.

Do I look like I have time to go to the park? Damn it all, Brody, I'm busy here.... Thanks to your no-good-louse-of-a-father, I have a family to support! Brody swallowed around the lump in his throat, aware that some pains faded but never really went away. "She said that she couldn't go places with me because she had to work," he said simply, trying to couch his answer in a way Kelly could understand.

His mother's reply had been the same, no matter what he'd asked of her, Brody recalled, sighing inwardly. She hadn't gone to see him play on sports teams, or win the computer science category in the state science fair. She'd made it to his college graduation ceremony, but had arrived late and refused to go out with him for lunch afterward. That had been the last time he had seen her, before she died. Brody knew he should be sad about her passing, and part of him was, but the other part of him felt no more at a loss than before. The truth was, his mother had never loved him, never known how. It was Roarke Taylor and Brody's other Irish relatives who had taught him how to be a family, and made him want to share the lessons now with Meg, Kevin, and Kelly.

"You look sad," Kelly told Brody, commanding his attention once again. She gave him a reassuring hug, which he promptly returned.

As much as he was loath to admit it, Brody noted as he held his little girl in his arms and stroked her hair, he was sad whenever he thought of his childhood and all the missed opportunities for familial closeness. And now, thanks to his own lapse in judgment, he was regretting all the time he had missed with Kelly, too. He'd thought he had been doing her a favor by not putting her and her brother in a situation where she was always being separated from him or Meg. After all, he and Meg had figured, the kids wouldn't miss what they had never experienced, right? Their way might have saved the twins the pain of custody arrangements and periodic separations, but it had also robbed them of so much, too. Brody hugged his little girl tighter. There was only one thing to do. He and Meg were going to have to find a way to make it up to the twins, Brody thought. And he would start by giving his children all the love he had in his heart, plus time and attention every day.

Finished with his drawing, Kevin came over to sit with them. "You wanta play with the building blocks?" he asked.

Kelly was already dragging them out. "I do," she said. "How about you, Daddy?"

"Count me in, too," Brody said enthusiastically. For the next half hour, the three of them worked to construct towers out of brightly colored plastic building blocks. As the twins giggled and talked and created to their hearts' content, Brody experienced a contentment of his own unlike anything he had ever felt. The only thing missing was Meg. And she would be joining them soon.

"Mommy sings pretty, doesn't she?" Kelly said.

"She sure does," Brody agreed. He'd been listening to Meg sing one love song after another all evening. Over the years, he'd heard a lot of singers, but few put their heart and soul into the music the way Meg did. When she was onstage there wasn't a person in the audience who wasn't mesmerized by her presence. Julia and Drew were lucky to have her performing at their wedding.

"I like the way Mommy sings, too," Kevin said, studying his latest creation from a sideways view. "It's real nice. Like a CD or something." He paused and looked at Brody seriously. "Mommy sings real good at school, too. We sing songs from *Mary Poppins* and *The Sound of Music*."

No doubt about it, Brody thought, Meg was talented. Amazingly so. She had sacrificed a lot to be with Kelly and give her a normal childhood.

He told her so, once her meeting was over, and the kids were bedded down for the night.

"You don't have to say that, Brody," Meg said, after he had complimented her on her beautiful voice.

Brody could see she was uncomfortable discussing her talent with him, probably because her ambition had been such a sore subject between them. He felt bad about that, because listening to her again and realizing how wonderfully gifted she was, he knew he had never given her the respect she deserved. It was time that changed, he decided abruptly. Time he put his own wants and needs aside and concentrated on what made her feel good about herself.

"It's true," he told her. He should be on his way by now, but he was unwilling to go just yet. Meg was stacking her music and filing it on the shelves behind her baby grand piano. "I always loved the way you sang."

"Thank you." She turned and sent him a shy smile that both invited him closer and warned him away. "I love singing."

"I know," Brody said, all too aware of the inanity of the conversation, the kind you would have with a stranger. He ran his fingers over the ivory keys. "It shows."

A restless silence fell between them. He paused long enough to shoot Meg a remorseful look. "I hate that you had to give up performing to be with Kelly and take the job here."

A cautious light sparked in Meg's eyes as she pushed in

the piano bench. Brody could see she wanted to believe he'd had a change of attitude; she just wasn't sure she should. He could hardly blame her.

"I haven't actually given it up," she told him pleasantly. "I'm going to be doing some master classes on stage work for the university. And I'm planning to try and do some summer stock next year, when Kelly and Kevin aren't in school and their schedule is more flexible."

Brody smiled, thinking about that. "They'd enjoy going to the theater and seeing you work." He moved around the piano, stopping next to her.

Meg tilted her head back and looked up at him. "You'll have to take them to the new offices of Taylor Software, too."

"I will," Brody promised. *And I'd like to take you, too. I'd like you to appreciate all I've accomplished.*

But wary of how those words would be received, he refrained from saying them. Silence fell between them once more. "Well, it's late," he said reluctantly, pushing away from the piano. He gave Meg a half grin. "I guess I better be going. I told Roarke's pilot I would meet him at the airport at nine-thirty."

Meg looked as sorry to see him go as he was to be leaving. "When will you be back?" she asked as she escorted him to the door.

"I'm not sure." Brody lingered in the entrance. "Could be tomorrow, could be a couple of days. It depends on how things go." He regarded her closely. "Is it a problem?" If so, he wanted to address it.

Meg shook her head.

Brody fished in his pocket and handed Meg a key. "In case Kev needs anything at our house while I'm gone, you can just go in and get it."

Meg nodded in agreement.

"You'll let me know if Kevin has any problems being

away from me?" Brody didn't want to borrow trouble, but he did want to be prepared.

Meg's eyes lit with maternal concern. "You think he might?" she asked anxiously.

Brody shrugged. "I don't know. He didn't have any trouble saying goodbye to me tonight, but Kev doesn't like it when I'm gone on business trips. There were times in Ireland when even Fiona couldn't comfort him. She'd have to call me in the middle of the night and I'd talk to him until he went back to sleep."

"How often did you have to travel?"

"At least three or four times a month," Brody admitted reluctantly.

A worried light came into Meg's eyes. "Are you going to continue to have to do that?"

Brody nodded grimly. "I'd hoped to delay any business travel until Kevin was settled in Seattle and I'd found someone to stay with him while I was gone. Obviously—" his lip curled wryly "—that's not happening. Although it should go a lot better this time since he's with you. His real mommy instead of just a nanny."

Meg looked as if she hoped that was the case.

"In any event," Brody reassured her, "you've got all my numbers, so I'm just a phone call away."

"Will do," Meg promised.

"And one more thing," Brody said, feeling happier than he had in years.

Meg looked up at him inquiringly. "What's that?"

"I want to say goodbye to you, too," he murmured, grasping her wrist and drawing her to him.

Meg gasped softly as she realized his intent, and then his lips were on hers, taking full advantage of her vulnerability to make her his. Needing her to know how much he was going to miss her, he continued to hold her tightly and embarked on a hot, languorous kiss. To Brody's pleasure, Meg reacted as if she were going to miss him just as badly.

Moaning softly, she went up on tiptoe, pressing her slender body against the length of his. He felt the pillowy warmth of her breasts cushioned against the hardness of his chest as she melted against him. Reveling in the hot, insistent demand of her body and the even sweeter thrust and parry of her tongue, he kissed her back even more deeply, until she felt every ragged edge of his need and responded avidly. Until she yearned for him as much as he wanted her, and Brody felt her tremble, go weak in the knees.

His arousal pulsing with desire, Brody cupped the soft curve of her hips and held her against him as they continued to kiss, sweetly and tenderly. A crazy mixture of emotions was running through him. The ones that were remembered, and the love that was new. Worry that he was once again moving too fast. That he would end up pushing her away, even as he tried to draw her near…

Meg hadn't meant to kiss him back. In fact, she had warned herself against doing just that. But the moment she had seen that look in his eyes and was in his arms again, she had been helpless to resist him. No one but Brody had ever made her want so desperately. No one else had ever been able to love her until all the hurts and despair and unhappiness of the past went away, until only the beauty of the present and the tantalizing magic of the future was left.

Feeling as if she had been waiting forever to rediscover the passion and the pleasure only Brody could give her, she let him pin her between his body and the door, let his tongue sizzle along hers, circling and flicking across the edges of her teeth, before dipping deep. And still he kissed her, as if the chance would never come again. As her lips moved beneath his, she became aware of his arousal pressing against her, demanding an intimacy she wasn't sure would be wise for her to give. Arrows of desire shot through her, weakening her resolve and adding to the need he had created, the need only he could ease.

"I want you to know how I feel," Brody murmured emphatically as he slowly, deliberately kissed her again. "I want you back, Meg." Wrapping both arms around her, he held her tight and buried his face in her hair. "I want you in my life. Not just because it's good for the kids, but because you're good for me. You keep me grounded, Meg. You help me realize what's important in a way no one else ever has."

"Oh, Brody," Meg whispered. She wasn't sure whether this was her wildest dream coming true, or a hint of even more conflict and sadness to come. All she knew for certain was that her heart was pounding as she rested her face against the solidity of his shoulder and struggled to regain what little equilibrium she had left. And she felt more recklessly hopeful and excited than she had in a very long time.

Drawing a deep breath, she pulled back to study the expression on his face. His dark eyes contained a wealth of support and understanding, and tenderness flowed between them as Brody pressed a silencing finger to her lips. "Don't say anything. Not yet. Just appreciate the new chance we've found with each other, Meg, and take it one day at a time."

Suddenly Meg knew this wasn't the last time they would be together like this. Rather, it was the beginning of a new chapter in their lives.

Maybe Brody was right, she thought, as her heart slowed into a steady, relaxed beat. Maybe they didn't need to decide everything in one night. Maybe if the two of them worked together, they could take things as they came.

After all, Brody was the father of her children. She and Brody obviously still desired each other. Maybe they weren't meant to be man and wife, but did that mean she had to continue to be as lonely as she had been? Or that they had to throw away everything that had been good—like their sex life—just because they had divorced? They were becoming friends again. Co-parents. Maybe one day, she told herself hopefully, they would find a way to be lovers, too.

"Is that your new motto?" she teased. She shot him a flirtatious glance as she opened the door, flipped on the outside light and walked him out as far as the porch. The rain had stopped—at least for a while—and the air had a fresh clean smell. Meg folded her arms in front of her and studied the toe of her shoe before slanting him a winsome glance. "Because I remember very well what it used to be—My Way or the Highway."

Brody grinned. "It may well be my new motto," he teased her back. "Although for the record…" he paused to playfully tug on a lock of Meg's hair "…I recall very well what yours used to be, too. Reach for the Moon—Even if You Can't Get There, You'll Land among the Stars."

Meg sighed ruefully. It seemed so long ago that she had been possessed with such tunnel vision. Maybe Brody had been right when he said she'd been fixated only on her career back then. Now her view of life was a lot broader, and less self-centered. She slanted him a glance, wanting him to know how much she had changed in the five years they had been apart. "I think these days my motto is more like Make Someone Else Happy and You'll Make Yourself Happy," she said seriously.

Brody tugged her toward him and kissed her again. Thoroughly. Tenderly. Sweetly. When he was finished, he drew back and gazed down into her face. "Well, you've done that for our kids. And me, too," he whispered. And then he was gone.

MEG HAD JUST SETTLED into bed with a good book when Kevin appeared in her doorway. He was rubbing his eyes sleepily and he looked upset. "I woke up," he said as he shuffled over to her. "And I didn't know where I was. Then I 'membered."

"Why don't you come and get in bed with me for a minute," Meg suggested tenderly.

Kevin crawled into bed beside her. She wiped the tears from his face and wrapped her arms around his little body. He snuggled against her, smelling of children's shampoo and sleep-warmed flannel. She stroked a hand through his hair and rubbed his back. "Do you feel better now?" she asked.

Kevin nodded, but Meg could feel him trembling and knew he needed a lot more comforting. For the first time in years, she was here to give it, and that filled her heart with joy, even as the knowledge of all the others times he had probably needed her, and she hadn't been there, tore her apart. "I miss my daddy when he's away," Kevin confided.

"Well, if you get scared, you come and find me," Meg said as she continued to rub his back. She wanted to be here for her little boy. Always. And that went double for when Brody wasn't around. "And I'll comfort you."

"Okay," Kevin promised. He wrapped his arms around Meg's waist and held her tighter. "It sure is good to have a mommy."

A lump formed in Meg's throat at the enthusiasm in his voice. "It's good to have a little boy," she murmured back, happy tears filling her eyes.

Kevin's face was pinched with worry once more. "Are you going to go away again?" he demanded anxiously.

"No, honey," Meg reassured him tenderly. "I'm staying right here in Seattle. And Kelly is, too. I promise."

"Daddy and me are, too," Kevin said with a relieved smile. "So that means we get to be a family." He tried but couldn't stifle another yawn as he cuddled up to Meg once again and held her tightly. "Can I sleep in here for a little while?"

"Sure," Meg said, hugging him back, wondering all the while how she'd ever agreed to be separated from her son. She was so glad he and Brody were part of her life again.

KEVIN HAD PUT his restless night behind him by the time the twins bounded out of bed the next morning, full of energy and their usual self-confidence. Together, they bombarded Meg with questions about everything from the projected weather for the day to the previous night's activities. "So what kind of wedding are Julia and Drew going to have?" Kevin asked as they sat down to breakfast.

Meg added milk to their glasses and orange juice to hers. "The wedding is going to be in a church—it's called Our Lady of Mercy—and the reception is going to be at an outdoor pavilion."

"Will there be flowers?" Kelly queried.

"And cake?" Kevin asked around a mouthful of French toast.

"Both," Meg said, smiling.

As she sat down to enjoy her breakfast, too, Meg couldn't help but think about her own wedding. She and Brody had planned it on a shoestring budget, under very privately stressful circumstances, but it had still been wonderfully exciting, picking out a gown and a tuxedo and inviting all their friends to Lake Tahoe. But looking back, Meg knew that she and Brody had let the theater of the moment overwhelm everything else. They had spent so much time planning the ceremony and trying to figure out how to do things beautifully but inexpensively that they had talked very little about the real reason for merging their lives. Perhaps if they had... But they hadn't. She sighed, pushing all the what-ifs away and turning her attention to the questions being asked by their children.

"Which do you like better?" Kevin asked curiously. "Getting married outside or inside?"

Meg knew if she were ever to get married again, it would probably be in a simple backyard ceremony with just family and a few close friends to witness it. Something simple. Heartfelt. And meaningful. "I think both types of weddings are nice," she said sincerely. "But I guess I'd still vote for outside."

"Do you have to get dressed up and have flowers and cake and everything if you get married in the backyard?" Kelly inquired.

"Oh, yes," Meg said, pushing the image of Brody as her groom from her mind. "Weddings are very serious occasions. So you should always get dressed up and look your best, whether it's a first wedding or a second."

"What kind of wedding does Daddy like best?" Kelly asked curiously.

"I don't know," Meg said, unhappy to have the image of Brody as someone else's groom in her mind. Like it or not, she admitted to herself, she did not want Brody to get married again. To Fiona or anyone else. "You'll have to ask him that question, guys," she said breezily. And, having had enough of wedding talk for the moment, she turned on the kitchen television to get the day's weather and traffic reports.

"DID YOU HEAR THAT?" Kelly whispered to Kevin as soon as Meg finished her coffee and went upstairs to get dressed for work. "Mommy wants to get married outside!"

Kevin cupped his hands over Kelly's ear and whispered back, "But we still don't know where Daddy wants to get married! And neither does Mommy!"

Kelly shrugged. As far as she was concerned, that was not a problem. "We just have to ask him!" she said.

CHAPTER EIGHT

THE DOORBELL RANG three evenings later just as Meg finished the supper dishes. She was stunned to find Brody on her front porch. "You're back!"

"Surprised?" He handed her a big bouquet of calla lilies—her favorite.

"Very." Trying not to think what the flowers meant, Meg smiled and ushered him inside. He'd just arrived and already she was tingling all over. "I didn't think you were returning until tomorrow morning." But she was very glad he was here now.

His lips curved in a smile. "I finished up earlier than I thought I would."

And rushed right home to all of them, Meg thought, satisfied.

"Daddy!" Kevin shouted as he and Kelly barreled into the foyer and launched themselves into Brody's waiting arms.

"We missed you!" Kelly announced jubilantly.

"I missed you, too." Brody hugged them close, looking blissfully content as kisses were exchanged all around.

As he let them down, Kevin looked up at him hopefully. "Did you bring something for us?"

Brody's triumphant laughter filled the house. "I sure did. Sit on the stairs and close your eyes and I'll go get it."

The twins complied while Brody stepped back onto the porch. Meg put down her flowers and waited, too. "Okay, you can open your eyes now," Brody said as he breezed back in the door, his arms laden with packages.

"Wow!" Kevin said as Brody handed him a complete set of Star Wars action figures and vehicles, complete with carrying case, and Kelly a video game box just like the one Kevin already had. "There are just two games and two controllers in the gift set," Brody explained, "but we can get you some more later."

"Can we set it up now?" Kelly asked, already tugging eagerly on the hem of Brody's sport coat.

"Sure," Brody said affably.

"Mommy, help me open this," Kevin demanded as he tore eagerly into his present.

Kelly beamed in overwhelming excitement. "This is like Christmas!"

Only it wasn't Christmas, Meg thought unhappily.

"No, it's not, silly," Kevin said. He regarded his sister with a condescending frown. "At Christmas we get lots and lots and *lots* of toys."

Exactly what Meg feared.

"You're piqued with me, aren't you?" Brody said an hour later when the twins were settled in front of the TV, playing a video game.

Because she didn't want to be a spoilsport, Meg had retired to the laundry room to work on her evening chores while Brody got the kids settled with their gifts. Still studying her cautiously, Brody leaned against the wall, watching as Meg sorted clothing to put into the washer. "You didn't like the gifts?"

Meg gently shut the door behind them, so they wouldn't be overheard by curious little ears. She turned back to Brody. "They were a bit much, don't you think?"

He shrugged, not about to apologize for his generosity. "So what? I can afford it."

"But I can't, Brody." And Meg didn't want to be put in

a position where she and Brody were competing, because when it came to lavish gifts, she would lose.

"Actually, Meg, you can. Or are you forgetting about the trust funds I set up for you and Kelly?"

Meg had received the papers from Brody's attorney via express mail while he was in Texas. The amounts he had set aside for them were indeed lavish. And though she appreciated what he was doing for Kelly, she had no desire to let it change her life, now or in the future. The money was a safety net as far as she was concerned, and that was all. "That's for Kelly's education," she stated firmly.

"And anything else your hearts desire," Brody insisted.

With a sigh, Meg stopped the pretense of sorting laundry and turned to Brody once again. "Kevin and Kelly need your time and attention, Brody," she reiterated gently. "They don't need more toys."

Brody's eyes darkened with displeasure. "The smiles on their faces just now say differently."

Folding her arms at her waist, Meg tipped her head up and regarded him just as contentiously. "If you keep this up, you'll spoil them to the point where they won't appreciate anything."

"Why shouldn't they enjoy the fruits of my labor?" Brody slid his hands in the pockets of his trousers and slouched against the wall. "I've worked darn hard so that none of us will ever have to worry about money again."

Doing her best to ignore how good it felt to have Brody with her again, Meg shouldered past him and turned her attention to the laundry once more. "Believe me, that wasn't on Kevin's mind when he woke up missing you the past three nights in a row."

Brody moved in front of her so she had no choice but to look at him. "You didn't mention that when I called from Texas," he chided, concerned.

"Because Kevin and Kelly were right there listening,"

Meg explained. And she hadn't wanted to make Brody feel guilty for being away on business. Flushing self-consciously and ignoring the jump in her nerves, she tilted her face up to his. "Look, Brody, I know you have to travel, that it's part and parcel of your work as CEO of Taylor Software. But bringing home extravagant gifts for the kids is not the way to make it up to them."

"Then what is?" he demanded softly.

Meg shrugged, aware of the sudden parched feeling in her throat. "Just spend time with the kids when you're here." Looking deep into his eyes, she risked alienating him even as she advised, "Let them feel your love. Don't try to buy their affection, because that just—"

"Reminds you of what your parents used to do to you?" Brody asked, when Meg couldn't—wouldn't—go on.

Meg nodded, the choked-up feeling in her throat growing worse.

Abruptly contrite, Brody shot her a beseeching look. "I'm sorry, Meg. I know you're right." He shook his head in self-remonstration. "I guess I just got carried away. I wanted to get them a souvenir from Texas. They didn't have anything suitable in the hotel gift shop, and I was in a hurry, so I went to the closest toy store. And before you know it, my arms were full of stuff for them."

That was so like Brody, Meg thought. But she could hardly fault him for wanting the kids and her to know he had missed them. "I just don't want to spoil them," she said gently.

Brody looked grateful for her understanding. "And I don't want them to ever have to do without, the way I did. But you're right, Meg. When it comes to big gifts like that, we should agree beforehand. So next time I'm on a trip, I promise I'll stick with a T-shirt or stuffed toy from the airport gift shop for each of them."

"Thank you." Meg smiled in relief. She reached over

and took his hand in a show of solidarity. "I want us to parent as a team."

"I do, too."

They regarded each other in happy silence. Finally, Brody grinned in a mischievous way that reminded Meg very much of Kevin, and chucked her beneath the chin. "Which only leaves us with one question," he added with a wink.

"And that is?" Meg queried, her heart already pounding as Brody slowly wrapped his arms around her waist and drew her close to him.

"What kind of souvenir do you want from me, Meg?" He rubbed his thumb across her lower lip and looked her in the eye, his expression suddenly, unbearably tender before he ducked his head and took her mouth in a searing kiss. "Will this do?"

Need pouring through her, Meg laced her arms about his neck and gave in to the feelings that had been plaguing her for days. "Oh, yes." It was—he was—exactly what she wanted these days.

THE PHONE RANG just as Meg was getting ready for bed the next evening. She wasn't surprised to hear Brody's voice on the other end. He had made it pretty clear the evening before that he was determined to do whatever it took to win her back. Including courting her incessantly. The surprising thing was, she wanted him to do just that.

"Just out of curiosity, how many wedding questions are you getting?" he asked at once.

Meg thought about the ground she and Kelly had covered in their marathon question-and-answer session on the drive home from school, during dinner, dishes and bathtime. Kelly was a tenacious child—both twins were—but Meg had never realized she could ask so many questions on one subject. There wasn't a detail they hadn't covered.

Knowing Brody was waiting for a reply, Meg confided, "I've been getting tons, including what happened when we tied the knot, and my wish list for any future affairs." Glad to finally have someone to share her parenting concerns on a daily basis, she asked softly, "What about you?"

"More than I thought I could answer, I'll tell you that." In the silence, Meg could almost hear him smile. "I gather you let them watch the wedding video while I was in Texas?"

Still buttoning her pajama top, Meg shifted the phone to her other ear and climbed into bed. "I didn't see the harm. I figured they would eventually get tired of it. And besides, I've got a backup plan."

"Can't wait to hear it," Brody teased.

"Tomorrow I'm going to pick up a copy of the video *One Hundred and One Dalmatians*."

Brody's answering chuckle was soft and sexy. "You know what that'll do, don't you?" he teased. "Make them start begging for a dog."

"Anything to change the subject," Meg said firmly, hoping her ploy would distract the twins and get them onto some other track. Meg tried not to wonder what Brody might or might not be wearing at that time of night. Was he in bed, like her? Getting ready to sleep? Stripped down to just his boxers?

Forcing her mind back to the conversation, she warned briskly, "And just so you'll know, I've already promised Kelly a dog, but not until she's eight and old enough to help out with the care on a daily basis."

"Ah, smart. I should have figured you'd know just how to handle that."

Meg warmed to Brody's praise, another comfortable silence fell between them.

"Well, I guess I better let you go," he said regretfully.

"I just wanted to touch base and find out how things went with you and the kids at school today."

Meg smiled blissfully. "I had a great day, and so did the kids, if you don't count Kevin's usual mischievous streak."

"What did he do this time?"

With a sigh, Meg recalled the chaos that had briefly ensued before Carmen got control of Kevin and her class once again. "He painted a mustache and horns on his self-portrait."

"Was his teacher amused?"

"Not really," Meg explained, "since it was an exercise in learning to follow directions. But the other students found it hilarious, including Kelly."

Brody's voice held weary resignation, "He's going to be a handful."

"Going to be?" Meg teased dryly.

"All right—is. Although I have to say, he's calmed down considerably since you came back into his life."

"I'm glad to hear that." Meg wanted Kevin to know he didn't have to clown around outrageously to get the attention he sought. It was there for the taking from both his parents now. And his twin sister.

Brody paused, his own relief apparent in his easygoing tone. "Seems like we worried needlessly about the way they'd take the news about us being a family, doesn't it?"

OR MAYBE NOT, Meg thought several days later, when the temper tantrum she had half been expecting erupted. She was finished for the day and was trying to get Kelly ready to go home, when Brody arrived to pick up Kevin.

"What do you mean you're not going home with me?" Meg asked, when Kelly refused to put her rain slicker on. There was no room for argument, since it was raining cats and dogs outside.

"I'm staying here tonight with Kevin." Kelly pointed to the kindergarten classroom.

"Honey, you can't sleep at the day care center," Meg said, beginning to be embarrassed as all eyes turned to the two of them.

"Yes, I can," Kelly insisted, her dark eyes flashing with Irish temper as she stomped one sneaker-clad foot. "Right here on the floor, on my mat and towel, just like I do at naptime."

"And I'm going to sleep here, too" Kevin said, folding his arms in front of him stubbornly. His face reddened beneath his freckles. "Every night from now on," he insisted firmly.

Carmen Perez, their teacher, smiled at Meg and Brody. A grandmother herself, the fifty-six-year-old teacher was experienced in both educating and parenting and the problems that came with both.

"Kevin and Kelly." Carmen got the twins' attention smoothly. "Your voices are getting very loud," she warned.

"I don't care!" Kelly stomped her foot again, even more dramatically. Beside her, Kevin followed suit as the remaining kindergartners watched, wide-eyed with apprehension.

Another parent arrived to pick up a child. "You know," Carmen said, "the events room is empty right now. Why don't you two take this in there, where you can work it out without so many little ears listening in. I'll gather up their things and bring them over to you."

"Thanks, Carmen." Meg turned to Kelly and took her hand. "Come on, sweetie."

Meg expected Kelly to comply, albeit reluctantly. Instead, Kelly did what she had never done before. She went totally limp on the floor. All eyes widened as the little girl pounded and kicked the floor and screamed unhappily at the top of her lungs. Kevin's eyes rounded, then he quickly followed suit.

Meg didn't know what to do.

She looked at Brody. "This has never happened before," she whispered.

"Wish I could say the same," Brody muttered grimly.

Carmen stood by patiently, waiting to see how Meg and Brody were going to handle this.

"Enough!" Brody's voice boomed throughout the room.

Kevin and Kelly jerked their heads up in surprise, and the other kindergarten students froze. With an expression on his face that said he meant business, Brody warned, "Kevin and Kelly, you have two seconds to get up and march yourselves into the events room."

Kelly wiped the tears from her face, amazed, because Brody had never said so much as a cross word to her before. "And then what?" she demanded tearfully, her lower lip trembling.

"Then," Brody said, helping Kevin gently but firmly to his feet, "the four of us are going to have a talk."

To Meg's relief, for once she didn't have to assume total control and responsibility for the situation. For once, she had Kevin and Kelly's father to lean on. And Brody did not disappoint in his ability to bring order to chaos as they walked quietly into the empty events room and shut the door behind them. In short order, he had everyone sitting in four chairs set in a circle, while Meg handed out tissues.

In a gentle but authoritative voice he began the impromptu meeting. "Okay, I want to know what is going on here and what started all this. Because this is not your normal behavior, Kevin. Nor yours, Kelly."

Kelly sniffed indignantly, looking glad to have a chance to air her grievances to such a captive audience. "It's just not fair that Kevin and I don't get to sleep in the same house all the time, and be together,'' she said sulkily. ''Everybody else that has a brother and a sister gets to be together.''

''Even if their parents are divorced,'' Kevin added, just as indignantly. ''Only me and Kelly don't get to be together. And it's just not fair. And things are supposed to be fair. Everybody knows that. Ms. Perez says it all the time. We have to be fair. You and Mommy are not being fair!''

''And that's not fair,'' Kelly added.

Brody put up a hand, temporarily commanding the twins to silence. ''Okay, we're getting the gist of it.'' He sighed and looked at Meg, at a loss how to solve this. ''It's Thursday night, so we have school and work tomorrow, but it's still early enough for us to go to one of our homes and have a family conference.''

''WE NEED TO TALK ABOUT the temper tantrum you two threw today,'' Brody said as the four of them gathered in Meg's living room.

''Because,'' Meg continued, looking each child in the eye, ''your daddy and I never want to see that happen again.''

''It isn't necessary,'' Brody said.

Meg reached over and squeezed Brody's hand in a gesture of solidarity, before picking up where he left off. ''What is necessary is for you two kids to tell us what else is on your mind. Because I have the feeling that what Kelly said at the day care is only part of it.''

''We think there are other things bothering you, too,'' Brody continued, backing up Meg.

Kelly's lower lip slid out petulantly as she studied her sneakers. ''I don't get to see Daddy.''

''You've been seeing lots of Daddy,'' Meg reminded her daughter.

"Not every night," Kelly complained unhappily, her dark eyes filling with tears. "I want to see my daddy every night, 'cept when he's on a business trip. I want him to show me how to do stuff on the new computer, and watch TV with me, and read stories, and play games and all kinds of stuff, and we don't get to do that every day," she summed up sullenly.

Kevin's lower lip trembled, too. "And I don't get to see Mommy cook stuff. And listen to her sing songs. And I want Mommy to read me stories."

Brody interrupted, looking upset. "I read you stories every night before bed."

"But you don't do the voices and act out stuff like Mommy," Kevin explained emotionally.

Meg had never been one to give in to temper tantrums, but this was a lot more than that. The kids were sending up an emotional SOS. She and Brody had to respond to it promptly, or deal with the consequences. She regarded Kevin and Kelly seriously. "I think you two have a good point."

"So do I," Brody concurred soberly as he and Meg exchanged concerned glances.

"We can't all live together in the same house," Meg said, forcing herself to ignore the way the kids' faces fell at her firm but gentle words.

"Why not?" Kevin interrupted unhappily.

"Because your daddy and I aren't married," Meg said. "But perhaps we can do a much better job of making sure you get to spend time with each other and us."

"Absolutely," Brody said, digging out his PalmPilot.

Meg got up to find her day planner. Together, they sat down. "How often do you want to do this?" she asked.

"How about we make sure we all see each other for at least an hour a day?" he said. "Unless I'm on a business trip, and then we'll make sure both kids talk to me on the phone every day. That way, no one will feel they're getting the short shrift.''

"We could take turns having the kids after school," Meg suggested. "Let them spend at least one night together on the weekends, and do things together sometimes."

"You mean all four of us?" Kelly interrupted, sounding unbearably excited.

Meg looked at Brody. "Sounds good to me," he said.

"To me, too!" Kevin shouted.

"Yeah," Kelly added blissfully. "Me, too."

For the next forty-five minutes, Brody and Meg worked to combine their schedules. "What do you want to do on your birthday?" Meg asked when they got to Saturday, October 11. Julia and Drew's wedding was in the morning, so there would be lots of time to celebrate later. "Something special, I presume?"

"We could have a party!" Kelly suggested.

"Yeah," Kevin agreed, "in the backyard at Daddy's house. 'Cause it's real big."

"But me and Kevin want to do the party," Kelly said, reverting to her independent self. "Can we?" she asked Meg and Brody excitedly. "Can we be in charge? And invite friends from school and church and Daddy's office? And figure out what cake to order and what kinds of decorations and everything?"

Meg could see Brody liked the idea, too. "I think it would be good for you two to do something together for someone else." Meg gave the twins an approving smile.

"WELL, THAT WENT BETTER than I thought it would," Meg said after they had finished dinner. The kids had gone upstairs to the playroom while she and Brody cleaned up the kitchen and shared a moment alone.

"That's because together we're the perfect parents," Brody teased as he broke up the pizza box and put it into the trash, while Meg rinsed the plates and silverware and placed them in the dishwasher. "You know how to see into people's hearts and deal with all the emotional stuff...."

Meg shut the dishwasher door and turned to face Brody. "And you know how to take charge when that's called for. I have to tell you, I really admire the way you cut short that giant temper tantrum today." Meg knew she wouldn't have handled it nearly so well on her own.

"I'm just sorry I didn't listen to you sooner," Brody said, coming to stand closer to her. He tipped his head down and continued in a soft, low voice meant to carry no farther than her own ears. "You told me this was coming. That sooner or later they would be acting out their unhappiness at the way we handled things years ago. I just didn't want to believe it."

They weren't even touching, yet Meg was already beginning to heat up inside. She continued in the most casual tone she could manage. "The important thing is that we dealt with it well—and together. And we'll just have to continue to deal with it, day by day, until the kids feel secure again." *Even if my being near you like this is stirring up all sorts of unwanted, forbidden feelings.*

Briefly, worry clouded Brody's dark eyes. If he was feeling the same wealth of desire she was, Meg noted unhappily, he wasn't showing it. Instead, his mind seemed solely on the problem at hand. "How long do you think that might take?" he asked her, concerned.

Meg shrugged and, ignoring the low thudding of her pulse, confessed in a low, guarded tone, "I don't know, Brody. I wish I did."

FRIDAY WENT without a hitch. Maybe because the kids knew they were going to spend the night together at Brody's house. Meg went over for dinner—take-out Chinese, à la Brody—then left around eight, as scheduled, and went home for a quiet evening alone.

Telling herself she was going to take advantage of the break from parenting, Meg put on her favorite music, ran a tubful of fragrant bubbles, lit a candle and poured herself a glass of wine. And while she was at it, she did the things she rarely had time to do these days, like deep condition her hair and give herself a facial. She had everything she needed for a perfect evening except someone to share it with.

Sighing, Meg shut her eyes and tried not to think about how much Brody's kisses had affected her, or how much she still wanted to make love with him. Not that this was any surprise, of course. She and Brody had been wildly attracted to each other from the very first. The chemistry between them was real and potent and lasting, and she knew she would discover it hadn't lessened the moment she welcomed him back into her bed.

There was no question in Meg's mind that lovemaking with Brody would be as thrilling and exciting as ever. The dilemma was, she mused as she soaped herself leisurely from head to toe, should she really let herself go down that path? She had managed without any sort of man-woman intimacy in her life for some time now. And she'd done so because she wanted her life to be simpler and devoid of the hurt a sexy man like Brody could wreak on her heart.

All that had mattered was Kelly. And keeping her safe and happy. Now Meg had Kevin to worry about, too. And both kids wanted her and Brody together as much of the time as possible. If Meg were honest, she wanted that, too.

So instead of putting up a firewall between herself and Brody, Meg realized as she stepped out of the tub and toweled herself dry, she was opening up to him more and more, and encouraging him to open up to her.

They were getting closer. She thought about him all the

time and even dreamed about him at night sometimes. Was he fantasizing about her, too? Meg wondered. And if that was the case, how much longer would it realistically be before the two of them ended up making love to each other again?

BRODY AND THE KIDS weren't even out of bed when the doorbell rang. Deciding no robe was needed over his pajama pants and T-shirt, Brody headed for the front door and looked through the viewer to see who could be ringing the bell at such an ungodly hour. Meg was standing on the other side. Raking a hand through his hair, he opened the door and asked, "Everything okay?"

He had to admit she looked gorgeous, standing there in the early morning mist, with the sun coming up behind her. Her auburn curls were in perfect order, and thicker and glossier than usual somehow. She was wearing tailored, dark brown slacks, sexy high-heeled boots and a crisp white shirt, open at the throat. A brown-and-white-patterned cardigan was tied over her shoulders, and she had a paper sack in her arms.

Brody glanced at his watch again. "I thought you weren't coming by until nine." They had promised the kids the previous evening, before Meg left, that they would do their errands together this morning.

Meg lifted the sack in her arms. "I thought I might cook you all breakfast. Waffles and bacon sound good?"

Brody's mouth was already watering. "That sounds great. Except I don't have a waffle iron."

"No problem." Meg breezed past him with a waft of deliciously sexy perfume. "Mine's in the car."

Behind Brody, footsteps sounded on the stairs. Seeing who it was, Kevin and Kelly came flying down the rest of the way. "Mommy! We missed you!" they said, hugging her.

Brody took the grocery bag from Meg. "I'll just carry this to the kitchen, and then go up and shower and dress," he said. Unable to resist, he cast another glance over his shoulder, marveling at how beautiful she looked. As if she were ready for a special date, not just a morning running errands. Had she done it for him? Or was that how she always looked on Saturday mornings these days? He admitted he hadn't a clue.

"Take your time," Meg said with a smile. "It'll take me a while to get used to your kitchen, anyway."

By the time Brody came down, Kevin and Kelly were dressed, and Meg was feeding them crisp slices of bacon and fluffy golden waffles garnished with strawberries and whipped cream. A glass of orange juice was next to his plate, and a freshly brewed pot of coffee sat on the warmer.

"This is magnificent," Brody said. It reminded him of Saturday mornings when they were married. Only then Meg had cooked in her pajamas, and they had headed back to bed for slow, wonderful lovemaking before continuing with their day.

But that wasn't going to happen this morning, he knew, thanks to a certain divorce decree and the presence of their chaperones, so Brody forced himself to be content with what he did have. A great breakfast, two wonderful kids and the company of one very beautiful, talented woman.

"WE WANT TO PICK OUT the cake for the party all by ourselves," Kelly said as the four of them walked into the bakery they had selected.

"Yeah, that way it's a big surprise for you and Daddy," Kevin said, slipping his hand out of Meg's and turning to the displays of sumptuous cakes in the refrigerated glass cases.

"Remember how much you liked your cake at the party at the theater?" Kelly chimed in, removing her hand from

Brody's. She looked at Meg, reminding her, "It was a surprise, too, Mommy. And that made you really, really happy."

"You'll both be real surprised," Kevin said, taking his role as party planner very seriously. "And real happy."

Meg looked at Brody.

"They're really getting into this," he said with an approving grin.

Maybe that wasn't such a surprise, Meg thought, given all the birthday celebrations they had missed the past five years. "They sure are," she said, smiling back.

Meg looked at the bakery owner, a pleasant woman in her midforties with dark hair and kind eyes. She introduced herself and Brody and the twins, then explained, "We're having a party, and we're going to let our children select the cake. It should serve forty." Meg handed over her credit card while Brody wrote out his name and home address on the order form, and the date the cake should be delivered. "We'll be right outside. You can just send them out when they're done," Meg said.

"But you can't tell Mommy and Daddy what we decide on," Kevin explained to the bakery lady patiently as Meg and Brody left the store. "Cause we really, really want it to be a *surprise.*"

"I guess that surprise birthday party they had for me at the theater made more of an impression on Kelly than I realized," Meg said, enjoying the sunny morning and the clear blue sky overhead. The mist had lifted and it was going to be an exceptionally beautiful day.

Brody grinned. "Maybe we should give them a surprise party at some point," he said.

"For their next birthday?"

Brody smiled down at her. Meg smiled back. As the awareness flowed between them, she wondered if he was thinking about kissing her as much as she was starting to think about kissing him. And what would happen if he did...

Before Meg could mull that possibility over any further, the door slammed to the left of them. Kevin and Kelly came barreling out, the bakery lady right behind them. "They placed their order," she reported. "We'll have it delivered to Mr. Taylor's home on Saturday, October eleventh. The total is on the bottom of the receipt, but there's no description—I didn't want to spoil the surprise."

"I'm sure it will be wonderful, whatever it is." Meg smiled.

The rest of the morning went smoothly as they finished their errands. The plan had been to part company once they returned to Brody's, with Meg taking Kelly home and Brody staying with Kevin. But Meg could tell by the way Brody was looking at her as they emerged from their cars that he was reconsidering their original plan, just as she was.

Why should they arbitrarily limit themselves to mere co-parents, or even friends, when they were still so attracted to each other, so in sync with each other in so many ways? Yes, Meg thought, there were still problems, but there was so much good, too. Their love for the children. The fun and sense of family they had when they were together like this. The feeling that as parents they could conquer anything.

And if that weren't enough, there was the sense of rightness she felt when he kissed her. And the yearning once again to be as close to him as it was possible to be.

"Sure there's nothing else I can help you with today?" Brody asked hopefully.

Yes, Meg thought, *my heart. Because even if it means I'm a fool, I'd really like to try again. See if we can't find some way to make it work this time.*

"A penny for your thoughts," Brody teased, his eyes

shining. Suddenly, he looked very much like he wanted to kiss her.

Meg leaned toward him, and he leaned toward her, just as a car pulled up in front of the house. They turned in unison to see a taxi park at the curb. Meg's breath lodged in her chest as a stunningly beautiful young woman in her early twenties got out and, eyes locked on Brody, headed straight for them.

"Fiona!" Kevin shouted. Excitement pouring from him, Meg's son raced over to give his former nanny a hug.

CHAPTER NINE

"MY DARLIN' KEVIN, how I've missed taking care of you!" the lovely young woman said in an Irish accent, swooping down to give her former charge a fierce hug.

The question was, had Brody missed Fiona? Meg thought with an unaccustomed wave of jealousy as introductions were swiftly made. If so, she could easily understand why. Fiona had satiny, coal-black hair that fell to her shoulders in a well-tamed cloud, beautiful green eyes with thick lashes even a supermodel would envy and a figure to die for. In addition, she was roughly the same age Meg had been when she had married Brody. Only Fiona, unlike Meg, had for the last five years devoted herself solely to taking care of Brody and Kevin. And would still be living with them had she not announced her love for Brody and tried to seduce him.

Still, Meg noted with relief, Brody looked more stunned than happy to see Fiona. So maybe Meg had nothing to worry about, after all.

Fiona released Meg's hand. She went toward Brody, giving him the same familial kind of hug she had given his son. "And I've missed you, too, Brody Taylor," she said in a soft, shy voice.

Brody hugged Fiona back impersonally, then stepped away, a rather pained smile fixed on his face. "What brings you here, Fiona?" he asked gently.

"Your uncle Roarke," Fiona explained as Brody unlocked the front door and motioned everyone inside. "He was more than generous, as usual."

"That sounds like him," Brody agreed as Fiona rolled her suitcase through the portal, brushing unnecessarily close to him.

Meg followed, resentment bubbling up inside her. Was Fiona planning to sleep here, too? she wondered. Not that Brody didn't have the room. His big house had six bedrooms and six baths. But still...

Beaming, Fiona parked her suitcase at the foot of the staircase, and holding on to Kevin, who had once again wrapped his arms about her waist, turned back to Brody. She looked him straight in the eye. "Roarke said you hadn't found anyone yet to take care of Kev, and he thought maybe you'd be needing me. Especially now that you're going to be traveling back and forth to Texas on business."

Brody shut the door behind them and led them all toward the rear of the house. "I told you before, Fiona, I would never ask you to leave family and home in Ireland," he said conversationally. "It wouldn't be fair."

Fiona slipped her hand around his elbow and beamed up at him. "You leave it to me, Brody Taylor, to decide what is fair and what isn't. I would happily make Seattle my home," she announced as she stepped into his spacious, state-of-the-art kitchen. "And in fact, that's exactly what I plan to do, whether you hire me back or not."

"What do you mean?" Brody asked, confused.

"I've contacted a child care agency here in Seattle. I've got several interviews lined up already and I plan to stay here until I actually get a job. I was going to check into a hotel, but Roarke said I would probably be able to stay here with you and Kevin, since you have plenty of room."

"Can she, Daddy?" Kevin asked happily, bouncing up and down. "Can Fiona live with us again?"

"Kevin, why don't you and Kelly go upstairs in your

room and play awhile?'' Brody suggested pleasantly. ''We'll come and get you when lunch is ready.''

''As long as I'm here, I'll be happy to prepare it for you!'' Fiona was already moving toward the stove.

''Wouldn't hear of it.'' Before Meg could stop herself, she was moving to block Fiona's way and acting as if she, not Brody, owned the place. ''You two go on into the living room, where you can talk privately and catch up on all your news,'' she said, pushing away the unsettling thoughts of what Fiona's presence might mean. ''I'll stay right here and whip up something for all of us.''

MEG WAS IN THE KITCHEN, heating two cans of alphabet soup and putting together a plate of peanut butter and jelly sandwiches, when Brody walked in twenty minutes later. ''Where's Fiona?'' she asked, disliking the tart tone in her voice, but unable to do anything to soften it. She was so jealous she could barely stand it. And not just because Fiona had been privileged to share the first five years of Kevin's childhood. It was because of the starry-eyed way the young Irish nanny looked at Brody, as if he was the only man on earth for her. *This was a woman who was still in love with her ex-boss.*

Brody moved closer, his tall frame blocking out the rectangle of sunlight pouring in through the wall of windows that opened up the rear of the house to the beautifully landscaped backyard. ''She went upstairs to play with the children until we call them for lunch.'' He looked at the juvenile fare, an odd expression on his face.

Flushing in embarrassment, Meg turned her face up to his and explained, ''I know the menu leaves a lot to be desired, but so do your pantry and fridge.'' She had done the best she could with what little she had to work with.

Looking as if the meager offerings didn't bother him in

the least, Brody shrugged. "I'm not much of a cook. You know that."

Meg only nodded.

Brody edged closer still. "But perhaps we could remedy that. We can go grocery shopping together later this weekend. You and Kelly could help me and Kevin buy what we need to adequately stock our kitchen."

At the implication, Meg's heart skipped a beat. Crossing her arms in front of her, she scolded herself inwardly. It was exactly the kind of activity that was leading her to think she and Brody might someday have a future together—beyond shared parenting. "Or Fiona could help you," Meg suggested pleasantly, doing her best to keep a civil tongue. Once again, she forced herself to smile as if she weren't disturbed by the sudden appearance of his young and beautiful Irish nanny. "I'm sure she's better versed in your likes and dislikes than I am."

Brody arched his eyebrows playfully. "You sound jealous."

Meg shot him a beleaguered look. "Realistic."

The familiarity between them deepened as Brody put his hand over hers. "I didn't ask her to come to Seattle, Meg."

Meg had the strong suspicion Brody wanted to do a lot more than just hold her hand. He wanted to take her in his arms and kiss her. Not about to let that happen now that Fiona was back in the picture, trying to finagle her way into Brody and Kevin's lives however she could, Meg withdrew her hand from his and moved away from him gracefully. "Yes, I know that," she said quietly. Fiona had done this on her own. As for Uncle Roarke, he was matchmaking again.

Her spine stiff, Meg turned to the stove and gave the alphabet soup another stir.

Once again, Brody edged nearer, watching her with that mesmerizing, yet disturbingly possessive smile.

"Fiona has every right to look for another job wherever she wants."

Meg had expected Fiona to make that argument, not Brody. "She has to do it here? In Seattle?"

Brody shrugged. "She wants to be close enough to visit Kevin."

"She wants to be close to you, too, Brody. And if you don't see that…" Meg stopped, bit her lip.

Brody clamped a hand on the counter beside her and leaned intimately close. "What are you really worried about here, Meg?"

"Isn't it obvious? I'm concerned she'll slip into something flimsy and corner you late one night and try and seduce you again!"

"She knows that's not going to happen—that I'm not interested in her that way."

"It didn't stop her before."

"She felt she had to try. Now that she has…" Brody gestured aimlessly as his words trailed off. He really didn't see it as a problem. "There's only one woman I want, Meg."

He lowered his head as if to kiss her, but Meg turned her face away. "I don't see how this can happen. Especially now, with Fiona clamoring to become part of your life again." *And you not resisting, either.*

Brody's face tightened. "And what would you have me do? Kick her out? Tell her she's no longer welcome in my home, even as a guest? She's like family, Meg. Especially to Kevin."

Meg knew that. For years Fiona had been much more of a mother to her son than she had been. Unwilling to let Brody see the anguish in her eyes, Meg turned her back to him and continued stirring.

Brody put his hand over hers, took the spoon from her and set it on the plate she was using for a spoon rest. With both hands on her shoulders, he gently turned her to face him. "I told her I'd do whatever I could to help her find another position, and when she does, she needs to take it. It's the least I owe her, Meg." He paused a moment to let that sink in, then, tightening his grip on Meg possessively, continued, "And I've invited Fiona to stay the weekend with us—she has come all this way, after all, and Kevin adores her. But come Sunday evening, I'm taking her to a hotel, where she will stay—as our guest—until she finds a job or decides to go home."

He was doing the decent thing, Meg realized. So why was she still upset?

Silence fell between them, tenser than before. Clearly, Brody wanted Meg's assurance that everything was going to be okay, that she accepted his decision to have Fiona as his houseguest. But she could not, in all conscience, give it. Not knowing what had gone on before. Not after seeing the adoration in Fiona's eyes when she looked at Brody.

His frown deepening, Brody stepped back. "I think you're reading way too much into Fiona's decision to move to Seattle. The truth is, she's always been enamored of the United States."

He sounded so confident. Too confident. Meg could feel her heart pounding anxiously in her chest. Anger stiffened her spine. "And I think, as usual, that you're not reading enough into the emotional aspect of the situation," she said right back, lowering her voice to a whisper. "You need to think about what Fiona's presence here today really means to you and to Kevin. For heaven's sake, Brody! She just chased you halfway around the world! You don't do that on a whim. She loves you, and she loves Kevin as if he were her own child!" It took every ounce of strength Meg had to keep her voice from breaking. "And he loves her, too."

"Of course I know that," Brody hissed right back.

Aware their voices were rising, he took Meg by the hand and led her swiftly across the kitchen and into the pantry. Giving her no chance to protest, he switched on the light and shut the door. "But I never once dated her. I never led her on or gave her any reason to think she would ever be anything more than my employee."

Meg leaned back against the mostly bare shelves and glared at Brody. "But that didn't stop her from falling in love with you, did it? It didn't stop her from loving Kevin and caring for him as if he were her own child." It hadn't stopped the three of them from forming a family of sorts.

"And what would you have preferred, Meg?" he demanded harshly, folding his arms in front of him. "That I had Kevin looked after by someone who didn't care about him, or want only the best for him?"

"No, of course not!" she replied, indignation rising.

Brody arched his brow. "Then...?"

"I just think..."

"Yes?" he prodded, still simmering with pent-up tension.

Meg stopped and put a hand to her lips. Brody wasn't the only one whose attitude was out of whack here. She, too, had been taking too much for granted. Thinking things might work out, deciding she had more of a stake in who visited her ex than she really did. The truth was, Brody had a right to be angry with her. Just as he had a right to receive visits from anyone he pleased without comment or reaction from her. Meg struggled to get her skyrocketing feelings under control. "Look," she apologized as sincerely as she could, exasperated that she wasn't able to be more emotionally removed from a situation that didn't technically concern her at all. "This isn't really my business, anyway."

Brody's dark brow climbed even higher. "You don't think so?" he remarked dryly as he slowly, deliberately closed the distance between them.

Meg drew a breath, aware her insides were as warm and liquid as if he had just made love to her, yet all he had done was stand next to her. She backed as far as she could against the shelves, until she felt the wood digging into her. "You and I have been apart for five years," she said as his arms went around her and tugged her close. Swallowing, she plunged on. "We have both had other relationships. It's to be expected." She almost sounded convincing to herself. "We're not monks and nuns here."

It was Brody's turn to look unhappy. Really unhappy.

He released her as abruptly as he had taken hold of her. "You're saying there's someone else in your life?" he asked in utter astonishment.

What had she gotten herself into here? The only man who'd even asked her out since she had moved to Seattle was her colleague Ted Isaacs. "I'm saying I was asked out on a date yesterday afternoon." She had initially turned Ted down again, but Meg supposed that could be remedied with a simple phone call.

Suddenly, she wasn't the only one looking jealous.

"For tonight?" Brody said shortly.

"Yes." Until now, Meg had had no intention of taking Ted up on his offer, but maybe dinner with the college professor was exactly what she needed. Anything to get her mind off Brody. "Ted and I haven't set the time, but…"

Impossibly, Brody's expression grew even grimmer. "Did you get a sitter for Kelly yet?" he asked as matter-of-factly as if he were inquiring about the weather forecast for the weekend.

"No." Meg wished Brody didn't look so good. Or that she didn't want to kiss and hold him quite so much.

"Then why not leave her here?" Brody asked pleasantly.

Another stab of jealousy struck, more potent than the first. "With you and Fiona?" Meg asked, pretending she could be unaffected by all this, too.

Brody studied her expression carefully. "Unless you have an objection to that."

What could Meg say? She had been the one who had just thrown down the gauntlet. She had been the one who had decided to go on a date with someone else in order to get back at Brody for having Fiona as his houseguest for the rest of the weekend. She spread her hands wide in a show of bravura better than any Broadway stage performance she had ever given. "Sounds great," Meg said cheerfully.

FORTUNATELY, Ted Isaacs was amenable to the last-minute change of plans. Unfortunately, although Meg did her best to participate enthusiastically in their date, her heart wasn't in it. No matter how hard she tried, her thoughts were with Brody and Fiona and the kids—her and Brody's kids!

"You seem preoccupied this evening," Ted said as he and Meg left the art house theater. "In fact, I don't think you heard one word of that movie we just saw."

Meg flushed guiltily because she knew he was right. Ted was cute, funny, intelligent and kind. A gifted professor, he also had the potential to be a great friend to her. But sadly, the chemistry needed for him to be something more just wasn't there. And Meg wasn't quite sure what to do about that. She didn't want to hurt his feelings. Nor did she want to lead him on and pretend there might be more dates after this one, because she had already made up her mind. She was not going to waste Ted's time when she knew she could never be the soul mate he was searching for. But not knowing how to end their date without destroying their friendship, Meg just smiled and said, "I was reading the subtitles."

Ted regarded her wryly. "The film we just saw didn't have subtitles, Meg. The subtitles were in the previews."

Meg had never felt so embarrassed. "Oh."

Ted placed a brotherly arm around her shoulders as they headed toward his sports car. "Suffice it to say, although you were a charming dinner companion, your heart was not in this date." He paused next to the passenger side and unlocked her door.

"I'm sorry." Meg pressed a hand to her chest. Now she really felt awful. She looked Ted straight in the eye. "I—"

He lifted a silencing palm. "No need to apologize, Meg. I had the feeling when I asked you out that there might be someone else."

That was the problem, Meg thought. There was someone else. From the day Brody Taylor had walked into—and then out of—her life, she had loved him and only him. She hadn't wanted to admit that to herself, but now she knew it was true. She leaned against the side of Ted's car instead of getting in immediately. "How can I make this up to you?" she asked, just as kindly.

Ted thought a moment. "You know Liza Culhane?"

Meg nodded. "She teaches the undergrad course on classic British comedies."

"I've been trying to get up the nerve to ask Liza out for weeks," Ted confessed shyly.

Meg could see this meant a lot to him. "You want me to fix the two of you up?" she asked cheerfully.

"Would you? Could you?"

Vastly relieved, Meg grinned. "I could sure try," she promised. Heck, she would do more than that, she would succeed!

"That's great." Once they were both in the car, Ted headed for Meg's neighborhood. The two of them traded stories about their teaching experiences, and in no time at all they were turning onto Meg's street.

Ted slowed in front of her house, frowning worriedly as he steered his jaunty little sports car into the driveway behind Meg's own sedan. "There's a man sitting in that SUV in front of your house."

"So there is," Meg said with a sigh. And unfortunately, she knew exactly who it was.

THE SOUND OF MEG'S low laughter and even softer, sexier voice made Brody's gut tighten with jealousy. He watched from his car as she said good-night to her date on the sidewalk. Brody couldn't make out anything they were saying, but there was no way he could miss the affectionate hug the two exchanged before they parted company. Meg glanced at Brody, acknowledging that she was aware of his presence, then turned back to her date and waved as he drove away.

His every muscle tensing, Brody got out of his SUV and sauntered toward Meg.

She turned to face him, a regal expression on her face. "So what brings you out this late at night?" She seemed to know there had been no emergency with the kids. "Or were you just here to spy on me?" she asked casually as she plucked her keys from her purse.

Brody saw no reason to deny he had been hoping to catch the end of Meg's date, especially when he had been caught in the act. He shrugged and slid his hands into the pockets of his khakis. "I noticed there was no good-night kiss between you and what's his name. In fact—" Brody narrowed his eyes disapprovingly "—he didn't even walk you to the door."

Meg flashed Brody one of her dazzling, stage-princess smiles. "I told Ted it wasn't necessary, since you were here to do it for him. That is why you were sitting here, isn't it?" She viewed him with cool determination. "Because you want to come in."

The knot in Brody's gut that had been there ever since Meg left him earlier in the day twisted painfully. "Yes. I want to come in.'' He wanted to correct her mistaken assessment of his relationship with Fiona.

Meg swept past him, her head held high. "Where are the children?"

Brody accompanied her up the walk to the porch, and watched as she unlocked the front door and went inside. "With Fiona. I asked her to stay with them while I came over to make sure you got home okay."

Meg stopped dead in her tracks and pivoted to face Brody. To his dismay, though she had been out all evening, she still looked as fresh and lovely as she had when she had appeared at his doorstep early that morning. Only now she was in a soft and feminine lilac-colored dress, with a V neck, fitted bodice and tea-length skirt. She had an ivory silk cardigan thrown on for warmth against the chilly night air. Her cinnamon curls had been swept up in a loose, sexy knot on the back of her head, and her ivory skin was as smooth and lustrous as the strand of pearls around her neck. Now she looked Brody straight in the eye, lifted a brow and dropped her evening bag onto the table in the foyer. "Hmm."

"So did you have fun on your date?" Brody continued.

Her chin took on that stubborn tilt he knew so well as she walked into the living room to close the blinds. "What do you think?"

"I think," Brody said as he followed her from window to window, appreciating the sway of her hips and the view of her womanly curves, "that you spent the whole evening doing exactly what I was doing."

Turning to face him, Meg folded her arms beneath her breasts. "Which was…?"

"Thinking of you."

Meg's pink lips curved in a taunting smile. "I understand you're jealous," she drawled, admitting no such thing.

"And you weren't?" Brody interrupted.

"But we can't indulge such petty emotions," Meg continued with a recalcitrant look.

Realizing there was a time for words and a time for action, Brody decided to indulge in the latter. "Then how about we indulge in this?" he proposed, taking her in his arms and lowering his mouth to hers. Meg murmured in protest, even as her body radiated heat. Knowing his ex-wife needed him—needed this—as much as he did, Brody spread a hand across her spine and deepened the kiss, running his tongue along the seam of her lips until she opened her mouth to his. His spirit soaring, Brody tasted the sweetness that was Meg. Wanting to feel connected to her again—not just physically, but in heart and soul—he turned his lips to the softness of her cheek, the slope of her throat, the curve of her ear. "Let me make love to you," he whispered persuasively.

"Brody…" Meg was silent a moment, and when he looked at her, her eyes were turbulent. It was as if she wanted him to want her, Brody thought, and yet didn't. As if she wanted them to be connected by the kids, by the sense of family they had found, yet she didn't. She drew in a ragged breath. "We've been down this road before, and the results weren't anything I want to suffer again."

Brody didn't want to go through more bad times, either. He figured he and Meg had endured enough of those to last a lifetime.

"No, we haven't," Brody argued back, just as resolutely. Aware he had never wanted a woman the way he wanted Meg, he cupped her face in his hands so she couldn't avoid his eyes. "We took a wrong turn, years ago. What I want now is to get us back on track, to find a way to love each other again."

Meg bit her lip uncertainly. "You mean physically," she said, excited color flooding her cheeks.

"I mean in every way…."

Meg meant to resist him, she swore she did, but the next thing she knew, Brody's lips were forcing hers apart, and she, too, was throwing caution to the wind. Following her instincts, she passionately returned his kiss. She knew it was risky, but he tasted so good, so undeniably male, and she could feel his erection pressing against her, hot and urgent. It had been a long time since she had felt so beautiful and so wanted. Desire trembled inside her, making her insides go all soft and syrupy. They had been apart so long, she thought as he coaxed response after response from her with his deep, mesmerizing kisses. And she had missed him so much, missed the closeness, the intimacy of being with him, and the thrill of being in his arms. And as the moments drew out, and they continued to kiss and hold each other close, she knew she wanted to feel connected to him again. Not just physically, but heart and soul. "I want to go upstairs," she whispered, knowing that if they were going to do this, she wanted to do it right.

Brody's dark eyes gleamed with a satisfied light as he gallantly bent down and tucked an arm beneath her knees. "Then your wish shall be granted," he teased. Lifting her in his arms, he carried her up the stairs and the short distance down the hall to her bedroom. Looking determined to let nothing stand between them, he let her down gently beside the bed.

Meg's heart was thudding heavily in her chest as she reached for the button on her cardigan. Brody shook his head. "Let me." He undid the button and guided the silk sweater off her shoulders, down her arms. The zipper on her dress was next. Feeling as if this was both familiar territory and their very first time, Meg stepped out of it. Brody's eyes darkened rapaciously as he took in the curves spilling out of her lace-trimmed bra. And then it, too, was coming off, and his hands were on her breasts, caressing and stroking until her nipples peaked. Shudders of desire swept through Meg, further weakening her knees as his mouth trailed a provocative path down her neck, his lips discovering the contours of her breasts, his tongue finding her nipples, laving them tenderly, again and again. A fire roared within her, and her skin tingled with the heat.

And then he was undressing her the rest of the way and dispensing with his own clothes. When he joined her on the bed, Meg was ready for him, but Brody was determined to take his time and make their lovemaking last.

"You see how it is between us?" he whispered persuasively as he slid upward, cupping her bottom in his hands and kissing her with the sensual thoroughness she remembered. "How it will always be?"

So hungry for him she could hardly bear it, Meg tucked her hand between their bodies. Their lips fused as her fingers closed over his arousal. She stroked his velvety skin, able to feel how much he wanted her in the hard, throbbing length.

"We'll get there," he promised, as his lips traced a scorching path down her body. "Right now I want to enjoy being with you again." He cupped her breast and lifted it toward his mouth, suckling her gently. The friction of his lips and tongue were almost more than Meg could bear. She arched up off the bed and her thighs fell open. Gently he stroked her, from the sensitive insides of her knees, to her thighs, to the sweetest, silkiest part of her, and then back again.

Meg sighed, and her head fell back in abandon as he worshiped her other breast, until both nipples beaded and ached and her insides were clamoring for more. Only then did his fingers seek the most feminine part of her. Holding her fast with one strong arm clamped around her waist, he stroked the damp, delicate folds, kissing her rapaciously all the while. Until she was trembling, shaking, and he slid lower yet, exploring her with lips and tongue. Until she could bear no more and was arching helplessly, crying out in pleasure.

His eyes dark, he watched as she shuddered helplessly, and then he was sliding back up the length of her body, as impatient as she was. "I want you, Meg," he whispered against her mouth.

"Oh, Brody, I want you, too," she whispered back. Reveling in the throbbing length of him, the bunched muscles, the heat of his skin, she wrapped her arms and legs around him and lifted her hips. And then she was opening herself up to him, accepting him all the way inside, as deep as he could go. He whispered her name with an emotion and a hunger she hadn't known he possessed, and then they were moving as one, kissing with an intensity that took their breath away.

Unable to contain the erotic sensations he was evoking, she pulled him deeper still, bucking and writhing beneath him, doing everything it took to make him lose control, too. As he slid toward the edge of oblivion, she took everything he offered and gave him everything in return. He possessed her now with deep, then shallow strokes, repeating the slow, deliberate act of lovemaking until her body was shuddering and urgency swept through her in sweet, undulating waves. She wanted him…so much. She wanted this. She had missed the closeness, the thrill and the intimacy of being in his arms, in his life, in his bed. She had missed him.

Meg's heart filled with tenderness as her body molded to his, her breasts rubbing against the steeliness of his chest, her thighs gaining heat from his. Her entire life she had wanted to feel connected to him, not just physically and erotically, but heart and soul. Tonight, for the first time, she did. And it was different for him, too, she could tell. It was more than fire and passion, or the simple longing for release. Tonight was about the two of them, connecting in a way they never had before.

Needing him as she had never needed him before, she thrust her hips upward, cloaking him in honeyed warmth. She surrendered herself, her heart, her soul, as they moved together, dancing toward the same distant point. Suddenly, there was no more thinking, no more speaking, only feeling, as they found the pinnacle and shuddered together in overwhelming release.

It was a long time before the haze of passion faded and the trembling that rocked their entangled bodies eased. And when it did, the reality of the situation returned, and Meg began to realize they had made a giant error in judgment, letting their physical yearning for each other override all the differences that were still keeping them apart.

Afraid she had acted way too impetuously, putting everything she valued at risk, she took a shaky breath and rolled away from Brody. As much as she loved making love with him, she despaired of being hurt by him again. "We can't do this," she declared emotionally, sitting up and dragging the sheet with her.

Brody blinked in confusion and rolled onto his side. "Why not?" he demanded, clearly perplexed.

Because it happened for all the wrong reasons. Because we were both jealous. Because neither of us has yet said a word about loving each other, and it takes love to make and sustain a marriage. But she didn't say that to Brody. Instead she explained stiffly, "Because we're not married anymore."

She scooted to the edge of her bed. Even if she was in love with Brody, as she suspected, it didn't mean he felt anything but desire and duty. What was it he had said when he'd told her about the trust fund? *You're the mother of my children, Meg. Of course I'm going to take care of you, too....* Was this part of that? she wondered, upset. Was he merely meeting "her needs" at the same time she satisfied his?

"What are you trying to tell me here, Meg?" Brody asked, folding his arms behind his head and lifting a curious brow. "That you're not willing to have an affair with me? Only a one-night stand?"

Meg shot him an annoyed look over one bare shoulder. She wished he didn't look so cozy on her pillows, so in control of the situation with his rakish, oh-so-satisfied, grin.

Brody nodded thoughtfully. "So I suppose that means," he suggested teasingly, content to stay just where he was, "that moving in with me is out of the question?"

CHAPTER TEN

MEG COULDN'T TELL whether he was serious or not. "Why would you even ask me that?" she demanded irritably. In her opinion, the subject was nothing to joke about. Moving in together was serious business indeed. Needing some physical distance between them, she stood, wrapping the sheet around her middle.

Brody followed her to the closet, where she shrugged on her thick yellow terry-cloth bathrobe. "Isn't it clear? The kids want us to be together. We enjoy being together. And most important of all, we've never stopped wanting each other. If we were all under one roof, we could give the kids a real sense of family unity. And think of the message it would send Fiona."

Meg was so upset by his last remark, she almost didn't notice he'd mentioned nothing about love. "I hardly want my presence used to send a message to your lovestruck ex-employee, Brody!"

"You know what I mean," he countered with a frown. He shrugged on his boxer shorts and sat down on the edge of the bed.

Yes, Meg did. That was the problem. Once again, Brody was doing what was expedient in his personal life—making things easier in the short run, rather than figuring out what would make things work over the long haul.

She sat down beside him. "Which is why we should table the discussion about moving in together, forget about making love again and go back to just being friends and parents."

"No," he argued, "that's why we should keep trying to effectively mesh our lives."

"For the kids?" Meg asked.

"And us."

Meg let her gaze drift over the length of him. She had never seen a more perfect male body, even on the New York stage. The fact was, he could turn her on just by being there. And when he tried to seduce her, as he had this evening, well, he was darn near impossible to resist. That was fine as long as they were getting along, but what would happen if she and Kelly moved in with him and Kevin, and once again she and Brody reached a point where they couldn't agree on anything, the way they had in the waning days of their marriage? What then? That would put her in a vulnerable, dangerous place. And the kids would be so hurt. "Splitting up with you was hard enough once, Brody."

He caught her wrist and tugged her down to sit beside him on the rumpled covers of her bed. "We won't break up," he said softly.

That's what he had said before, when he had talked her into marrying him. Meg swallowed around the growing knot of emotion in her throat. This was such a risk. Worse than all the turmoil she had endured as a kid. "But what if we do?" she persisted stubbornly.

Brody turned her so she had no choice but to face him. "Why are you resisting what's obviously meant to be?" he asked gently but curiously.

Meg let out a little sigh, already able to feel herself weakening, and he had just started his why-we-should-do-this pitch. She didn't want to compare the two of them to her parents, but she couldn't seem to help it. "Because I'm trying to be sensible here, Brody," she said, looking him firmly in the eye. "I'm trying to keep us both from getting hurt. I'm trying to keep the kids from being hurt. If they even suspect we're sleeping together or have some sort of relationship going, apart from just being their parents—" Meg's voice caught. She couldn't go on. The thought of raising the twins' hopes about a remarriage, or worse, having them be caught between two warring parents, was unbearable. She didn't want them hearing the kinds of ugly words she had....

"You love your father more than you love me. Just admit it...."

"Fine. Side with your mother! Let her use you as a pawn against me! See if I care!"

"You can't agree with us both, Meggie. You're going to have to take sides on this, make a decision.... Now, where do you want to spend the Christmas holidays?"

It had been such a miserable way to grow up, Meg thought.

Brody caressed her cheek with the pad of his thumb and looked deep into her eyes. "How would the kids know we were involved again?" he asked her pensively. "We won't tell them. They wouldn't have to know. We're perfectly capable of being discreet about our lovemaking. We'd have separate bedrooms. When we wanted to make love to each other, we could hire a sitter, meet here, or even at a hotel or a private apartment we'd keep just for that purpose, if that's what you want. You know money is no object for me these days. If we want to, we can work that aspect out."

"I'm sure we could, as long as we were under separate roofs and had our own places to go to when we were out of sorts with each other."

Brody gave her a crooked smile. "You're assuming the worst again, Meg," he chided her gently. "Maybe we won't be out of sorts. And if we are, the same goes. You can always come here, or we'll go somewhere else to argue, away from the kids, if it ever comes to that. And I am not for one second saying it will.''

Meg paused. He was making a tempting case. And yet she was far from convinced his idea was a good, never mind workable, one. Even when she had tried not to know the specifics of the latest disagreement between her folks, she had figured out what was going on. Just as she was sure Kevin and Kelly would. And that knowledge had been just one more burden for her to carry, especially since many of the arguments between her parents had revolved around her and the custody agreement.

Meg didn't want to risk having the twins carry around that kind of guilt. Or suspicion. ''They'd sense we weren't being honest with them, Brody. All it would take is one look from you—like you gave me when you came here tonight—and they would know there were sparks between us, and their hopes would be unfairly raised. Brody, I couldn't bear it if we put them through another breakup. They don't recall the first one. But I remember all too well my own parents' split when I was six. It was brutal.'' She shook her head, recalling that miserable time. ''And it never ever got any better.''

Brody's jaw hardened stubbornly. As always, he dismissed her concerns as irrational. ''We're not your parents, Meg. We are not going to make their mistakes.''

She nodded. ''You're right. We've worked hard to keep the bitterness out of our divorce.'' And for five years, she thought mournfully, deprived each other of a child and their children of a parent. ''And up to now, we've succeeded. Probably because we kept so carefully to the setup we worked out—only contacting each other through letters.'' Allowing themselves no child-custody issues that would lead to bitterness or acrimony that would inadvertently involve the twins.

"We were protecting ourselves, Meg," Brody countered smoothly.

Protecting our hearts, you mean....

"Because we thought we couldn't make it as a couple or a family." He paused and took her hands in his. "Now we both know differently. I know it's only been a few weeks, but we are making it as a family now, in a way we couldn't seem to do before."

Meg tried not to be swayed by the comfort of his hands holding hers. "Maybe as a divorced family that still adheres to carefully negotiated rules," she allowed, warning herself to be cautious.

Brody's eyes darkened and he frowned. "As a family, period, Meg."

She looked at him honestly. "I just don't want to screw things up," she whispered, wanting so much to simply throw caution to the wind and be with Brody again.

"We won't." He squeezed her hands reassuringly. "Trust me. We won't. But you're right. We should keep our renewed closeness from the kids until we're ready to live under the same roof all the time and be a family again in every sense. We don't want to tell them anything until we've worked everything out to the last detail."

Nevertheless, Brody made sure he, Fiona and the twins sat next to Meg during Sunday services at the Seattle church he and Meg had decided to jointly attend, and then stopped her afterward, as the twins skipped on ahead to stand in line and say hello to Reverend Bollick. "I promised the kids I would take them to the park this afternoon, if that's a good time for you."

"Actually," Meg said, determined not to deprive Kelly of any more time with her daddy, even as she protected her own heart, "if you and Fiona wouldn't mind taking both kids yourself, it would really help me out." She needed

some time alone—to think. And it would spare her the awk-
wardness of having to observe Fiona's love-struck glances
at Brody. "I've got to finish the plans for the kindergarten
performance coming up," she told him, which was true.

"I could help you with that," Brody offered quickly.

"I know." Meg smiled, glad he was such a can-do kind
of guy. But she didn't want him volunteering to help her
just because it was the easiest, most convenient way to
spare him the company of his houseguest for the afternoon.
"And I will need your help later, when it comes time to
make up the programs," she explained patiently.

"But right now you need your space," Brody guessed,
not bothering to hide his disappointment.

Was she that transparent? Knowing church was no place
to have this discussion, Meg quickly glanced around her.
Kevin and Kelly were talking animatedly to Reverend Bollick, whispering something in his ear—heaven only knew
what! After a moment's hesitation, Meg turned back to
Brody and Fiona.

"You don't have to answer," Brody countered abruptly,
disappointment on his handsome face as he read her actions
the wrong way. "What time do you want Kelly back?"

Meg pushed her guilt aside. She was doing what was best
for both of them here. And she wasn't going to let Brody,
with his romantic notions, make her feel otherwise. Besides,
she wasn't asking all that much. Just a few hours to mull
things over, and at the same time get caught up on her work.
"How about after supper?" Meg asked cheerfully. *Or after
you've settled Fiona in her hotel?*

Brody agreed, and they headed toward Reverend Bollick
to say hello and gather up the kids. A few minutes later
they parted company in front of the church, the children
going off with Brody and Fiona, while Meg headed back
to her home alone.

BRODY DIDN'T STAY LONG when he and Kevin dropped Kelly off later that evening. Nor did Meg ask him to. She figured they needed their time apart to sort out their feelings.

On Monday, Meg taught the kindergarten class their new program. She had cooperation from every student except one, who also happened to be the most talented singer and dancer in the class. Kevin couldn't—or wouldn't—learn the routine with the rest of his class. By the time their music period had ended, every kid had the lyrics and the accompanying choreography for "A Spoonful of Sugar" down pat. Everyone except one. She sent the rest of the children back to class with Carmen Perez, then asked to speak to Kevin alone.

"I noticed you were having difficulty today," Meg said.

Kevin stood first on one foot, then the other. His face was a telltale red as he shrugged his small shoulders nonchalantly and fibbed, "I just couldn't learn it, Mommy." As he continued the ruse, he avoided looking directly into Meg's eyes. "I guess you're going to have to teach me by myself."

Meg was about to call her son on his duplicity when she caught the hopeful gleam in his eyes. *He's only doing this because he wants to spend more time with me.* After five years away from each other, she found she could not deny him the heartfelt, if sneaky, request. She pulled up a chair and sat down in front of him so they were at eye level with each other. "When did you have in mind?" she asked with a casual smile, doing her best to contain the joy she felt bubbling up inside her at the thought that her little boy was beginning to feel as close to her as she did to him. Soon she would be as much a mommy to him as she was to Kelly.

The hope on Kevin's face increased tenfold as he climbed onto her lap and wrapped his arms around her neck. "Maybe tonight?"

Meg hugged him back, delighting in his sturdy body and

little-boy smell as she ruffled his hair affectionately. "I think that could be arranged. But I'll have to talk to your dad to make sure." According to the calendar she and Brody had designed for the month of September, Brody had the kids alone at his place tonight.

Meg gave Kevin a kiss and a hug and then took him back to the kindergarten classroom.

When Brody arrived, Meg drew him into the events room and explained what had happened during music class. "I think Kevin just wants some one-on-one time with me," she concluded.

To Meg's relief, Brody had no problem with that, and was in fact eager to help her work out the new logistics. "How about coming over to my place tonight for dinner?" he said, all traces of his previous pique gone. He perched on the edge of her tall stool, one foot propped on the rung, the other on the floor. He was wearing an olive-green blazer, open-collared shirt and slacks. His black hair was combed away from his forehead in the sophisticated style she liked. And he smelled delicious, like a mixture of soap, shaving cream and spicy cologne. His glance moving over her lazily, he brought her up to speed on the plans he had already made for the evening ahead of them. "I've promised the kids fried chicken from the take-out place down the street. So if that's okay with you—"

"It is," Meg said.

He nodded. "I'll pick up dinner and we'll eat, then you can work with Kevin on his song and dance routine, and I'll tutor Kelly on the computer."

"OH, GOODY, Fiona's here again, too!" Kelly said as Meg pulled in the driveway to Brody's home, and Kevin and Fiona came out the front door. "She's a lot of fun, Mommy. She really likes the park, too, you know."

Meg's heart did a funny little jig in her chest as she

smiled and waved at the dark-haired Irish beauty lovingly hanging on to her son's hand. A carefree smile fixed on her face, Meg removed her keys from the ignition and dropped them into her shoulder bag.

Brody hadn't said anything to her earlier about Fiona joining them for their family dinner this evening. If he had, she probably would have asked to work with Kevin at her home. Alone. But he hadn't, and now she just had to deal with it.

Smiling, Meg shut the rear passenger door and started toward Fiona and Kevin, who were busy exchanging hugs and high fives with Kelly. Meg waved self-consciously. She wished she had on something more appealing than her threadbare jeans and a long-sleeved white university T-shirt with Drama Department written on the front and Diva! on the back. But it was too late to change now, just as it was too late to take her hair out of the bouncy ponytail or put her makeup back on. She was just going to have to go in there, casual as she was.

Besides, after what she had told Brody the other night about going back to being strictly friends why should it matter if Fiona was back in his life?

Meg had set the ground rules. Now, she instructed herself sternly as Kelly skipped back to her side, she had to get a grip.

A smile plastered on her face, she walked up to Fiona.

"Hello, Meg." Fiona smiled at her in an easy-going manner Meg could only admire. If the situation were reversed—if she were Fiona and had a crush on Brody—Meg didn't know if she would be able to be so affable toward his ex. Unless, of course, Fiona had been told—by Brody—that there was nothing to worry about where Meg was concerned. That their relationship was over, at Meg's request.

Fiona shooed the twins ahead of them, toward the front door. "Come along inside. Brody is upstairs changing clothes. I was just making some tea.'' Fiona held the door wide, as if she, not Brody, owned the place. "I know how Brody favors his, of course, but I don't know if you even drink it.'' Fiona looked at Meg expectantly.

Meg reminded herself this was no time or place to be showing her jealousy. "I love tea, as a matter of fact, both hot and cold. And I like it with a little bit of lemon if you have it.'' She followed Fiona into the kitchen and stopped dead in her tracks at what she saw. The miniblinds that had complemented the modern kitchen with its stainless steel appliances, white cabinets and sleek, black marble countertops were gone. In their place were Irish lace curtains.

"What do you think?'' Fiona asked, smiling.

Kevin bounced up and down. "Fiona made us curtains as a surprise!''

"I can see that.'' Meg's smile was beginning to feel a little frozen. "And they're beautiful.'' The problem was they just didn't fit the style of the kitchen. Nor had Brody ever favored lace, at least as far as Meg knew.

"As well as homey,'' Fiona agreed, with a proud glance at her handiwork. "In fact, they're just like the ones in Brody's cottage back in Ireland. Except made to fit these much larger windows, of course.''

"You must have worked around the clock to finish them,'' Meg said, stepping nearer for a closer look. As much as she was loath to admit it, the stitchwork on the Priscilla curtains was absolutely amazing. A pro couldn't have done a better job. Meg turned back to Fiona in admiration. "Did you do these in your hotel?''

"Back in Ireland, before I flew over here. Uncle Roarke brought me the measurements. It was my housewarming gift for Brody and Kevin. I hung the curtains yesterday, after church. Didn't he mention it to you?'' Fiona asked, looking quite pleased with herself.

"No. He didn't.'' But then, Meg hadn't given him a

chance, and she hadn't encouraged Kelly to talk about the time she had spent with Fiona and Brody on Sunday, either. Ignoring the stab of uneasiness, Meg inquired, "So, how are your interviews going? Any luck there?"

Fiona made an apologetic face. "I haven't actually had any yet."

Which meant what? Meg wondered. That Fiona wasn't really trying to land another job, so much as reinstate herself as Kevin's nanny? Or that opportunities in the States weren't as easy to come by as she had hoped?

Brody headed down the stairs and into the kitchen. He, too, had changed into jeans and a navy Taylor Software T-shirt. "Hi." Brody nodded at Meg, looking as happy to see her as she would have been to see Brody, had Fiona not still been here. "I see you two made it," he said cheerfully.

Meg nodded, really uncomfortable now, both with Brody's seeming naiveté where Fiona was concerned, and her own possessive feelings toward him. "I didn't know you were having company this evening," she commented as pleasantly as she could manage.

Brody looked at Meg cautiously. "Fiona stopped by to get some additional copies of my recommendation and letter of reference for her. She needs them for her interviews later this week."

"And I had one more reason, as well," Fiona explained happily. "I had to finish Kevin and Kelly's surprise for you."

Meg felt herself tense even more.

"Yeah," Kevin said. "We asked Fiona to help us yesterday at the park, when Daddy was getting us ice cream."

Kelly nodded swiftly. "'Cause we needed Fiona to sew."

"Sew what?" Brody asked, his brow furrowing.

"Just a moment and I'll show you," Fiona said. She disappeared up the stairs.

Meg looked at Brody. Brody could only shrug.

Short minutes later, Fiona came back down. In her hands was a long white veil, attached to a tiara.

For Brody, the day could hardly be any more surreal. Every time he tried to gently get Fiona to move on with her life, every time he thought he had done so, she turned right around and showed up again. And now she was standing there with what looked like an Irish lace wedding veil clasped in her hands.

Kevin and Kelly clapped hands and jumped up and down.

"Oh, it's pretty!" Kelly exclaimed.

"Is this for playing dress-up?" Brody interrupted, still trying like heck to figure out what was going on.

"Hardly," Fiona said, more than a little miffed at his query. "It's a wedding veil, Brody. For your bride!"

Once again, Brody had a sinking feeling in his gut. As if he had just stepped into a vat of quicksand. Catching Meg's look of equal dismay, he turned his full attention back to Fiona. "What bride?" he asked warily.

At his obvious confusion, Fiona's face fell.

"You didn't think…" Brody started unhappily. To his left, Meg stood looking aghast.

Fiona's eyes glimmered suspiciously. "The twins said that you were going to ask someone to marry you, and soon," she related in a low, tremulous voice. "They said you needed a wife, that you were tired of living alone, and that you and Kevin both missed me terribly. And that you didn't want me to go back to Ireland, you wanted me to stay here. With all of you."

And Fiona, bless her naive, hopelessly smitten heart, Brody realized, had taken it from there. Swearing inwardly, and berating himself for not having ended Fiona's employment much sooner, before she got herself so emotionally entangled in his life, Brody turned to the kids. He couldn't wait to hear their reasoning about this.

"You're going to need a baby-sitter for us when you go on your honeymoon," Kevin explained helpfully. "And Fiona baby-sat for us on Saturday, and we liked it...."

"Yeah," Kelly added, linking hands with her twin in a show of solidarity. "One of Mommy's friends at the theater got married and her two kids had to stay with a friend who was their baby-sitter while their mommy and new daddy were gone."

Brody was beginning to resent Meg's theater friends. They seemed to have been the inspiration for all of the twins' ideas.

"But I'm not getting married," Brody explained patiently, speaking to both Fiona and the twins. *Not yet anyway,* he amended silently. Not unless Meg changed her mind and got involved with him again, and then said yes when—and if—he did propose. And right now, given the fact that she looked ready to bolt out the door at any second, that was no sure thing.

"But you could get married to Mommy," Kelly said.

"Yeah." Kevin seconded the motion. "Just like before. So we got you a veil for when that happens."

Brody turned back to Fiona. She blinked, determined, Brody thought, to hide her tears.

"You know, I think the time difference is more of a bother than I realized," she said in a thick low voice, her sweet nature coming through. She thrust the veil at Brody, then turned her back to all of them. "Why, in Ireland right now it's the middle of the night! I think I need to go back to my hotel and try and get some sleep."

Meg glared at Brody, urging him to do something. Anything. And he knew Meg was right. No matter how pushy Fiona's actions, or how misguided the kids', Fiona hadn't deserved to be hurt like this. No one did. "I'll drive you, Fiona," Brody promised kindly, "just as soon as you're ready to go."

BRODY RETURNED from the hotel with their dinner of take-out fried chicken and all the trimmings. The kids, sensing they had done something very wrong, even if they didn't understand exactly what, were subdued. "I learned my music, Daddy, and all my choreography," Kevin announced as soon as they sat down together. "Mommy taught me."

"That's good," Brody said approvingly.

Kevin studied Brody as he spread his napkin on his lap. "Are you mad at me, Daddy?"

"Concerned," Brody corrected.

Kevin's brow furrowed in consternation. "How come?"

"I'm concerned because I think you and Kelly hurt Fiona's feelings," Brody explained.

"We didn't mean to!" Kelly protested.

"I know that." Brody did his best to explain the situation to the twins, so they wouldn't make the same mistake again. While he spooned coleslaw and mashed potatoes on both children's plates, Meg spread butter and grape jelly on their biscuits. "But when you asked Fiona to make a wedding veil, Fiona got the idea that the veil was for her."

The twins looked surprised and perplexed. "But Fiona's not going to marry you," Kevin insisted. "She can't marry you! She's not my mommy. She was my nanny. Nannies aren't the same as mommies."

Brody knew that. The question was, did either woman? "The point is," he said firmly, ignoring the flush of embarrassment on Meg's cheeks, "you can't just go around asking someone to make a wedding veil without talking to me first." *And especially not before I've won your mommy's love and asked her to marry me again.*

"Why not?" Kelly asked, perplexed.

Because it was like putting the marketing brainstorming session before the development of the actual product you were going to sell, Brody thought. Meg needed romance. She had made that pretty plain to him. And he needed time to be able to woo her so she would fall in love with and eventually remarry him.

"You can't do that because it's a lot of work for someone," Meg said, smoothly picking up where Brody had left off but deliberately avoiding his eyes, "And it's not very good manners."

"Oh," Kevin and Kelly murmured in unison.

Finally, a subdued Kelly asked, "Does this mean you won't help me learn that counting game on the computer after dinner, Daddy?"

"No. I'll help you," Brody said with a comforting smile, letting his children know one thing had nothing to do with the other, and that his forgiveness for their mistakes was something that could be counted on. Always. Just as his love could be. And then later, Brody added silently to himself, when he and Kelly were finished with their game, he and Meg were going to talk.

CHAPTER ELEVEN

"WHAT ARE WE GOING TO DO with the veil?" Meg asked, as soon as the kids were upstairs playing with toys and she and Brody were alone.

His empty coffee cup in hand, Brody led the way into the kitchen. Meg perched on one of the stools at the center island while he took the glass carafe off the warmer and refilled both their cups. "I don't know." He walked around to her side and took the stool next to hers. "Fiona told me adamantly that she doesn't want it back."

Meg turned her gaze to the dark night outside, and shrugged. "Well, it's way too lovely to give to the kids to play dress-up." She paused, thinking, then looked back at Brody and said, "Maybe you should just hang on to it, and return it to Fiona later, for her use or someone else's."

"Either way, it's going to be tricky," Brody said, as if he too had considered all possible solutions. "Because anything I do or say on the subject could easily be misinterpreted by Fiona. Experience has shown me that." He frowned, perturbed. "Maybe if I were blunt...."

Meg took his free hand in a light, warning grip. "You can't do that."

Brody turned his wrist and slid his palm beneath hers, linking their fingers together intimately. "Being nice doesn't seem to be getting us anywhere." He paused significantly. "But I don't want her hurt."

"Maybe you should ask your uncle Roarke to talk to her," she suggested.

Brody withdrew his hand from hers and shook his head. "That won't work. Roarke's been wanting me to see Fiona as wife and mother material for some time."

Meg sighed and tried not to feel too disillusioned. Shouldn't she have expected this? "In other words, no matter what, you don't expect Roarke to stop his matchmaking."

Brody's dark eyes took on a brooding glint. "Not unless he sees that you and I are serious again."

"But we're not," she protested, sliding off the stool.

"Speak for yourself." Brody wrapped his arms around her waist and brought her into the open V of his spread legs. Lowering his mouth to hers, he delivered another heart-stoppingly sexy kiss. Meg melted against him, trembling, even as she tore her lips from his. "Brody," she whispered urgently, "please, the kids—"

"The kids," he whispered back, just as significantly, "are otherwise occupied right now."

Time seemed suspended as he delivered another kiss. Suddenly, there was just the two of them, just this moment.

"See?" A whisper sounded behind them. "I told you they were kissing!"

Meg and Brody broke apart. Meg was embarrassed beyond belief to be caught in Brody's arms. Brody, on the other hand, didn't seem to mind being caught kissing her. "I thought you two were supposed to be picking up Kevin's room," he said sternly.

"We put all the toys away," Kevin protested.

Brody looked as disappointed about that as Meg felt. "Already?" he asked.

Kelly smiled happily. "You've been kissing a long time."

Long enough, Meg thought, to give rise to all sorts of romantic fantasies. Two minutes in Brody's arms, and all she wanted to do was make love with him again and again, consequences be damned. And worse, the kids seemed to sense that. If this was what it felt like after just a few weeks of each other's company, what would the coming days bring?

Kevin climbed up onto one of the stools next to them and asked, "Is this a date?"

Kelly climbed up on the other side of Meg and Brody. She swung her legs back and forth. "'Cause people kiss at the end of dates."

Meg and Brody exchanged a glance. "How do you know that?" Meg asked.

"One of my friends at school told me."

Kevin regarded them patiently. "So is it or isn't it a date?" he asked.

"It's not," Meg said, at the same time Brody replied, "It sort of is."

The kids grinned.

Well, Meg thought, *that was helpful.*

HANNAH RICHARDS was in the day care office near closing time the following evening when a young man walked in. He was around eighteen or so. Tall, blond, with vivid blue eyes much older than his years.

"I'm Hannah Richards." She rose from behind her desk. "Can I help you?"

"Yes. I'm Will Tucker."

They shook hands. "Amy Tidwell's boyfriend," Hannah said. "She talks about you all the time."

"Yeah." Will's face lit up shyly. "I really like her, too. Anyway, Amy and I were supposed to meet at Caffeine Hy's when she got off work today. That was half an hour ago. She hasn't shown up."

"You're right. Amy was scheduled to get off at five to-night, but I don't think she's left the building yet. Why don't you have a seat, and I'll go see if I can find her for you."

"Thanks." Will smiled. "I appreciate it. And Ms. Richards? I hope you don't mind me coming over here like this. I know you wouldn't want boyfriends visiting staff while they're working. But I had to make sure Amy was okay because it's not like her to stand me up like that."

"I understand, Will. And I'm glad you did double-check." Hannah gave the teen's shoulder a reassuring pat. "I'll be right back."

Hannah searched the first floor classrooms and kitchen. Thinking Amy might have gone into the bathroom behind the dining area to freshen up before her date with Will, she walked in there and heard the sounds of someone getting sick. Hoping this wasn't the start of a flu bug that would go through the entire day care center, she waited until the retching subsided, and then rapped on the stall door.

"Do you need help in there? Do you want me to run and get Kathy Verbist?" Hannah was sure the staff nurse would know what to do.

"No. There's no need to bother Mrs. Verbist. I'll—I'll be all right," Amy Tidwell called from the other side. Seconds later, the stall door opened. Amy emerged weakly and headed for the sink.

Because she looked as if she needed the support, Hannah put an arm about Amy's waist and handed her some paper towels when she had finished rinsing her mouth and thoroughly washing her hands.

Noting Amy was still looking rather shaky, Hannah asked gently, "Are you ill, Amy? Because if you are, you shouldn't be here. We don't want staff coming in sick. At the first sign of not feeling well, you should tell us—even if you've already shown up for work that day."

"I know," Amy said quietly. She slumped against the

sink and closed her eyes. Tears leaked from beneath her lashes and streamed down her face.

To Hannah's frustration, nothing else was forthcoming. But then, Hannah thought, maybe she didn't need to be told what was going on. She had noticed the signs. The high school senior had been looking pale and drawn for two weeks now. Amy was unbearably sleepy at times, and nauseous at others. And most telling of all, she was keeping to herself as much as possible. "You don't have the flu, do you, Amy," Hannah said quietly, recognizing the signs full well.

Amy opened her gray-blue eyes. They were full of despair.

"You can confide in me," Hannah encouraged the high school senior softly. "I promise you, Amy, whatever you tell me will remain just between the two of us unless you decide otherwise."

Amy bit her lip. She looked as if she wanted to speak what was on her mind and in her heart, but was afraid to.

"But I have to tell you," Hannah continued matter-of-factly, "even with those baggy clothes you're wearing, if the problem is what I think it is, you won't be able to hide it much longer."

More tears flowed from Amy's eyes as she plucked at the clean fabric of her jeans.

Hannah could see the young woman needed a friend. "How far along are you?" she asked gently.

Amy blew her nose. "Four m-m-months."

Hannah's heart went out to her as she handed Amy a tissue. "Have you told your father yet?"

"No. And I can't. You have to promise me that you won't either, Hannah. Because he would absolutely *freak out* if he knew."

Hannah knew that was probably true. Russ Tidwell was a wealthy Seattle businessman. He ran a tight ship at his company and his home. And he had high expectations for Amy. Unfortunately, Amy had no mother to turn to, since hers had died when she was very young. That meant that Russ and Amy were going to have to deal with this together. "Your father might surprise you, Amy—adversity often brings out the best in people."

"I don't think so," Amy said resentfully. "Not in this case, anyway."

Hannah sighed. "What does Will Tucker have to say about all this?" she asked curiously.

Amy's lower lip quivered. "I haven't told him yet, either."

"You don't think he'll be responsible?" Hannah had only met Will briefly, but he had struck her as the extremely responsible type. And there was no doubt he cared about Amy as much as she cared about him. His actions had demonstrated that.

Gulping hard, Amy dabbed her eyes before continuing in a low, choked tone, behaving as protectively toward Will as he had behaved toward her. "Will has plans, Hannah. He wants to go to college and get a good job. If I told him, he'd probably insist on doing the 'right' thing and give all that up and go to work on the fishing docks full-time. He wouldn't want his own kid having a dad who walked out on him the way his did."

It was clear from the affection in her voice how much Amy cared about her baby's father. "And you don't want that for Will," Hannah guessed.

Amy shook her head as fresh tears flowed. "It's bad enough my own life has been turned upside down, without doing the same thing to Will," she sobbed.

Hannah folded the younger woman in her arms and let her have a good cry. When she had finished, she gave Amy more tissues and waited while she wiped her eyes and blew her nose. Deciding to focus on first things first, Hannah asked, "Have you been to a doctor?"

"No," Amy mumbled, flushing guiltily.

"Well, you're going to have to go to one right away," Hannah said firmly, more than a little upset about this. "Do you want me to take you?"

"No, I can call my own family doctor."

"All right, but I want you to promise me," Hannah continued gently, "that you'll come to me if you—or your baby—need anything at all."

"Thanks. I d-d-didn't know what I was going to do," Amy confided as she collected herself and headed for the door, with Hannah.

"Well, not to worry." Hannah put her arm around Amy's shoulders and gave her a comforting squeeze. "We'll get it all worked out. In the meantime, Will is here. He's waiting for you in the office."

"We weren't supposed to meet here," Amy said.

"I know. But he got worried when you didn't show up."

While Amy went off to get her things and meet Will, Hannah lingered to talk to the other teachers before heading back to the day care office. Her mind stayed on Amy, however, and it was still on Amy as she headed home for the day. Their situations were so remarkably similar, Hannah thought wistfully.

She, too, had been raised in an upscale, privileged household. And she lived with a secret, too, Hannah thought as she tucked her honey-blond hair behind her ears, put on her sunglasses and drove toward her high-rise condo. Only her secret dated back to her junior year of college in Dallas, Texas, and the bad-boy cowboy Jack McKay. She had fallen hard for him and really let herself go wild. Unfortunately, Hannah thought sadly as she turned her car into the building's parking garage, like Amy, she had ended up pregnant and unmarried. And just like Amy, she had been scared out of her mind, as afraid to tell Jack as Amy was to tell Will. Not that she'd expected Jack to do the right thing by her and the baby, Hannah thought resentfully. No, Hannah had been afraid Jack would not want to settle down. And rather than have him hurt her, Hannah had done the responsible thing and given her son over to a private adoption agency to be placed in a warm and loving family with two parents who wanted and adored him.

It had been a torturous decision, and a very hard time for her, Hannah recalled, depression swamping her anew. But she knew she had done the right thing in giving her baby away. She just wished she could see her eight-year-old son now and know for certain where he had been placed and with whom, and that he was healthy and happy and well cared for.

But it wasn't possible. The agency's policy was to keep the adoptions private to protect all the parties involved. And she had agreed to that when she'd signed away her parental rights and left Dallas and Jack McKay and their baby behind her. So she would just have to trust that she'd made the right decision, because like it or not, Hannah realized sadly, there was no going back.

"SO EXACTLY HOW MUCH kissing is going on between the two of you?" Julia Stanton teased Meg late Friday afternoon in the upstairs hall.

Meg flushed as she followed Julia toward a changing table. "How did you hear about that?"

Julia laid her infant son on the table. "I think the question is who in the day care center hasn't heard about it," she informed Meg wryly as she plucked a clean diaper from the stack. "Kevin and Kelly have been telling everyone that you and Brody have been kissing each other all week, and that this means you're going to get married again someday real soon."

Meg's face got even warmer as she grabbed a can of diet soda from the fridge along the wall. "We didn't know they had seen us, except the one time."

Julia's eyes widened. "Meaning it's true—there has been more than once?"

Knowing she had to confide in someone, Meg nodded, "Every time we're alone, it just seems like…"

"You're in each other's arms," Julia guessed, as she cleaned and powdered Jeremy's bottom.

This was embarrassing. Meg wasn't normally the kind of woman who had trouble controlling herself or her emotions. Usually, she saved all her excess emotional energy for her performances on stage, or her teaching. But with Brody, it was different. He brought out the woman in her. And he made her feel special—and vulnerable. The special, she liked. The vulnerable she didn't need.

"That's the way it is for Drew and me," Julia confessed softly. "We can't keep our hands off each other."

"Good thing you're getting married then," Meg teased.

Julia smiled blissfully. "We're really looking forward to you singing at our wedding."

"BEFORE YOU GO," Meg said, catching Brody's arm at the bottom of the stairs and steering him into the living room, "you and I need to talk."

Brody sat down on the sofa where Meg directed. It had been a busy evening. Meg and Brody had worked on e-mail reminders and the programs for the kindergarten music performance slated for the following week. They'd also supervised the twins' baths, read them their bedtime stories and tucked them into bed. "What about?" he asked curiously, able to tell from the look on Meg's face that something was up.

"Something happened at school." Meg dropped down beside him, "Julia Stanton told me that Kelly and Kevin have been telling everyone that you and I have been kissing—a lot—this week."

He and Meg had stolen a few kisses, Brody admitted. Kisses he'd initiated. But she hadn't seemed to mind until now. "How do they know that?" he asked cautiously.

"Big ears. Big eyes." Meg looked at Brody directly. "I guess they've been keeping closer tabs on the two of us than we realized."

Brody studied her, wishing he could take her into his arms and kiss her worries away. But knowing she was unlikely to appreciate that remedy, given the problem they were discussing, he merely said, "And this upsets you."

Meg nodded. "A little. I'm worried at how quick the kids were to leap to conclusions about our future. I don't want their hopes raised, only to be dashed again."

It was a risk, restarting their romance. But in Brody's view it was a risk worth taking. "They're not going to be dashed," he said firmly.

Meg sighed wistfully. To Brody's disappointment, she wasn't as sure as he was. "They will be if it doesn't work out between us again."

Brody took her hands in his and clasped them warmly. "We're smarter now, Meg," he reassured her softly. "And wiser. Wise enough to realize we've got to keep this romance of ours out of sight of our kids."

That was an idea she seemed to like, Brody noted with satisfaction. "What are you suggesting?"

Something he had been wanting for days now, but had held off on for fear of pushing too hard, too fast. "A date. Just the two of us. Tomorrow night. We'll call Amy Tidwell, see if she wants to baby-sit. We could go out and have a grown-up dinner in a grown-up place."

Meg's lips curved in anticipation. He could see she was softening, and not just about the date. There was a part of her that wanted to feel only optimistic about the two of them. "No more Chester Cheese pizza?" she teased.

Like Meg, Brody had eaten at the twins' favorite pizza emporium, known more for its video arcade than the food, once too often in the past few weeks. So he suggested Meg's favorite instead. "How about seafood?" he asked eagerly. "Are we on?"

Meg didn't have to think about it for more than two seconds. "You bet."

KEVIN WAS VERY EXCITED when he learned that Amy Tidwell was going to baby-sit them again, and so was Kelly. This fit right in with all their top secret plans, even though their mother and father and even Amy didn't know it. But that was okay, Kevin thought, because this was a good secret.

"So, let's go over the rules one more time," Amy said the next evening before Meg and Brody headed out the door.

She ticked off the items on her fingers one by one. "The snacks are in the fridge, the list of approved TV channels and videos is on the coffee table and bedtime is at nine o'clock tonight, since it's Saturday."

Kevin's mother smiled at Amy as if she had just done something really great. "Right," Meg said. Looking as happy to be going out as he and Kelly were to be staying behind with their baby-sitter, Meg and Brody kissed the twins good-night and slipped out the door.

As soon as they were gone and the coast was clear, Kevin turned back to Amy. "We needs lots of flowers," he told her urgently, knowing that Amy was old enough and smart enough to help them get everything they needed. "They're for Daddy's birthday party. Mommy and Daddy are letting us make the plans for it. We even got to pick out the special cake all by ourselves."

"That's neat," Amy said, looking impressed.

"But we also need some more stuff," Kelly continued as she hopscotched back and forth across the living room carpet. "Like a bouquet of flowers for Mommy—just like the one she was carrying when she married Daddy before we were born, 'cause that's *her* surprise. And a lot of chairs, so people can sit down if they want."

"Yeah, you get real tired if you have to stand up forever," Kevin added seriously.

Amy looked at Kevin first, then Kelly. "Am I supposed to help with that?" she said, a stunned expression on her face.

Kevin and Kelly nodded. "Do you know where we could get some extra chairs?" Kevin asked eagerly. "'Cause we're going to have the party in the backyard and we don't have enough chairs even if we bring out all the ones in the kitchen."

Amy stood there quietly, considering a moment. "Well, we could call everyone who's invited to the party and ask them to bring a couple of lawn chairs. That would work."

"Can we e-mail them?" Kelly asked.

"Well," Amy said slowly, "I guess, if you have the addresses of the people who are coming."

"Will you help us type it?" Kelly asked. "It takes me and Kevin too long to find the right letters all by ourselves."

"Sure," Amy said, grinning the way big people did when they thought what a little kid was doing was cute. She sat down in front of the computer and used the mouse to point and click until she brought up the e-mail screen. "Okay, tell me what you want to say to everybody."

Kevin and Kelly had to talk it over, but finally they decided on a message.

Come to our party Saturday night, on October 11. It's in Daddy's backyard because it is bigger and it will hold more people. You can bring a birthday present for our Daddy if you want, but you don't have to. We need lots of flowers and more chairs for people to sit on, and some music. Thanks a lot. Love, Kevin and Kelly

Amy finished typing the message, then said, "Exactly who is invited to this party?"

Kevin and Kelly told her the names of their friends and the teachers from the day care who were being invited, as well as the minister at their church. They didn't have the e-mail addresses of the people at their dad's office, since this was their mother's computer.

"I'll ask Uncle Roarke or Fiona to help me," Kevin said.

"Sounds good," Amy murmured. As quick as a flash, she used the address book to send out all the messages they could, then made up a list for Kevin to give Roarke or Fiona.

When that was done, Kevin and Kelly smiled at each other. "This is going to be the best surprise party ever," Kevin declared.

Amy tilted her head and suddenly looked confused. "I thought you said your mom and dad knew about this and were letting you help plan it," she said worriedly.

"They do!" Kelly told her. They even sent out invitations by mail!"

"So the e-mail we just sent out was just a reminder," Amy said.

The twins nodded.

"Then how can the party be a surprise?" Amy asked, even more puzzled.

"Because they only know about the *birthday* part and the cake they let us order," Kevin explained as he sat on Amy's lap.

"Yeah," Kelly chimed in, coming to stand beside her.

"They don't know about the rest. About the very special present from us."

Amy wrapped her fingers around her long, sandy-blond braid. "Are they going to like it?"

"Oh yes. This present is going to make us all very, very, very, *very* happy!" Kevin announced as he turned to his twin sister and gave her a high five.

CHAPTER TWELVE

"THAT'S GREAT, Uncle Roarke, but I can't talk right now because I'm on a date...with Meg. Fine. Tomorrow. And you're right. That is good news." Brody slid his cell phone back in his pocket and sent Meg an apologetic glance. "Sorry about that," he said softly.

"What was so important Roarke had to call you at this time of night?" Meg asked.

Whatever she was feeling about the interruption to their date was well hidden. In the past, he wouldn't have cared whether she was ticked off at him or not, as long as his business continued to go well. Now he did. Maybe because there was so much more at stake. He leaned over to pour her more wine. "That Austin software company accepted our offer, which means we've just doubled the size of our engineering staff and product line."

Her lips curved up as she lifted her glass and offered him a congratulatory toast. "Wow."

"Yeah." Brody couldn't contain the pride he felt, even as he relished the impressed look in her eyes. He touched the rim of his glass to hers, watched as they both took a sip of their cabernet. "Anyway," he continued, "Roarke didn't want to wait until tomorrow to tell me."

Meg nodded, seeming to understand the satisfaction he felt, just as Brody's cell phone rang again. This time they both frowned at the interruption. This evening was supposed to be about the two of them, their future. As he put the phone to his ear, Brody muttered grimly, "This better be important." To his chagrin, it was.

"What's wrong?" Meg asked him anxiously the moment he got off the phone with Amy Tidwell. Despite the fact they were barely halfway through their entrées, Brody was already signaling for the check and pulling out his wallet. "Kevin and Kelly are sick."

By the time Meg and Brody got home and took the children's temperatures, Kevin's was 104 and Kelly's was 103.6. Amy was beside herself. "They told me before they went to sleep that their throats were hurting a little bit, but they seemed fine otherwise, and I figured it could wait until you two got home. Then when I felt their foreheads, they were really hot. Did I do the wrong thing?"

Meg and Brody exchanged looks, then Meg said gently, speaking for both of them, "You probably should have called us right away, Amy, just to let us know. We wouldn't have minded having our dinner interrupted." And, Brody thought, they would have instructed Amy to take the twins' temperature then, instead of waiting.

"I've never seen anyone get so sick so fast," Amy said, as Meg and Brody bundled the kids up and took them out to the car.

"Little kids can spike a high fever pretty quickly," Brody explained, knowing this wasn't the first time—and probably wouldn't be the last—the twins had done so.

"And that would have happened whether we'd been home or not," Meg added comfortingly as she paid Amy for sitting and walked her to her car. "So don't beat yourself up about this." She gave the teenage girl a hug. "We're not upset with you. Next time you'll know."

Meg and Brody drove the kids to the pediatric minor emergency center, which was open twenty-four hours a day. To their relief, the center wasn't very busy and they were seen right away. Kevin and Kelly were both extremely cranky and tearful, especially after the throat swabs were taken.

"Looks like strep throat," the doctor said. He gave them each a shot of antibiotics, acetaminophen for the fever, and grape-flavored liquid antibiotic to take home with them.

Once they were back at Meg's, Brody helped her put the kids back to bed. And then it was just the two of them. "I don't want to leave you to handle this alone," he told her sincerely, not sure what her reaction was going to be to his suggestion. "Especially since we're going to have to keep an eye on them through the night."

To his relief, Meg looked as happy to have his help as he was to give it. "I suggest we take shifts," she said.

Sounded good to Brody. Especially since he knew the twins would feel better having both their parents nearby. "I'll go first," he offered. After the tumultuous end to their evening, Meg looked like she needed some sleep.

"YOU WERE SUPPOSED TO wake me at four," Meg scolded from the doorway of the kitchen as she tightened the belt on her flannel robe. It was nearly 6:00 a.m. She'd ended up having a straight six hours of sleep. As far as she could tell, Brody had had none.

He shot her an appreciative look that reminded Meg he had always liked her in flannel pajamas as much as a sexy negligee. He had joked it wasn't the wrapping but what was underneath that interested him. Obviously, Meg thought, her cheeks warming at the look in his dark eyes, nothing much had changed on that score.

Brody was sitting at the kitchen table, drinking coffee. He still had on the shirt and slacks he'd been wearing the night before, but had dispensed with the tie and jacket. His black hair was rumpled, falling onto his forehead in sexy disarray. Morning beard rimmed his handsome face, giving him a faintly roguish look. But his dark eyes were exceedingly gentle, as only Brody's could be. "Things were going okay," he said quietly.

Meg poured herself some coffee from the freshly brewed pot on the warmer, and splashed in a generous helping of cream and a tiny bit of sugar. "When did they last have acetaminophen?" she asked.

Brody pointed to the chart he had left in the center of the kitchen table. "At five this morning. Kevin's temp was 101 and Kelly's was 101.7."

As she sat down across from him, Meg's knees nudged his under the table. "That's better on both scores." She reached over and touched his forearm. "You look tired. Why don't you get some sleep?" she suggested gently.

Brody nodded and pushed himself to his feet. "I'd like to stay close to the kids, at least until their fever breaks and we know for sure they're on the mend."

Meg was glad he'd said that, because she was no more eager for him to go than he was to leave.

"And then I'd like to continue our date," he told her, getting slowly to his feet and drawing her up to stand beside him. "With no business interruptions or family emergencies this time."

Meg's spirits rose at his low, teasing tone. "Me, too."

He lifted her hand to his mouth and traced the inside of her wrist with his lips. She stared into his handsome face, aware her heart was beating double-time. Lower still, she was aware of that telltale, fluttery feeling.

"I was really looking forward to a good-night kiss," Brody continued sexily as he pressed his lips to her temple, then behind her ear.

Meg trembled and felt the traitorous weakening of her knees. "Just a kiss?" she murmured back playfully.

Brody shrugged his broad shoulders laconically. "Or two or three or four." He stroked the pad of his thumb across her lower lip, and it was all she could do to stifle a moan.

Only the thought of their tiny chaperones kept her from taking this moment to its eventual, much-wanted conclusion. "Any more of that and we'd end up making love again," she whispered as she splayed her hands across the hardness of his chest. Lower still, she could feel his arousal pressing against her.

"I know." Brody wrapped his arms around her and held her tight. She reveled in his warmth and closeness, the overwhelming tenderness he had displayed toward her and the children through the night.

He let out a low, ragged sigh of regret and reluctantly loosened his hold on her. "I guess I better head for the sofa," he said.

"Why don't you take my bed?" Meg suggested softly, knowing exactly how tired he must feel.

He lifted an eyebrow, as if wondering exactly what her impulsive offer meant in terms of their relationship.

"You'll be more comfortable there," Meg whispered in a voice that radiated passion. "And I'm up for the day."

His gaze lovingly roved her face, lingering on her lips, before returning to her eyes. "You're sure you want me between your sheets?"

Meg tried to suppress the image of Brody sprawled out comfortably in her bed, and her growing desire to join him there. "That's a loaded question," she teased, then pressed a silencing kiss to his lips. Gently she pushed him in the direction she wanted him to go, trying not to lament the fact that events still seemed to be conspiring to keep them apart. She would have liked the chance to climb into bed with him, and if not make love, at least cuddle with him for a little while. But first things first. After keeping watch over the twins all night long, he had to be exhausted. Like so many other things, talks about the future were simply going to have to wait for a better, more private time. "I'll take over from here," Meg stated firmly.

Brody's arms tightened around her. "I know what you're thinking," he said as he pressed a reassuring kiss to her temple. "You're thinking the time is never right for us. But it will be, Meg. And soon. I promise."

"I hope so." She rose up on tiptoe and kissed him back. Fiercely, passionately. Then tenderly and sweetly. "Because that's a promise I'm going to hold you to, Brody Taylor." That said, she took him by the hand and led him to her bed for the sleep he had earned.

"SO HOW ARE THE KIDS?" Alexandra asked on Monday afternoon when Meg came into the office to let them know she was clocking in.

"On the mend. They still have about seven days of antibiotics left, but they should both be back in school by Wednesday."

"That's great." Alexandra finished signing for a delivery of diapers, juice and formula. "Who's taking care of them today?"

"Brody." Meg held the door for the delivery man as he left, then turned back to Alexandra. "He's working at home, so they're both over there."

Alexandra opened her vegetarian lunch and spread it out on her desk. Because they were short-handed that day, she was going to cover the phones in the office while she ate lunch. "It's nice you two can help each other out like that," she said as she opened her carton of soy milk and stuck a straw in the top. "A lot of divorced couples aren't able to be so cooperative."

"Brody and I both want what is best for our kids." Meg thumbed through the notes and messages in her mail cubbyhole. Finding nothing urgent, she turned back to Alexandra. "Is anyone else sick?"

"Not so far." Alexandra rapped her knuckles on her desktop. "Knock on wood." The phone rang and she picked it up, pleased to hear the familiar voice of her aunt Mary Rose Cullen. "Hi, Aunt Mary Rose! What's happening in Montana these days?" Alexandra asked cheerfully as Meg waved and headed out to teach a class.

"Nothing good, I'm afraid."

Alexandra sat back down. Mary Rose and her husband had been like parents to her since she was six, the year her parents had died in the fire. "Have you heard from Brad?"

"He calls every two or three weeks on his cell phone and checks in, but he refuses to tell us where he is or when he's coming home," Mary Rose told her unhappily.

Brad was seven years older than Alexandra, and of all the Cullen offspring, the "adopted" sibling she was closest to. Probably because they were both restless and free-spirited at heart. "Do you think he's still embarrassed about his wedding to Jo Millen being called off at the last minute?"

"I don't know what he feels. He won't discuss the situation with us. I thought he might have confided in you."

"Not yet, but if he does get in touch with me, I'll see what I can do to help," Alexandra promised. "In the meantime, try not to worry. After all, it's not the first time he's taken off like that. Brad always packs up and heads off for a few days of solitude whenever he has things to sort out."

"That's true," Mary Rose agreed. "But he's never sworn to stay clear of all women before."

Alexandra pooh-poohed that notion immediately. "He'll get over that when he gets over his broken relationship."

"You think so?" her aunt asked hopefully.

"I know so. Brad is too big and strong and sexy to be lonely for long. Why, I bet even now he's got a few women chasing him."

Mary Rose chuckled, her usual good humor returning. "You're probably right about that. Kind, good-looking cowboys don't have to struggle for dates."

"He'll be fine," Alexandra soothed. "Brad just needs a little more time to lick his wounds. Once he does, he'll be as good as new."

"In the meantime," Mary Rose cautioned, "if that son of mine does show up there in Seattle or gives you a call—"

"I'll be sure one of us lets you and Uncle Walt and the rest of the family know he's all right," Alexandra promised. It was the least she owed the Callens. They had given her a home and love and a sense of family when she had none. As for Brad... Well, the two of them had always been close, so maybe his mother was right, Alexandra mused. Maybe this time Brad would show up in Seattle before heading back to Montana and the Split Rock Ranch.

"YOU LOOK TIRED, Meg," Brody said Friday evening as he carried the orange plastic tray, brimming with food, over to their table. They had decided to let the kids play first, and then eat, so Meg sat watching the twins romp in the indoor playground attached to the restaurant.

"I'm exhausted." Meg unwrapped her grilled chicken sandwich. "I think it's been the longest week of my life."

Brody nodded as he added more mustard to his double-decker cheeseburger. "It's not easy having the kids get sick, and nursing them through an illness."

Meg shook her head as she tasted a french fry. "I don't know what I would have done without you this week. If you hadn't been here to take them days, when I had to go to work—"

Brody waved at the kids, who were having a blast going up and down the circular slide, then turned back to her. "You would have called in sick, and they would have gotten substitute teachers to fill in for you."

"You know what I mean." Meg gave Brody a look. "Because you could work at home and watch them this week, I was able to go to work without worrying myself to death.''

''Is that what happened in New York when Kelly came down with something?'' he asked curiously.

Meg nodded, forking up a bite of garden salad. ''If she was really sick, of course, I would ask my understudy to go on, and I stayed home and took care of her myself. But when it was just the sniffles or a sore throat with no fever, I had to leave her with her sitter and go to work. And that was hard. I always felt so guilty.''

''Me, too.''

''You couldn't work at home in Ireland?'' she asked in surprise. From the tone of his letters to her, she thought that everything had been exceedingly rosy there.

Brody frowned unhappily. ''Uncle Roarke didn't approve of men skipping work for anything other than the most dire of situations. Wives—and in my case, nannies—were supposed to do the nursing. And since Roarke was putting up the money and Kevin was well cared for by Fiona, and occasionally Aunt Norah, I went to work.''

Meg smiled, guessing the next. ''And then you worried the whole time.''

''You got it.''

A companionable silence fell between them as Meg thought about how much Brody had changed, for the better, since their divorce. ''I take it you're planning to run things differently in the Seattle branch,'' she said.

Brody nodded. ''We have to offer flextime and the work-at-home option to stay competitive with other Seattle companies. Uncle Roarke understands that.''

''Otherwise—''

''There's no way anyone would work for us. Not when they could go somewhere else in Seattle or the Silicon Valley and have those same benefits.''

"Does it bother you, having to bend to your uncle Roarke's wishes on things?" Meg asked.

Brody shook his head. "Without his generosity, I wouldn't have had the opportunity to start my own company."

"You could have gotten the funds."

"Maybe," he allowed. "But not without bowing and scraping to whoever gave me the money—whether it was another individual or an investment banking group. If the money is loaned to you, then you have to answer to the person giving you the loan. That's just the way it is. So, better that it was family, who genuinely cared about me and Kevin, who were controlling the purse strings."

Meg nodded. "That makes sense." They both turned to the kids and saw they were beginning to tucker out, which meant they would be wanting to eat in the next ten or fifteen minutes.

"Anyway, at least you have the weekend to rest up," Brody consoled Meg.

At that she could only grin. She shook her head ruefully. "I wish that were the case." At the sympathy in Brody's eyes, she confided easily, "You remember the mother who was an artist at kindergarten night? The one who offered to paint the plywood props for the performance Monday night?" Brody nodded. "Well, she had an emergency appendectomy yesterday. Her husband called me this morning. The props are all cut out and drawn, but they're only half-painted. He's got his hands full caring for her and their three kids, so he brought the props and the paint by my house this evening, before Kelly and I came over. I'm going to be painting most of tomorrow. Fortunately, there's no rain predicted, and you'll have Kelly and Kevin, so it should go pretty smoothly."

"You want some help with it?" Brody asked.

As much as she wanted to spend time alone with him

again, Meg knew she couldn't ask Brody to pitch in after the week they'd both had nursing the kids. Given the purchase of the Texas software company, he probably had a lot of work of his own to catch up on. And it would be impossible to get the painting done as quickly as she needed to with the kids underfoot. "I'll be fine," she assured him, thinking this was yet another opportunity to spend time with Brody that was blown. "Thanks, anyway."

LATE SATURDAY MORNING, Meg was halfway through the props when Brody strolled around the side of the house and into the backyard. Like her, he was dressed in his oldest pair of jeans and a T-shirt that had seen better days. Although she had told herself repeatedly since they had made love that she didn't have to have him in her life these days and could function perfectly fine on her own, there was no denying the joy she felt as she saw him sauntering confidently toward her.

"Where are the kids?" she asked, smiling. She knew it was selfish, given the children's affection for Kevin's ex-nanny, but she hoped Fiona hadn't once again stationed herself at Brody's place. Meg didn't like having the beautiful young woman around Brody, and that went double when it was in an intimate setting like his home.

Brody grinned back at her in a way that made her insides melt with pleasure. "Hannah Richards and Alexandra Webber took them roller-skating. Then they're going out to lunch and to a movie. We're officially free until six o'clock this evening. So—" he braced his hands on his waist, already sizing up the job ahead of them "—we'll just hope we can get everything done here that needs to be done by then, so we don't end up trying to watch Kevin and Kelly and paint at the same time."

Meg hadn't asked him to help her complete this task, and in fact had warned him away from it, but she was glad he was here, anyway. This was one time she hadn't really wanted him to listen to her. She handed him a brush.

"How did you manage to work that out?" Meg asked, doing her best to disguise her relief that he hadn't automatically turned to Fiona, who was still in Seattle looking for work.

"Simple." Brody shrugged, his broad shoulders straining against the soft worn cotton of his shirt. "I just called Hannah and Alexandra last night and told them you needed help. They had their choice of painting or playing, and they chose playing. So tell me what to do."

"See the numbers penciled in on the cardboard cutouts?" When Brody nodded, Meg continued, "Well, the numbers correspond to the paint colors we have here. Seven is red, three is green…. They're all on the sheet I have tacked up over here."

"Ah. So we're painting by numbers."

"You got it."

Brody rolled up his sleeves. "I think I can handle that."

For the next hour, they worked diligently, painting a musical staff with the C-major scale written on it, a big medicine bottle and a spoonful of sugar, an umbrella and a chimney, a nanny and an umbrella and two life-size children dressed in clothing circa 1910.

Meg and Brody chatted about everything and nothing, until all the cutouts were three-quarters done. "We probably better let what we've painted so far dry before we finish them, to keep the different colors from smearing," Meg said, putting her brush down and stretching. She turned to Brody, aware she hadn't been this happy since the glowing early days of their marriage. Smiling, she paused and wiped a streak of green paint from his cheek with a cloth, then stepped back. Swallowing around the sudden tightness in her throat, she asked cheerfully, "Are you hungry? Do you want some lunch?" It was the least she could do for him.

"Sure." Brody followed her inside and stood next to her at the sink as they washed up. "If it's not too much trouble."

No trouble at all, Meg thought. In fact, she was never happier than when she was cooking and caring for those she loved. And the person at the top of her list, she was stunned to realize, was Brody Taylor. Wondering what had gotten into her, she opened her refrigerator and peered inside. "That depends on how you feel about Italian sub sandwiches and Diet Cokes."

Brody lounged against the counter, his gaze trailing lazily over the length of her. "Pretty damn good, as it happens," he replied cheerfully. "Can I help make 'em?"

Brody offering to help her prepare the food? He had always said he couldn't cook, period, and had refused to try and learn anything except how to dial for delivery or go out to a restaurant. Stunned, Meg slanted him an approving look. "You have changed," she drawled.

His eyes darkened as he hooked his hands around her waist and murmured huskily, "I've been waiting for you to notice." The next thing Meg knew, she was in Brody's arms. He brushed the hair from her face. "I want to make love to you, Meg."

Her heart took on a slow, heavy beat. "I want that, too," she whispered back.

Brody looked behind them, in the direction of the small laundry room off the kitchen. It had space for a washer and dryer, a broom closet and shelves, but not much else.

"Then hang on." Eyes sparkling mischievously, he tucked his arms beneath her bottom and hoisted her up so her weight was settled against his torso, her legs wrapped around his waist. He carried her easily into the laundry room and shut the door behind him.

A small half-moon window set high on the outside wall illuminated the room with golden sunlight that filtered down on them. Brody set her on top of the washing machine, and pushing her knees apart, stepped between them. Meg saw the hunger in his gaze and surrendered to it, to him. And then his lips were on hers in a kiss that sent her spirits soaring and her body thrumming. Tangling her fingers in his hair, Meg pulled him closer yet. He smelled like paint and sun and man. Overwhelmed by the pleasurable sensation, she guided him closer yet, returning his kiss with everything she felt for him.

And Brody was just as relentless in his pursuit of her. She felt his hands slide beneath her shirt to her bra. He unclasped it, pushed the fabric aside and cupped the weight of both her breasts in his hands. Then her shirt and bra were coming off. His eyes held hers with the promise of the lovemaking to come as he ran his thumbs over the tender crests. Meg had never felt sexier or more voluptuous in her life as his head lowered. She hitched in a breath, watching as his lips moved over her skin, exploring, until she shut her eyes and gave in to the tantalizing sensation.

Soon they were kissing again, hotly, rapaciously, and then her jeans, too, were coming off, and Brody was repeating the sensual exploration until she no longer knew where his body ended and hers began. She only knew she wanted them together. Now.

She helped him off with his shirt, running her hands across the hard muscle and smooth skin. He kicked off his jeans and boxers. He'd driven her mad with desire. Now she slipped down off the washer and used her hands and mouth to drive him to the brink, until he, too, could take no more. Lifting her in his arms, he shifted her back onto the washer and wrapped her legs around him. And then he was plunging inside her, making her his.

Meg's heart swelled with love, even as she trembled with pent-up desire. She gasped and moaned as they kissed, and he obliged her with slow, deliberate thrusts. She met him with an abandonment of her own, her hips rising instinctively as he possessed and took and gave. And then there was no more thinking, only feeling, the hot golden rush of pleasure, the exquisite, shattering release and the slow, satisfied fall back down to earth.

It was like the old days, Meg thought, her passion for him flowing through her anew. Only it was better this time. Much, much better. Because this time she knew it wasn't just a physical thing. Or the infatuation of a whirlwind romance. Or the enforced intimacy of a "shotgun" marriage bringing them together and pushing them into each other's arms. This time she knew she was head over heels in love with him. The question was, how did Brody feel about her?

CHAPTER THIRTEEN

BRODY LOUNGED in the bathroom, watching as Meg put on her clothing, splashed water on her face and ran a brush through her curls. It wasn't hard to see what she was doing, he thought, amused. Although he doubted she wanted to admit it to him or anyone else, she was trying to erase the aftereffects of their lovemaking. And it was impossible.

"They're going to know," Brody told her lazily, coming up behind her. He wrapped his arms around her waist and buried his face in the fragrant softness of her hair. Meg smelled like soap from the shower they had just taken together, and lotion and the uniquely feminine essence of her skin.

Meg turned to face him. Leaving her lower half pressed against him, she tilted her face up to his and looked into his eyes. "Who's going to know?"

Brody smiled. If being with her like this, making her his again, wasn't heaven, he didn't know what was. He threaded his fingers through her hair. "Hannah and Alexandra and anyone else who sees you."

"I don't see how," she murmured, her eyes a soft, misty green.

"You're glowing," he told her, pressing a kiss to her temple.

Smiling, Meg stepped back. No longer the tempestuous, guarded, independent-to-a-fault diva he remembered, she splayed her hands across his chest and kissed his lips. "So are you," she quipped playfully, unashamed of the ardor they had both displayed in their lovemaking.

"Which is completely understandable," Brody countered, kissing her again, slowly and lingeringly. "There's no way I could look anything but completely besotted after making wild, passionate love to the most beautiful woman on earth." Whether she wanted to admit it or not, Meg had been his since the first time they had made love together, and even throughout the long years of their divorce, she had remained, at heart, his woman and his alone. He knew he had remained her husband, too, at least in spirit. He could feel it in the possessive way she held him, and in the intensity with which she returned his kisses and caresses.

Meg ducked her head shyly, resting her head against his chest. "I'm not the most beautiful woman on earth."

Brody tucked his hands beneath her chin and lifted her face to his. "In my eyes you are," he told her huskily, not about to pretend something of major significance wasn't happening to them. Because it was.

The conflict and apprehension Meg still felt was mirrored in her eyes. "Oh, Brody..." she whispered.

"What?"

"I know how right it feels when we're together like this."

No kidding, Brody thought. "But when we're apart?" he queried. "What happens then?"

Meg bit her lip uncertainly. "I get scared we've slipped back into being a couple again because we're together so much of the time with the kids, and because making love to each other is so familiar and comforting." She paused, worry clouding her eyes. "I never stopped caring about you, Brody. And I know in your own way you still care deeply about me, too."

She was making their love sound platonic, familial—not

the passionate emotion he would always feel for her. Fear knotted his gut.

"But I don't want us to fall into a relationship simply because we never gave ourselves a chance to be a whole family the first time, or had someone to share the responsibility of parenting with," Meg continued sincerely.

Brody swallowed around the growing ache in his throat. "I'll be the first to admit it's great to have you here to help me with Kevin, or take over when I have to go out of town."

Meg smiled appreciatively. "And it was nice for me when you were able to help me care for the twins and stay home with them when they were sick." She searched his eyes. "But I don't want to repeat our mistakes, and I worry that that isn't really enough to build a lasting relationship on."

As much as Brody wanted to, he couldn't take away the trauma and uncertainty of Meg's childhood, any more than he could erase the pain that lingered from his own. Their parents' unhappy marriages had scarred them, left them wary of commitment. As young adults, they had been unsure there was such a thing as everlasting love. So when it came to their wedding vows, they'd avoided making sappy promises or wild declarations of love and chosen a "sophisticated" approach. Yet when the first problems came, they had been quick to protect themselves and their hearts and part company, telling themselves all the while it was for the best. Now, five long, lonely years had passed, forcing both of them to grow up. And to realize that in every marriage, problems arose, causing some unhappiness and pain and even, at times, abject misery. But problems could be solved, and the marriage hadn't had to end, Brody thought fiercely. He knew now the two of them should have put their mutual anxiety aside and toughed it out. They should have worked out their problems together, no matter how long it took or how hard it was. If they had done that, there would have been no divorce. No lost years or unreciprocated love. But there was still time to remedy that and make up for lost time. And somehow he had to get Meg, who was still struggling with her uncertainty, still fearing their happiness would be snatched away again, to realize that, too.

Wrapping his arms tighter around her, he anchored her against him and reassured her firmly, "What we have is a great foundation upon which to build a life together, Meg. And I think deep in your heart, you feel that way, too." *Or you would, if you put your fear aside and took the risk.*

But to Brody's dismay, Meg said nothing. Instead, she simply held on tight, her breath warm against his chest, her body cuddled against his. Brody told himself not to feel disappointed. Meg had always been the more cautious of the two of them when it came to letting herself feel anything.

Finally, she looked up at him. "The only thing I know for certain," she murmured with a troubled sigh, "is that we can't keep sneaking around like this. Making love on the sly every time the two of us happen to end up alone together, just because it's convenient and easy."

Not to mention wildly satisfying. Nevertheless, Brody knew she needed more from him. He needed more from her, too—a lot more, in order to be truly happy. "I agree," he said, just as firmly. He lowered his head and kissed her soundly. "This is no way for two grown-ups and responsible parents to act." He threaded his fingers through her hair, trailed a hand down her face. "I think we should stop the subterfuge and tell the world that we're getting involved with each other again, and start dating publicly."

A wary look in her eyes, Meg stepped away from him. "We talked about this."

Brody lifted a dissenting brow. "Did we?"

Meg's lips set stubbornly. "I don't want to raise the hopes of the twins, only to crush them again."

"Neither do I," he agreed, his patience fading as he followed Meg out into the master bedroom.

"So we can't tell them," Meg said bluntly, pivoting to face him once again. "We can't tell anyone."

Brody studied her silently. "Are you saying you never want to sleep with me again? Like you said the last time?"

"No."

Hope rose within him. "Then you do?"

Meg's breath hitched. "Yes."

"But only in secret." Brody didn't bother to hide his mounting frustration.

"Until we're sure this isn't just a convenient affair," Meg stipulated in a low, subdued voice.

Personally, Brody didn't know how much more sure they needed to be. He knew he wanted and needed Meg more than he had any woman in his life. He knew she was the only woman for him. The problem was, she wasn't nearly as willing to believe that. He just had to be patient, Brody schooled himself sternly. Give her time. And room enough to come to the same conclusion he already had—that the two of them were meant to be together.

"Okay," he said quietly, looking her straight in the eye. He was determined to make their relationship work this time, whatever it took. "We'll do it your way," he promised with a reassuring smile.

Meg blinked as if she didn't quite believe what she was hearing. "You mean that?" she asked hoarsely.

Brody nodded and took her into his arms again. "But having made that concession, there's one I want you to make," he told her sexily.

"And that is…?" Her eyes glimmered in anticipation as understanding dawned.

"I want you to make love with me again." Brody swept

her up in his arms and carried her to the bed. He laid her down gently and stretched out beside her, amazed at how hungry he was for her. "And I want to do it now, while we still have time," he murmured, kissing her deeply and feeling her kiss him back.

This wasn't everything he wanted from her. But for the moment, it was enough.

"I DON'T UNDERSTAND how it can be a surprise party if your mommy and daddy already know about it and even helped you two order a cake," Hannah said as she and Alexandra lingered over post-skating ice-cream sundaes with the twins.

"It's a surprise," Kevin explained seriously, "because they don't know everything that is going to be at the party. They only know part of it."

Hannah looked at Kelly, who seemed just as excited. "Well, what else is going to be there?" she asked, knowing enough about the twins' penchant for mischief to be worried about the possibility of more double trouble.

"Well, we don't know yet...exactly," Kelly said. "But there's a surprise for sure."

"Maybe two," Kevin said, grinning at his sister conspiratorially in much the same way they had before letting the classroom gerbil loose at naptime.

Alexandra and Hannah looked at each other uneasily. This was not good.

"Let's back up here a minute," Alexandra said. "We all got the e-mail notice that Amy Tidwell helped you two send out last weekend. It asked us to bring extra chairs and flowers to the party for your dad. Right?"

"Yes. Because Mommy likes flowers a whole bunch, and Kevin and I get in trouble if we just go in someone's yard and pick them," Kelly explained.

Both women's eyes widened. "Did you do that?" Hannah asked.

"No. But we talked about it," Kevin told her as he played with the rainbow sprinkles on top of his sundae. "And Mommy said we couldn't do that, because it wouldn't be right."

"And then she said Daddy didn't need flowers for a birthday party, but we don't think that's right," Kevin explained with five-year-old logic.

"Yes." Kelly backed up her brother adamantly. "They need flowers because it's a very special party."

"Okay." Hannah and Alexandra made note of that. "Is there anything else you need for your party?" Alexandra asked.

"Well, more food." Kelly licked the chocolate syrup off her spoon, then leaned forward earnestly. "Mommy said we only need cake and ice cream, but *we* want more food."

Hannah didn't find that request so unreasonable. In fact, she was impressed at how hard the twins were working to be good hosts at Brody's birthday party. "I think we can arrange a potluck, and you're right, people are always hungry at parties."

"And music," Kevin added, waving his spoon in the air. "We need music."

Alexandra shrugged. "That's easy. We'll just bring the karaoke machine from school and play some CDs."

"Anything else?" Hannah asked as she pushed her dish aside.

"Well," Kelly said, "there's a couple more people we wanted to invite to the w—the party."

"Just tell me who you want to be there, and I'll ask 'em," Hannah promised.

"Well, our Sunday school teacher, Ms. Henning, and we already asked Reverend Bollick at our church."

"So is that it?" Hannah asked.

Kevin and Kelly nodded. "Just don't tell Mommy and Daddy 'bout all the extra stuff," Kelly said.

"They're up to something," Hannah warned Alexandra after they had dropped both Kevin and Kelly off at Meg's house.

Alexandra ran a hand through her short red hair. "I think so, too. But it couldn't be anything bad, could it?"

"I don't see how." Hannah shrugged as she stopped at a traffic light en route to her place. "It's just a birthday party."

"Still," Alexandra sighed, "their secret surprises make me nervous."

"Me, too," Hannah admitted. Her own parents' divorce when she was nine gave her insight into why the twins wanted so desperately to be one big happy family again, if only for the party. "But in this case I think the twins just want their parents to be pleased with their efforts and have an exceptionally good time. I mean, they're not asking for water balloons or squirt guns or fireworks. I think they figure that if they add all the extra stuff and make the party extra special—"

"Their parents will get back together again?" Alexandra guessed.

Hannah smiled. "Have you been getting those vibes, too?"

"Oh, yeah." Alexandra sighed wistfully. "Did you see the way Brody and Meg were looking at each other when we dropped the kids off?"

"Like they're secretly in love?" Hannah asked.

Alexandra nodded. "Do you think they'll remarry?"

"I don't know." Hannah shrugged and pulled into a shopping center with a variety of small specialty stores. "Once burned, twice shy, and all that. But I have to tell you, I hope so. I think it would be the best thing for both of them, not to mention the kids. In the meantime, since we're here, let's do our bit," Hannah said as she turned her car off. "A few more invitations, additional food and music coming right up."

To MEG'S DELIGHT, the children recalled everything during the first-ever musical performance at the Forrester Square Day Care on Monday evening. They breezed through the choruses of the popular Disney tunes. Singing exuberantly to "A Spoonful Of Sugar," swaying and dancing perfectly to "Chim Chim Cheree," and even recalling all the lyrics and choreography to "Do-Re-Mi." By the time they reached their finale of "A Dream Is A Wish Your Heart Makes," there wasn't a dry eye in the house, including Meg's. She was so proud of the kids for pulling it all together so quickly and professionally she thought she could burst. "Great job!" she said, giving them all a hearty thumbs-up over the thunderous applause of the parents. "Great job!"

Still smiling, Meg turned to the audience of family and friends crowded into the school events room and took her bow along with the kids. It was only when they were dismissed, and she was accepting congratulations from various parents, that Meg realized Brody's uncle Roarke had been in the audience, and that he had brought Fiona with him. Judging from the look on Brody's face as he moved to insert himself between Roarke and Meg, it had been a surprise to him, too. But the practical part of Meg knew she shouldn't have been surprised. Roarke had never felt Meg was the woman for Brody. Doing her best to hide her feelings of unease, she finished talking to the parents, then made her way over to the assembled family with all the grace she could muster.

"Congratulations, Meg." Roarke kissed Meg's cheek with his customary bravado. "Wonderful job here tonight!"

"I thought so, too." Fiona beamed.

If Fiona was jealous of her, Meg noted in reluctant admiration, she wasn't showing it. Instead, Kevin's ex-nanny looked every bit as confident and comfortable in the awkward situation as Meg longed to be.

Kelly and Kevin came up to Meg and latched on to her, one on either side, giving her a reprieve from Fiona's sweet gaze. "Didn't we all do good?" Kevin asked, grinning from ear to ear.

"You did magnificently!" Brody exclaimed, hugging both his kids, and then, ever so discreetly, Meg. She leaned into his embrace gratefully, appreciating his warmth and strength, if only for a few seconds. "I was really impressed."

"Thank you," Meg said, giving Brody a quick glance that told him everything she couldn't say in front of everyone else. That she was glad he was here. That she was happy he was proud of her. That it felt good to be together again, even secretly. Too soon, however, their moment of intimacy was interrupted.

"Oh, Kevin, we're all so proud of you." Fiona knelt and gave her former charge a hug. "And you too, Miss Kelly." Fiona warmly embraced Kelly, too, then straightened to face Meg. "You did an amazing job," Fiona told her with obvious sincerity. "I've never seen children of this age perform so well."

"Thank you," Meg said humbly. "But I deserve only part of the credit. The kids in the class are really talented, and they tried so hard." It had made her job as an instructor much easier.

"But it's the teacher who makes them want to try so hard," Fiona said, looking at her with respect. "And you're obviously very good at what you do."

"Thank you," Meg said, appreciating the compliment in the spirit it was given. For reasons that had everything to do with her feelings for Brody and nothing to do with rational thinking, Meg wanted to dislike Fiona. At the very least resent her for coming to the children's performance and the school where Meg taught. But she couldn't do that. For one thing, no one knew Meg and Brody were involved again. For another, as the only "mother-figure" Kevin had had in his life for most of his first five years, Meg had to admit that Fiona deserved to be there as much as anyone else. And Meg couldn't overlook the fact that Kevin wanted her there, too.

"How is your job search coming?" she asked, forcing herself to put her petty jealousy aside and be as nice to Fiona as Fiona was being to her.

"I've interviewed with three Seattle families. I think two are going to offer me a live-in position."

"But?" Meg prodded, sensing Fiona's hesitation.

"I'm just not sure I would feel as comfortable in those homes as I did in Brody's." Fiona turned to him. "And I heard you are going to be traveling a lot more again, to Texas this time, and thought I might be of assistance, were I not employed elsewhere, so if you need me, I wanted to let you know that I'm still available and could come and live with you and Kevin again. Immediately, if necessary."

Brody looked as stunned by Fiona's unexpected offer as Meg felt. They had both been under the impression Fiona had given up the idea of being Brody's woman when he had cleared up the wedding veil misunderstanding. Obviously, Meg thought, beginning to feel resentful toward Kevin's ex-nanny again, that had not been the case. Despite her determined show of civility, Fiona was still hoping Brody would ask her to be part of his and Kevin's life again. Perhaps permanently this time. And Uncle Roarke was encouraging her in that regard.

"Actually," Meg interrupted, gently but firmly, "Brody and I have already made arrangements. I'll be taking care of Kevin in Brody's absences."

Fiona looked crestfallen.

"Well, shall we all go out for pizza?" Brody asked, moving on with forced cheer. "I know the kids must be starving."

"YOU LOOK…IRRITATED," Meg said to Brody the next morning, when the two of them met for a quick cup of coffee at his office before Meg's first class of the day. She had wanted to meet for breakfast, but Brody hadn't had time. And judging from the stacks of papers and telephone messages on his desk, his workload was as heavy as ever.

"I am." Brody scowled as he sat back in his leather swivel chair.

"Why?" Meg opened the bakery sack and pulled out two pastries to go with the coffee Brody's secretary had poured for them.

"Over half of my newly acquired Austin employees are refusing to move to Seattle, even though I've offered them substantial raises and full moving and living expenses for the transition." Brody shook his head. "I just don't get why any of them would refuse such a generous offer!"

Meg shrugged. "Maybe there are more important things than money." She knew that was still the case with her.

Brody shot her a critical glance. "You sound like them."

And you sound like you used to when we were married, Meg thought. But then, maybe that was par for the course, she told herself. Maybe this was just how CEOs behaved. Maybe they all wanted what they wanted, when they wanted it, damn the consequences. Just because Brody was reverting back to past behavior in his professional life didn't mean he would also return to his dictatorial ways in his personal. "How do they explain their refusal?" she asked gently.

Brody shrugged, looking even more frustrated. "For some, the sticking point is their extended families. For others, it's their kids' schooling. Some don't want to sell their homes. Some object to the weather!'' Ignoring the pastry on his desk, Brody got up and began to pace. ''And it's ridiculous, given the fact that my company can provide so much more for them in terms of salary and perks over the long haul than the old management could. Plus, the schools are good here. The weather is something you can get used to. You can fly home to visit extended family. And there are plenty of comparable homes for sale here.''

''It's not really the same, though, is it? I mean, Seattle and Texas.''

When Brody only looked annoyed, Meg tried again. ''Maybe they're just happy where they are.''

''Close-minded is more like it,'' Brody muttered.

A tense silence fell between them. ''What happens to the employees who refuse to go?'' she asked.

Brody's jaw hardened. ''They quit the company. There is no severance package. The terms of their employment include moving to Seattle immediately. If they refuse, they're out.''

Whoa. Meg wondered if he knew how unreasonable he was being. ''Can't you keep an office open in Texas, let those who want to, stay there—at least for a while?''

He shook his head. As far as he was concerned, the matter was closed. ''I don't want to be traveling back and forth all the time. Besides, to effectively integrate the two U.S. teams, we need to have everyone in one location. But I don't want to talk about this.'' Brody relaxed his shoulders. ''I'd rather talk about what happened last night.'' He came toward her and took her in his arms for a brief kiss. Drawing back, he looked down into her face, his ruefulness apparent as he murmured softly, ''It wasn't exactly the end to the evening we had planned last night, was it?''

''No, it wasn't,'' Meg admitted with a sigh as Brody escorted her over to the sofa in the corner and dropped down beside her. They had thought—with Roarke supposedly still in Texas—that it was going to be just the four of them going out for a celebratory pizza. Instead, it had been six. And an awkward six at that.

Brody tucked an arm about her shoulders and brought her against his warm, sheltering body. "Roarke should have told me he was planning to come to the performance. And that he was going to bring Fiona. Because if he had, I would have asked him not to bring her."

Meg looked down at her hands. As much as she wished otherwise, their own feelings weren't all that counted here. "Kevin enjoyed having Fiona there last night."

Brody made a dissenting sound as he slid Meg onto his lap and turned her until she was facing him. He tightened his hold on her possessively as he looked deep into her eyes. "Kevin is five and too young to understand the ramifications of the situation."

At their nearness, Meg drew in a tremulous breath. "Which are?"

"That by inviting Fiona last night, and encouraging her to try and become a part of Kevin's and my day-to-day life again, Roarke is fueling Fiona's fantasies that someday she might be a real mother and not just an ex-nanny to Kevin."

"Not to mention your wife," Meg said dryly.

Brody nodded, reluctantly admitting this was true.

A more companionable silence fell between them. "So what happened when you got back to your house last night?" Meg asked curiously, relieved that they were laying all their cards out on the table for the other to see.

He shrugged. "We dropped Fiona at her hotel, and then I took Roarke back to my house. I put Kevin to bed, and then Roarke and I had a brandy and smoked cigars."

Meg made a face. "Sounds manly."

"I had a talk with him, Meg," he said, massaging the

back of her wrist with slow, sensual strokes. "He's not very happy with me right now."

"Why? What did you say?"

Brody's expression grew stern. "I told Roarke that he needed to butt out of my love life."

"Oh, my. That sounds…"

"Ugly?" Brody lifted his brow, guessing at her thoughts.

"Yes," Meg admitted, studying his pained expression, "sort of."

"Well, it was. But Roarke got the message."

Meg was relieved about that, even as she began to worry. She bit her lower lip nervously. "Roarke's not going to do anything crazy, is he? Like pull your funds?"

"I don't think so, but even if he did, I wouldn't care. I want him as family, Meg, but I also want you and Kelly and Kevin, and if I have to make a choice, well—" he squeezed her waist "—I've made it. The three of you are it for me."

Meg smiled. She had wanted to be first in Brody's life for what seemed like a very long time. Now, finally, it appeared she was. "Oh, Brody…" She leaned up to kiss him passionately, despite the fact they were in his office and could be interrupted at any time.

Brody kissed her back just as passionately, until all she wanted was to find a place where they could be alone and make love the way they had on Saturday afternoon—as if there was only the two of them, this moment in time. But she knew, even before the phone on his desk buzzed and Brody had to excuse himself to talk with his Austin management team, that that wasn't going to happen. Not today, anyway, with their packed schedules and responsibilities. So she whispered goodbye to Brody and went on to the university to teach her morning classes, then headed over to the day care. When she walked into the office to pick up her messages, Katherine, Alexandra and Hannah smiled at her.

"So how was your morning?" Katherine asked with a sly grin.

"Fine." Meg paused. "Why do you ask?"

The three women shrugged. Finally, Hannah said, "The twins told Carmen you were seeing Brody this morning at his office."

"And?" Meg guessed by the way all three women were trying to get a look at the ring finger on her left hand that there was more.

"They also told Carmen you would probably be getting married again real soon," Katherine confided reluctantly.

Meg's eyes widened in amazement. The twins weren't supposed to know she'd had an impromptu date with Brody this morning! She had called him while Kelly was upstairs brushing her teeth and getting ready for school. And how and why had they jumped to that particular conclusion, anyway? She and Brody had made it plain they weren't talking about remarrying.

"It's okay, Meg," Alexandra soothed.

Her expression matter-of-fact, Hannah agreed. "Everyone here knows that you and Brody still have a thing for each other."

Meg realized that was true. According to Julia Stanton, the twins had told everyone at the day care center days ago that she and Brody had been kissing and hugging. The gossip had just been upped a notch, thanks to Kelly and Kevin's misinterpretation of events.

Katherine nodded. "It's obvious whenever you and Brody are within fifty feet of each other that something romantic is going on. So it's only natural the twins would pick up on it, too."

And jump to conclusions, Meg noted unhappily. Which was exactly what she had *not* wanted to happen.

CHAPTER FOURTEEN

"WHERE ARE THE KIDS?" Brody asked Thursday evening, when he came over to Meg's to pick up Kevin and take him home. A staff meeting with the new employee managers had run late and kept him from joining the three of them for dinner. When he had called to let Meg know he wouldn't be there, she had said she understood his absence. Now, looking at the carefully controlled expression on her face, he wondered if she had been truthful. Maybe she thought he was once again choosing work over his relationship with her.

She hadn't been happy Tuesday morning when he'd had to cut short their tête-à-tête at his office, or Wednesday, when he'd had to nix an evening with her and the kids to meet with an up-and-coming creator of educational software he was trying to sign exclusively to his company. He had asked Meg to join them for dinner and see him alone afterward, but she had cited her own workload and the need to be with the twins that evening, and had refused. At the time he had accepted her reasoning at face value. Now he wasn't so sure. Meg was giving him the kind of smile she reserved for casual acquaintances as she ushered him inside, and he wondered if her unusually subdued attitude might be something to worry about, after all.

"They're upstairs, watching our wedding video again."

That didn't seem to be welcome news to Meg, though personally, Brody thought it was kind of cute. He followed her into the living room. Several boxes of music were on the floor and she seemed to be in the process of sorting it into stacks. Meg frowned as she added the score of *South Pacific* to a stack of other Rodgers and Hammerstein musicals.

Her eyes darkened unhappily as she reported in a dejected tone, "They can't seem to get enough of it."

Brody shrugged and leaned back against her cherished piano. "That's understandable, I guess. They really want us together again." When Meg said nothing in response, he continued pumping her for information. He wanted to understand her mood. "Anything else on your mind? You look a little blue." He paused. "You're not nervous about singing for Julia and Drew's wedding, are you?"

"No." Meg emptied out one box, set it aside and picked up another, lifting it onto the piano bench. "I'm looking forward to that."

Feeling both baffled and annoyed that she wasn't helping him out here, he stuck his hands in the pockets of his slacks and made another stab in the dark. "Are you overwhelmed because the birthday party you and the kids are giving me is happening on the same date?" It was a lot to do in one day. "Because we don't have to hold it that day. We could contact everyone we've asked and let them know we've changed the date to the following weekend, or even Sunday afternoon, if you'd prefer."

Meg held up a hand and gave him a pleasant, level look. "I'm fine with having the party Saturday. Besides, we've already ordered the cake," she added with a weary sigh.

Brody edged closer. "The cake isn't supposed to be baked until Saturday morning, so it shouldn't be a problem to change the order if we call first thing tomorrow."

"I know." Meg bit her lip, the troubled look coming back into her eyes again. "But the kids are really looking forward to it."

Brody studied her. "So you want to keep the birthday party scheduled for Saturday evening?"

"Yes."

"Then what's the problem?" he demanded, loathing the impatience in his tone, but unable to help it. He didn't like playing games, especially games in which he didn't know what the rules were, and that was exactly what it felt like they were doing.

Meg took his arm and steered him into the dining room, away from the stairs and any possibility of being overheard by the children. "I'm upset because you were right." With a sigh she sat down on the window seat and briefly explained what had happened at the day care.

Brody shrugged, not really seeing why that should be so upsetting. He didn't care who knew how he felt about Meg.

"So, our little secret is out," Meg continued. "Everybody knows we're getting involved again, and the twins are convinced we're going to remarry."

Getting involved? They *were* involved. Head over heels involved with each other. Deciding not to quibble about semantics, however, Brody merely sat down next to her and said, "I don't mind if people know I want to be with you. Or that the kids would like it a lot if we got married again." And frankly, he didn't see why she did.

Meg shot right back up again. He was perplexed to see she looked offended. "Well, I do—very much!"

He'd been expecting something like this all along, some irrational emotional reaction on Meg's part. He'd just hoped it wouldn't happen. Again. "And why is that, Meg?" he asked wearily, wondering if it was just talk of their romance at the day care that was setting her off, or something deeper and less easily addressed.

"Because all the sly looks we're getting and the secret smiles, and the occasional teasing from the staff is adding

fuel to the fire and setting the kids up with false expectations about what might or might not happen in the future.''

Brody didn't like the sound of this. It seemed as if Meg
was putting walls around her heart once again and bracing
herself for the worst. When she was a kid, it had been
necessary for her to keep her guard up at all times. He knew
that. But she had never needed to do that where he was
concerned. He'd hoped she had finally realized that. Now
he wasn't so sure. ''Have the twins said anything to you?''
Brody asked.

''Not directly, but they've told Carmen Perez and some
of the other adults at the day care, and I accidentally overheard them talking to each other tonight after they started
watching the video. They said they can't wait for us to get
married again. They really believe it's going to happen,
Brody.''

And that, it seemed, was breaking her heart.

Giving him no chance to reply, she turned on her heel
and swept out of the dining room, through the kitchen and
into the garage.

His exasperation mounting, Brody followed her, shutting
the door to the house behind them. The light was on, and
some fifteen boxes were piled in the garage with the name
of a storage company on the sides. ''Why do you consider
that a problem?''

Meg went over to the stack and picked up a pair of scissors sitting on one of the boxes. ''Because we've *been* married, Brody,'' she reiterated, cutting through the tape.

Brody moved to stand beside her, wishing she would let
him help her instead of pushing him away. ''And we cut it
short way too soon,'' he said gently, loosening his tie. He
hoped if they just talked this through, Meg would see how
silly she was being.

''We weren't just married.'' She opened the box, exposing a stack of self-help books for single mothers. "We were unhappily married."

His own temper simmering, Brody watched as she picked up a couple of the books, then dropped them back into the box. "That was then," he stated evenly. "This is now. We're older, more mature, less selfish."

She shook her head sadly and looked up at him as if she couldn't believe his naiveté. "But a lot of our fundamental problems remain the same."

He took her arm. "Such as?"

"Money is more important to you than it is to me."

Stung, he dropped his hold on her and stepped back. "Someone has to care about it!"

Meg clamped her lips together stubbornly. "You know what I mean."

"What I know is that you're looking for excuses because you're afraid to make a real commitment to our relationship."

"Now you're talking as if we're negotiating a business deal," she scoffed.

"If you're accusing me of wanting everything spelled out plainly, then you're right," Brody admitted in a flat, uncompromising voice. "That is what I want."

Meg glared at him. "How romantic."

"Romance didn't get us anything before except a heap of trouble, Meg." He was looking for something deeper. He had hoped that she was, too.

Meg's glance held thinly veiled contempt. "Because romance fades?" she queried in a sarcastic tone.

Why was she persisting in misunderstanding him? "Because the bottom line is that sooner or later, every couple has to be practical. And our stopping all this subterfuge and nonsense and living under the same roof would be practical."

"So we're back to the easiest, most convenient thing to

do, right, Brody?'' Meg's eyes glittered with resentment. ''When you asked me and Kelly to move in with you and Kevin, you were just skipping on ahead a little, getting to the bottom line.''

Her sarcasm sent his own temper soaring. ''It sure would save a lot of money that could be put to far better use!''

''No doubt,'' Meg snapped back. ''Unhappily for you, I am not going to marry or move in with anyone to save on my utilities and rent payments.''

Brody didn't know how this conversation had gotten so far off track. Their difficulties weren't about money, or the lack of it, and they never had been. Aware that he was panicking because Meg was erecting defences again, he forced himself to calm down, and said a lot more empathetically, ''Look, Meg, I understand you want to protect the kids.'' *And yourself.* He took her by the shoulders, forcing her to look up at him. ''But hiding our feelings for each other is *not* the way to do it.''

Her eyes glistened. ''What would you have us do then?'' she demanded in a hoarse, anguished voice.

Brody gave her a look that let her know her fear was pointless. ''I'd start by being honest and have us go public with our situation. Let everyone including Kelly and Kevin know we're seeing each other again, and that it's serious. And we could start with me taking you to Julia and Drew's wedding as my date.''

Instead of being delighted by the idea, as he had hoped, Meg looked even more anxious. ''Then people really would talk!''

The romantic speculation of others was just a small part of the problem, Brody knew. His and Meg's real quandary was their mutual fear of making the same mistake twice. He knew the first time he had pushed her into marrying him, he had focused on the reasons why it had been the right thing to do, instead of their feelings for each other.

Given the emotional volatility of the situation, it had seemed safer to approach it that way, to convince her to marry him for practical reasons.

In hindsight, he saw what a terrible mistake it had been. Because his we-can-do-this,-it-isn't-really-such-a-big-deal attitude had only served to reinforce her anxiety that theirs was an ill-thought-out union that would never last. Not over the long haul, anyway. He dropped his hands from her shoulders and stepped back. "They're making assumptions about us now," he countered just as firmly. "And most of the reason they are is because they think we're trying to hide our relationship and pull something over on everyone, and they're right. We aren't being honest with anyone." *Including ourselves,* he thought. Because the truth was, he was still in love with Meg and always had been. And he had thought she was in love with him.

"It's no one else's business what you and I do in our private lives!" Meg said irritably.

"You're right, but that's neither here nor there. Our friends are only human, Meg." Brody paused to let his words sink in. "People are naturally curious, especially when they sense something very good or very bad is happening to people they like. I don't fault them for that. If I were Katherine or Alexandra or Hannah, I'd be reacting the same way. Smiling whenever I saw the two of us together, and even dropping the odd comment to let us know it's okay, that we don't have to hide our feelings."

Brody could see Meg wanted to agree with him, but something—some nameless fear or anxiety—was holding her back. "That might be okay if it weren't for the kids." She turned her attention to another box. "But we have to consider what's right for them, too."

Closing the distance between them, Brody took her in his arms once again. "You want to do what's best for them, Meg?" he stated practically, smoothing a lock of hair from her cheek. He waited until he had her full attention before continuing. "Then forget dating, forget moving in with me, and just marry me."

MEG STARED AT BRODY, unable to believe what he had just said. This time it was clear he was serious, but it still felt more like a solution to their problems than a declaration of love. This was her worst-case scenario, with Brody once again casting about for an honorable solution that would silence the speculation and make their kids happy. And although those were laudable goals, they were not enough to sustain a marriage. Not the kind of marriage they both deserved. "You can't be serious," she said, trying not to show how crestfallen she felt.

"I'm dead serious," Brody told her solemnly, looking as determined to have his way with her as ever. "If you want people to stop talking, then marry me as soon as possible, and you and Kelly can move in with me and Kevin. The kids will be happy. We'll be happy. We'll be married and a family again, and there will be no more reason for anyone to gossip about us. Period. And you and I won't have to worry about what the future holds, because we'll know what it holds for us—one happy family."

Spreading her palms across his chest, Meg pushed him away from her. She was so hurt by his attitude she could barely breathe. "We can't get married just to make things easier."

"No, you're right," he said sarcastically, his exasperation showing plainly in the taut lines of his face. "We should stay apart, keep trying to see each other under the radar, keep disappointing the kids, and be miserable and lonely to boot. That's a *much* better plan."

Meg hunched her shoulders and glared up at him. "You know what I mean."

Brody sat on a stack of boxes. "No, I don't." A tense

silence fell as he continued to look at her. "I've explained to you why we should get married again ASAP," he said as calmly as if he were laying out a business plan. "It's your turn to explain to me why we shouldn't."

If there was one thing Meg hated more than being told what to do, it was being put on the defensive. Feeling as if she wanted to punch something, she went over to one of the boxes and tried to rip the tape off the top. Aware that Brody was still sitting there smugly, she pushed the words through her teeth. "I say that, Brody, because we don't have any proof that our relationship will work now any better than it did in the past." *Because I don't have a commitment of love from you.*

"And we're never going to get any proof our union will work, Meg," he said calmly. "Not beforehand, anyway. We're going to have to go forward on a leap of faith. Just like we did before."

When we failed…

And why did we fail?

Because love was not part of the equation.

Feeling unbearably self-conscious under his watchful gaze, Meg grabbed the scissors and cut the tape on the box. "Why does it have to be *now?*" she argued truculently, still hoping Brody might eventually see the light and be able to give her the love she needed from him.

He sent her a determined smile. "Because that's best for all of us, that's why."

Bristling at his confidence, she ripped open the box and found more books she didn't feel like shelving right now. She shoved the box aside with her foot, then turned back to Brody and challenged with a sweetness meant to cut him to the quick, "So as usual, it's your way or the highway, right, Brody?"

He flinched at the mention of his old motto according to Meg. The motto that had caused them to split in the first place, when she'd refused to do as he ordered. Lips set grimly, he slowly got to his feet. "I never said anything about breaking up with you."

Meg gulped at the deep unhappiness on his face. "Not yet, you haven't." But she hadn't come right out and refused his proposal yet. Determined to keep herself from bursting into tears, she added the flip comment, "The evening is still young."

Another silence fell between them, even tenser than the first. Brody's mask of civility fell away and he looked as ticked off, frustrated and misunderstood as she felt. "I've been meeting you halfway for weeks now. It's your turn to give some, Meg."

With Brody, it was always her turn to give. To meet his terms. "I've been giving, too," Meg pointed out just as resentfully. "Getting involved with you again within a matter of weeks was a big sacrifice on my part." One he didn't seem to recognize. Feeling even more unhappy, she stepped closer and jabbed a finger at his chest. "But you don't see it that way. Just like you don't see that all of this is happening way too fast."

Brody studied her quietly. "So in other words," he summed up contemptuously, "you're not willing to commit yourself to me or our family. Or believe that if we just stick together, instead of walking at the first opportunity, we could have the kind of happy home situation both of us always wanted."

Meg balled her hands into fists, struggling to contain her fear and frustration and hold back her tears. The problem was they hadn't honored their promises to each other back then. They hadn't put each other's needs first the way they had vowed they would. And they certainly weren't doing so now. But not wanting to get into all that with him, she merely said, "You're asking too much, Brody." Just like before. Why couldn't he be patient and give her all the time and understanding she needed to make this work? Why did it have to be on his accelerated time schedule?

"And as usual," Brody said, before stalking out of the garage angrily, "you're willing to give way too little."

"This is it then?" Meg asked, following him out into the driveway.

"You've given us no other choice," Brody said grimly. "Because I'm not going to do things with you halfway again, Meg. Not anymore. Not again."

"ARE YOU AND DADDY fighting?" Kelly asked Meg Friday evening as Meg helped her into a pretty dress.

"No," Meg fibbed, even though she felt as if her heart was irretrievably broken, "of course not. Why would you even ask that?"

"Because you're not going to the special dinner with me and Kevin and Daddy and Uncle Roarke tonight."

"I told you, I have to go over to the church and run through my songs for the wedding tomorrow morning. As soon as you leave, I'm going there to practice with the pianist."

"You need to check out the 'coustics?"

"Acoustics. Yes, I do. I need to know how loud I have to sing, and how my voice is going to carry in the chapel, and I need to make sure the pianist and I are perfectly in sync, so we give the most beautiful performance ever for Drew and Julia."

Kelly sighed, looking all starry-eyed and romantic again. "I wish me and Kevin could go to the rehearsal."

"You'll see the wedding tomorrow," Meg promised. "As well as a tiny bit of the reception." How long the children stayed depended on how long they could behave.

"Then we have to go back to Daddy's house and take naps so we'll be all ready for his party tomorrow night."

Meg smiled. "Right."

"Well, I guess that's okay," Kelly said as she sat down to put on her patent leather dress shoes. "But I still wish you and Daddy were being nicer to each other."

"We've been nice!" Meg protested.

Kelly made a face as she carefully worked the metal prong through the hole in the ankle strap. "Too nice," she said, conjuring up a fake smile. "Me and Kevin know pretending when we see it."

She and Brody had made a mistake thinking things would be different this time, when essentially nothing between them had changed. She knew it, felt it, understood it. So why, Meg wondered miserably, as she finished getting Kelly ready for her dinner with Brody, did she still feel so bad?

MEG WAS STILL CONFLICTED when she showed up at Our Lady of Mercy Church on Saturday morning, well ahead of the other guests. She warmed up with the pianist, then went to the anteroom where Julia was to dress, and helped her into her wedding gown.

"You look so lovely," Meg told her. Seeing her reminded Meg of her own wedding day, how happy and thrilled she had been then. How full of hope for their future.

"Thank you," Julia said, looking absolutely radiant as Meg helped smooth the beautiful satin over the layers of petticoat underneath. "I feel—"

"Serene? Because that's the way you look."

"I guess I am," Julia confessed shyly as she pulled the sleeves up over her shoulders and made sure the bodice was in place. "I know promising your life to someone is a risky thing to do, but I'm really committed to Drew and to our marriage. So I know in my heart, no matter what difficulties lie ahead, everything is truly going to be all right, that together there is no challenge we can't handle."

And there lay the difference between her and Julia, Meg

thought. Even as a first-time bride on her wedding day, Meg had not felt the same assurance about her marriage to Brody.

When she said nothing, Julia turned to study her. "You're thinking about your own wedding day, aren't you. You still love Brody."

Meg wasn't sure how to reply. "It's complicated," she said finally.

"Then explain it to me," Julia prodded with a smile.

"Brody and I initially got married for all the wrong reasons."

"I understand that," Julia said gently. "But what does that have to do with the way you feel about each other now?"

"MOMMY LOOKS SO PRETTY, Daddy," Kelly whispered. "Doesn't she look pretty?"

Meg did look incredible, Brody thought as he watched her make her way to the front of the congregation and begin to sing the half-dozen songs Julia had asked her to perform as the guests were being seated.

Kevin tugged on Brody's sleeve and whispered from the other side. "She sings pretty, too."

"I know," Brody murmured back, squeezing the hands of both their kids.

Meg was a beautiful woman, inside and out. It was just too bad, for all their sakes, that she wasn't interested in making a life with him. If he could change the way she felt, Brody thought wistfully as her voice filled the church with lilting, romantic music, he would do it. But how? he wondered. Hadn't he already tried every way possible? And failed big time. Still, he mused, maybe he shouldn't give up. Especially when he was still sure that deep down, Meg did love him. The question was how to make her realize that?

The service began, and before they spoke their vows, the priest instructed Drew and Julia to take a moment and express to each other and the people gathered there to witness their union what was in their hearts.

Drew took Julia's hands in his. "I can't imagine being without you, Julia," he said. "You've brought meaning, love and joy to my life...."

Julia regarded Drew, tears sparkling in her eyes. "You are my friend, my partner, my love. I am so looking forward to sharing my life with you...."

Before Brody had met Meg, when he'd heard people utter such emotions, he'd thought it all hopelessly corny. A way to get what you wanted from someone, and little else. But now he knew that people really did feel such strong emotions when it came to those they loved. Meg and the kids were his reason for living. Maybe Meg was right, Brody mused as he looked down at the twins, who were raptly watching every single detail of Drew and Julia's wedding. Maybe it was time he stopped trying to have everything his own way. Maybe, Brody reasoned thoughtfully, Meg hadn't been running from commitment. Maybe he was driving her away with demands she wasn't yet able to meet.

SITTING THERE WATCHING Julia and Drew pledge their hearts and their lives to each other, Meg realized so many things.

Brody would always be ambitious. But these days his dedication was tempered by his love for his family.

Years ago, he had been unable and unwilling to stand up to Roarke. Now, finally, he could.

He still spent money more freely than she did, but he had earned his money the hard way. And he had agreed not to overindulge their children in material things, while giving freely of his time and attention so they would feel secure and loved.

Kevin and Kelly weren't the only ones who yearned to feel that way. And Brody wasn't the only one who had needed to change. For years, Meg had been using her own parents' inability to get along, even after the split, as the reason for her wariness of close relationships. The real source of her anxiety went much deeper. She had been perfectly content to coast along, day to day. Never allowing anyone to get too close, never investing much of herself in anything but her work onstage. Only there, when she was pretending to be someone else, had it been safe to let her emotions flow free.

Brody had changed all that. He'd made her want to feel intensely all the time. He'd tempted her to love with all her heart and soul. And whenever she was in his arms, in his bed, she had.

Away from him, it was a different story. Not wanting to be too dependent, or risk committing to anything that would ultimately be taken away from her, she had put her guard back up.

And that, too, had worked—until she had become pregnant with the twins. Then she had felt trapped. Scared. Like it or not, her whole heart had been involved in her pregnancy and her marriage. But she hadn't been sure Brody's was. And rather than give him a chance to show her what was in his heart, she'd shut him out until their divorce was as inevitable as her parents' had been.

Now he was back in her life.

Back in her heart.

She was still afraid of making a foolish mistake that would have repercussions on all their lives. But for the first time, her yearning to be his and her need to be with him were strong enough to propel her back into his arms, his life, for good this time. No more trying to convince herself she didn't care, when she did. No more letting her fear of being hurt keep her from enjoying a full and love-filled life.

Only one question remained.

Was it too late?

Or was there still a chance?

There was only one way to find out, Meg decided. And she would do so at the first opportunity....

"MAGNIFICENT PERFORMANCE, Meg!" Alexandra said after the ceremony had concluded, and pictures were being taken at the front of the church.

"Oh, thank you," Meg replied. She was trying to thread her way through the crowd of people to Brody and the children, but every time she took a step, someone else came up to her to compliment her singing.

"No kidding," Hannah agreed, giving Meg a congratulatory hug. "I was just enthralled. I've never heard any of those love songs sung so gorgeously."

"It was as if you put your whole heart in every word," Katherine agreed.

Meg had.

"Like you were singing directly to the audience," she continued warmly.

Actually, Meg had been singing those love songs to only one person. Unfortunately, that person was heading away from her, she noted nervously, not toward her.

"Thank you so much." She smiled, trying her best, without being rude, to excuse herself from the guests gathered around her.

Carmen Perez, the kindergarten teacher, reached out to take Meg's hand. "Kelly and Kevin are so proud of you, Meg. They're running around telling everyone that was their mom up there singing!"

And meanwhile, there went Brody, Meg noted, even as she murmured yet another polite thank-you for the compliments coming her way. Her ex-husband was striding toward a taxicab parked at the curb. Out of the corner of her eye,

Meg watched as the rear door opened and Fiona stepped out. She spoke to Brody quietly for several minutes, smiling up at him raptly all the while. Brody looked very happy to hear whatever she was saying, and when Fiona had finished, he wrapped her in what looked like a warm, heartfelt hug. They talked some more, this time with Brody doing a lot of the talking, then Fiona nodded agreeably and reached up to hug Brody again.

Meg watched numbly as Brody leaned down to speak to the driver through the open window. The man got out, removed Fiona's suitcases from the trunk of the cab and set them at the curb. Brody handed him several bills, then gallantly carried Fiona's suitcases over to his SUV and put them inside. Smiling and talking incessantly all the while, Fiona accompanied Brody over to where Kevin and Kelly were standing with several other children. Where, Meg noted with a perilously sinking heart, Fiona was greeted just as enthusiastically.

Had Brody just offered Fiona her job back? Meg wondered, watching as her children jumped up and down in glee. Had Fiona just accepted? Or was something else going on between the two?

Meg turned away from the intimate scene, telling herself it was none of her business what was happening between Brody and Fiona. Not even if Brody was once again choosing the easy way out and rehiring Kevin's beautiful nanny. There was no reason, Meg scolded herself inwardly, that she should feel so depressed. No reason she should feel so betrayed. Not even if Fiona were still jockeying to become Brody's wife and Kevin—and Kelly's—stepmother.

CHAPTER FIFTEEN

"YOU'RE SURE YOU DON'T want to come with us?" Hannah asked, as she, Katherine and Alexandra prepared to leave the reception. "We're just going over to Katherine's to hang out for a while. And as long as Brody has the kids at his house, napping—"

"Thanks." Meg held up a staying hand, doing her best to hide her sagging spirits. "But I've got to go home and change clothes and wrap the kids' and my present for his birthday party this evening." She also wanted to spend some time alone, absorbing what she had just seen. Roarke had been correct in his assessment of the situation, Meg realized sadly. Fiona had been right there, waiting for everything between Brody and Meg to fall apart. And as soon as it had, she had moved right in.

Heck, Meg thought resentfully as she pulled into her own driveway, Brody was probably still with Fiona right now. Helping her move into his home....

Hurt and confused, Meg trudged inside and went straight upstairs. Tears misted her eyes as she stripped off the pastel yellow dress, high heels and panty hose she had worn to the wedding, and put on her most comfortable bathrobe, an old pink chenille wrap with big fat tulips embroidered on it. It wasn't a particularly flattering garment, but it was warm and cozy, and it had seen her through the preperformance jitters in many a backstage dressing room. And that kind of comfort was exactly what she needed.

Determinedly she slid her feet into comfortable pink

scuffs and tromped back downstairs to make herself a cup of soothing peppermint tea before she had to go to Brody's backyard birthday party. And pretend to be oh so happy in front of their children and all their friends, when in reality—because of her own foolishness and fear—her heart was breaking all over again.

The doorbell rang just as Meg walked into the kitchen. Wondering who it could be, she headed back out to the foyer, looked through the viewer and saw Brody standing on her stoop. He was still wearing the dark suit and tie he had worn to the wedding. In one hand, he held a paper sack from an arts and crafts store, and what looked to be two trench coats were looped over his arm. Her distress increased as she thought about all the things they had said to each other the last time they were alone, things she now regretted terribly. Cautiously, she opened the door, as unsure of his mood as she was about what the future held for them.

"I want to talk," he said simply.

So did Meg, but only after she'd had time to carefully formulate what she was going to say. She couldn't afford to make any more mistakes where the love of her life was concerned. "Where are the children?" she asked, then feared, given the tête-à-tête she had witnessed at the wedding reception, she already knew.

Looking suave and confident as ever, Brody sauntered in at her invitation. "Kelly and Kevin are both back at my house, sleeping. Don't worry," he continued with a reassuring smile as he looped the coats over the banister and set the paper bag down on the floor. "Fiona is with them."

And that was supposed to make her feel better? Meg thought. She stared at him, knowing she had never felt more full of regret in her life. Calling on every bit of strength she had, she forced her voice to sound casual. "She's working for you again, I take it?"

"No." Brody's eyes locked on hers. "She took a job with another family—back in Ireland."

Meg frowned, perplexed. "I thought she was going to stay here in Seattle."

"That was the plan," Brody admitted candidly. "Unfortunately, she didn't factor in how homesick she was going to be. She wants to return to Ireland, to be close to family."

Relief flowed through Meg. "Is that what she was talking to you about at the reception?" Brody nodded. "How do you feel about that?" she asked.

Brody's shoulders lifted in a shrug. "I'm happy for her, relieved for me. I never wanted to hurt her."

"I know that," Meg said.

"Anyway, she agreed to wait and take a flight tomorrow so she could say bye to the kids. I asked her to baby-sit them while I talk to you."

Wishing she were still dressed in her wedding clothes instead of the ratty old robe, Meg asked, "About…?"

"The way we ended up Thursday night. I want to reconsider a few things."

So did Meg. She could only hope that finally they were on the same page.

Brody picked up the bag from the arts and crafts and handed it to her. "Look inside."

Her heart pounding, Meg pulled out two Marx-Brothers-style, thick black plastic eyeglasses with attached mustaches and fake noses. She stared at them, perplexed. She had no idea what he was trying to tell her. Or why he had showed up on her doorstep carrying two trench coats, one obviously well used, the other so new it still had the price tags hanging off it. She returned her attention to the glasses. "These look a little big for the kids," she said.

Brody grinned even as he reached for her, a hungry gleam in his eyes. "They're not for the kids."

"Okay, now I'm really not getting it," she murmured ruefully.

He tucked his hand beneath her chin and looked deep into her eyes. "They're for us."

Meg blinked. "At Halloween?"

"Anytime you want to use them," he said. Shifting her hair aside, he whispered conspiratorially in her ear, "So we won't be recognized."

Meg was beginning to be very warm every place their bodies touched. And even the places they didn't. She tilted her head up to his, aware she had never had so much at stake in her entire life. She wanted so much for them. A happy marriage, a life with their children, an everlasting love and a closeness that would comfort and sustain them for the rest of their lives. She could only hope he wanted those things, too.

"Why wouldn't we want to be recognized?" She didn't know why, but as she searched his face, she was suddenly whispering, too.

Affection glimmered in Brody's dark eyes. "I don't know," he teased softly, tenderly stroking his hands through her hair. "Maybe because we're having a clandestine affair?"

Meg's heart took on a slow, thudding beat as the meaning of his words sank in. Unable to help herself, she moved another half-step closer, wrapped her arms about his waist and tipped her head up to his. "I thought you were opposed to that." She felt as if she was going to cry again, out of happiness this time.

"I was a fool, okay?" he acknowledged in an unsteady voice, drawing her even closer. Gently he traced a finger down her cheek. "I had no right to be putting demands and restrictions on you or us, Meg," he apologized sincerely, and the conviction in his voice let her know he meant every word from the bottom of his heart. "This isn't a corporation and I'm not the CEO. We're partners, Meg, each with an equal say. And what you want counts as much as, if not more than, what I want. Because most of all I want you to be happy. So if you want us to take our time and sneak around and keep our love a secret, I'm all for it,'' he offered with a teasing wink. ''Heck, I'm thinking it might even be fun.''

''It won't be easy or convenient,'' Meg warned, even as she leaned in close, savoring his warmth and his strength and the essence that was him.

''I don't care. I just want you in my life and in my arms again, Meg.''

The tears Meg had been holding back slipped down her face as her heart filled with joy. A feeling of euphoria surged through her. Against all odds, despite the mistakes they had made and their stubborn refusal to admit their true feelings, she and Brody were working things out, after all. They had a future together. She had never felt more hopeful about what lay ahead. ''Oh, Brody. I love you so much,'' she murmured, cuddling closer. There. She had finally done it. She had spoken the words out loud.

Brody grinned. He looked down at her as if he had known it all along. ''I love you, too,'' he confessed, filling her heart with joy. He held her close and pressed his lips to hers in a long, slow kiss that made her tremble. When they finally drew apart, he swept a hand down her spine. His touch was warm and possessive and felt oh-so-right to Meg. ''So does that mean you're not kicking me out of your life?'' he asked her gruffly.

Meg smiled, knowing her world had finally righted once again. ''I'm not kicking you out of my life.'' And to prove it, she gave him a long, lingering kiss. ''But I do have something to tell you,'' she said, drawing a deep breath. ''I've changed my mind, too.'' She knew it was a risk, approaching him this way, but she had to do it. "I do want to get married, Brody. As soon as possible."

Brody blinked in stunned amazement. "You're not just saying that?"

"No. Because I realized something today," she told him seriously. "I realized you were right. I never did commit to you and our marriage all the way. But no more, Brody. I love you with all my heart, and for once, finally, I'm not afraid to tell the whole world."

They kissed again, even more poignantly, and then went upstairs together to make sweet, passionate love. Afterward, Brody held her close and stroked her hair. "I guess we're both going to need new mottos," he murmured.

"You're right," Meg teased. "Our old ones aren't going to work anymore." They had both changed, and their personal credos needed to reflect that.

"I've got one in mind for myself," Brody said.

Her body still humming from their lovemaking, Meg asked, "What is it?"

Taking her free hand, Brody pressed it to his lips. "Sometimes, if you want to change something in your life, you might have to change your attitude. I've changed mine. From now on, I'm putting you and the kids first. Nothing happens in this family unless it's good for all of us. And I mean that, Meg. Heart and soul."

That sounded so good to Meg. For too many years, she and Brody had put themselves—and their fear—first. It was time that stopped. "Okay, I've got a new one, too, then," she said confidently.

Brody's eyes lit up. "What is it?"

It was kind of corny, Meg knew, but the meaning was exactly right for the way she was feeling now. "Don't be afraid to go out on a limb. It's where the fruit is."

"I like that." Brody clamped his arm around her waist

and rolled so she was lying on top of him. "And I like the idea of you being out on a limb with me even better."

Meg grinned as their bodies began to simmer again. "And as long as we're going out on a limb…" she said, then leaned down and whispered her idea in his ear.

Brody grinned wickedly, his passion for her clear. "My sentiments exactly."

As PLANNED EARLIER with the kids, Meg walked Brody around to his backyard at precisely seven o'clock that evening. "Surprise!" everyone yelled, along with Kevin and Kelly.

Meg and Brody grinned. It hadn't mattered how many times they had explained it to Kevin and Kelly, the twins had insisted this was a surprise party, even though Brody already knew about the celebration in advance, and in fact had been instrumental in planning many of the details. So, bowing to five-year-old logic, he and Meg had finally just gone along and now acted as stunned as the twins expected them to be by the crowd gathered in the backyard.

"Are you amazed?" Kevin ran up to Brody and clamped both his arms around his father's legs.

"Absolutely," Brody confirmed with a happy grin as he lifted Kevin into his arms for a proper hug, then did the same with Kelly. He gazed at the balloons tied to the fence and the bushes. "Did you two do all this?" he asked.

"Yeah," Kevin and Kelly said. They took Meg and Brody by the hand and led them through the assembled guests to the other end of the beautifully landscaped yard.

Once there, Meg and Brody were truly speechless. Assorted shapes and colors of lawn chairs were set in rows, with a center aisle. There was a long, linen-covered table off to one side, and in the center of it sat a three-tiered white cake with a bride and groom on top. "See, it's a birthday party *and* a wedding!" Kevin explained.

"For you and Mommy!" Kelly added.

Katherine was the first to come forward. She looked about as stressed out as it was possible to look. "We didn't know until we got here exactly what the full plans were," she said apologetically.

"There's plenty of food!" Hannah announced brightly, trying to lighten the mood. "Everyone brought a contribution—it's all in the kitchen."

"And presents," Alexandra added helpfully. "Although those are birthday gifts for Brody."

Silence fell abruptly over the yard. No one, it seemed, knew quite what to do. Or say. Even their minister, Reverend Bollick, looked as taken aback as everyone else. Everyone except Meg and Brody, who reached for each other's hands and burst out laughing.

"We were afraid you would be angry," Amy said.

"Actually, it's perfect," Meg explained. "Because Brody and I made a stop on the way over here."

Brody reached into his pocket and pulled out a velvet-lined box. He opened it up for everyone to see.

"What is it?" Kelly asked, standing on tiptoe, along with her brother.

"Wedding rings," Meg replied gently.

"One for Mommy and one for Daddy," Brody told them. He and Meg knelt down at eye level with the twins. "You see, Mommy and I decided this afternoon that we were going to get married. We can't do it officially until next week, because we have to get a marriage license and then wait for three days for it to become valid."

"You mean you can't get married tonight?" Kevin asked. His face fell.

Kelly's lower lip trembled and she looked near tears. "We got the minister here and everything. And your dress and veil, and Daddy's bow tie and his tuxedo."

"Well…" Meg and Brody looked at each other uncertainly.

"I guess we could have the wedding rehearsal here tonight," Meg suggested thoughtfully after a moment.

"And do it officially in the church later in the week," Brody agreed. That way, they wouldn't have to disappoint the kids.

"Great idea!" Reverend Bollick declared with a wink. "That is, if you don't mind having an audience."

"I don't," Brody said. He wanted everyone to know how much he loved Meg and she him.

"Neither do I," Meg said.

Cheers erupted around them.

"Congratulations," Fiona said. And Meg could tell by the look on the ex-nanny's face that she really meant it. Maybe, Meg thought, Fiona had finally recognized what everyone else had—that Meg and Brody were in love, and that their family was meant to be together, today, tomorrow and forever. That knowledge left Fiona free to go on with her life, and her future, too. And for that Meg felt very relieved.

All their friends came forward to offer their congratulations, and Brody grinned at them all. "See?" he said, spreading his hands wide. "Great minds do think alike."

While everyone waited, Meg and Brody went upstairs to dress in separate rooms. He got into his tuxedo, and Meg got into the long white dress Kelly had brought from Meg's closet. Reverend Bollick officiated and the run-through was as beautiful as Kevin and Kelly wanted it to be. The twins watched, their eyes shining with happiness, as Meg and Brody practiced saying the vows they would repeat for real later in the week.

"I, Brody, take thee, Meg…"

"To have and to hold…from this day forward…as long as we both shall live."

"And here, Brody, is where you kiss the bride," Reverend Bollick advised as the wedding rehearsal drew to a close.

And to the cheers of everyone gathered around them, Brody did.

* * * * *

FORRESTER SQUARE,
a new Harlequin series,
continues in October 2003 with
ALL SHE NEEDED
by Kate Hoffmann...

After Dani O'Malley's childhood friend died, she found herself guardian to three scared, unruly kids. Dani tried desperately to cope, but she was a single businesswoman who grew up in foster homes. If it weren't for Brad Cullen, she'd be lost. Who would have thought that this cowboy would have such a way with kids...and with her?

Though Brad would much rather have been left alone with his ranch as his only responsibility, when the children's aunt and uncle sued for custody, Brad knew he could never let Dani lose the kids...when marrying her would make them a family.

Here's a preview!

"MISS O'MALLEY?"

"I'll be out in a few minutes," she shouted.

"I—I think you'd better come out here now."

Dani cursed softly, then yanked the bathroom door open. Louie the doorman stood outside, an apologetic smile pasted on his face. "Can't the woman wait?" Dani asked.

"She says that she's here about Evie Gregory. And she has to see you immediately." He cleared his throat, then lowered his voice. "She has three children with her, and the little one has very sticky hands."

At the mention of Evie's name, Dani's breath caught in her throat. Her heart ground to a stop, and for a moment, she couldn't think. Slowly she walked down the hall, telling herself that everything was all right. But in her heart, she knew that something had happened to Evie. She'd had an odd feeling all week long, but had written it off to exhaustion. When she reached the living room, she took in the scene in front of her.

An elderly woman sat on the sofa, her plump figure straining her rumpled clothes. Evie's three children sat quietly beside her, their expressions dull and emotionless. With an effort Lucille Wilson stood, clutching her handbag in front of her. "Are you Danielle O'Malley?"

"What's happened to Evie?" Dani demanded, her voice trembling. "Why are her children here? Is she all right?"

"Evie died last week," Lucille Wilson said, as if she

were commenting on the weather or the price of chicken at
the supermarket.

A tiny cry slipped from Dani's throat and she clutched
the back of a chair to keep her knees from buckling. "No,"
she murmured. "I just saw her last month. She said she was
getting better."

"The doctors gave her three months," the woman said.
"And that was six months ago."

Dani glanced at the children. Jack, Evie's twelve-year-
old son, stared at his shoes. Rebecca, who was just five,
wept softly, her face streaked with tears. And the baby, two-
year-old Noah, didn't seem to understand what had happened. He clutched a ragged teddy bear and crawled back
and forth between his siblings, whining for attention.

Hesitating slightly, Dani approached Jack, then bent
down and placed her hand over his. "I'm so sorry," she
said, tears filling her eyes. "Your mother and I were best
friends. She was the only friend I ever had."

She fought the urge to retreat to her bedroom, to crawl
into bed and let the grief overwhelm her. Instead, old instincts returned and she hardened her heart. Their friendship
was never meant to last. Dani had been surprised they'd
managed to keep it going this long. But the rationalization
didn't help. Evie was gone, and Dani had no one left in the
world who meant anything to her.

"Well, I suppose that's it then," Lucille Wilson muttered. "I've packed all their things. The bags are down in
the lobby along with the baby's car seat and a portable crib.
I'll ship everything else next week." She waved an enve-
lope in the air, then dropped it on the coffee table. "This
is a copy of Evie's will and a letter from her. She changed
the will a couple weeks before she died. My husband, Fred,
and I were supposed to take the children. We were all ready
to take them. Had our house all fixed up. But I guess Evie

thought you'd be a better mother to these three than a blood relative. I don't think she was in her right mind. My husband and I plan to contest your guardianship. You'll be hearing from our lawyer.''